Dutch Schreiber moved into the Apache slowly, warily, taking his time. He had pushed anger out of his mind and his eyes were coldly calculating. This was a job he needed to do, a man he needed to kill, and there was no rage or passion in him. Nothing but purpose.

Torres blinked, then rushed suddenly and swung his knife up in a flashing arc. Schreiber moved to one side and watched the blade miss his stomach by nearly a foot. He smiled thinly. "Take your time, Indian. We got all day."

Torres pressed in, holding his knife at waist level. Schreiber circled him, staying barely out of reach. Torres jumped toward him, jabbing the point of his blade at Schreiber's chest. Dutch caught the steel on his own blade, then stepped inside the Apache's outthrust arm and ripped his knife across the Apache's stomach. Torres gasped and blood seeped, then flowed freely from the gash.

Schreiber said, "This is different than butchering women, Indian. You're goin' to get butchered up some yourself."

Also by Dan Kirby:

SHOWDOWN AT CIBECUE CREEK

SCHREIBER'S CHOICE

DAN KIRBY

CHARTER
NEW YORK

A DIVISION OF CHARTER COMMUNICATIONS INC.
A GROSSET & DUNLAP COMPANY
51 Madison Avenue
New York, New York 10010

SCHREIBER'S CHOICE

An ACE CHARTER Original

First ACE CHARTER printing: November 1981

Published simultaneously in Canada

Manufactured in the United States of America
2 4 6 8 0 9 7 5 3 1

CHAPTER ONE

On Castle Peak, flanking the western edge of the White Mountain Reservation, on a clear day a man could see more than thirty miles to the blue mist that rose like a ghostly shroud from the devil's cauldron called Salt River Canyon. Particularly if that man was an Apache.

Nochelte sat motionless on his horse on the peak and looked down the sweep of the land, empty except for the intrusion of the weathered log cabin half hidden in a pine grove a mile below. The cabin had once belonged to the Dutchman, but he had left it, and the new owner had died yesterday. The emptiness was good to see and Nochelte raised his eyes to the mid-morning sun and thanked the Great God for it.

He was a slight man, small in stature even for an Apache, and pale almost to being white, but he was the fire that kept the Apache kettle boiling. He was the Prophet. He was the chosen one, destined, he knew, to return this country to the people called Apache.

The emptiness below was deceptive. Over the hump of a small butte ahead lay Cogar's ranch. Beyond that, across the great canyon, were white settlements and many ranches. Looking eastward the White Eyes were even more numerous with their towns and forts and small farms. The tranquility of the morning was deceptive, also, for death lay in the willow grove along Reno

Creek a half mile below. Neither breaking the emptiness of the land nor adding to it, a half-dozen vultures beat their dark wings against the sky as they circled the willow grove on the creek.

Down there in the shade of the grove, Nochelte knew, lay the body of an Americano. Beside him, his stomach blown open by a pointblank rifle shot, was an Apache boy. The White Eyes would not notice the loss of the Americano. Another would take his place tomorrow. But it would take an Apache squaw nine months to produce another Apache boy, and ten years to bring him to the size of the dead one. And time was running out for the Apache.

Now the land was no longer empty. There was movement in the trees along the creek. A rider moved out of the cover across a bare spot of rock forming the east bank of the creek. A square-set man on a dun horse, picking his way, stopping now and then, searching the ground, staring at the vultures, then moving on. It was the Dutchman, the man called Schreiber. Nochelte's eyes narrowed. The Dutchman would find the bodies, he would read the signs, and he would know how the Americano had died.

Nochelte half turned his horse and looked around at the six Apache warriors behind him. One of them, a young, deep-chested, muscular man, naked except for breechclout and deerskin leggings, pulled his horse around and rode toward Nochelte. Around his neck was a leather thong and from the thong a woman's scalp hung down the man's broad back. The hair was long and silky and almost black except for a single snow-white streak that ran the length of the softly waved tresses. As the warrior rode forward the gentle breeze and morning sun rippled and glinted upon the scalp making it seem somehow alive.

The warrior stopped short of Nochelte, facing him. He said, "We must kill the Dutchman. He will have the Army upon us and we are not ready."

Nochelte regarded the young warrior impassively. Finally he said, "The Dutchman will see how this thing happened and he will know the Americano deserved to die. He will tell the horse soldiers this."

The warrior gestured impatiently. "He will see the squaws and children leaving the reservation, moving south toward the border. He will know what this means."

Nochelte shrugged. "I do not think the Army will listen to him. The soldiers are enjoying the peace we have given them for a long time now. They have sent many of their troops away and they are using but few of our own people as scouts. They will stay fat and content and hope that the Apache warriors will follow their squaws and children into Mexico and leave this land to the White Eyes." Nochelte smiled slightly. "You have another reason for wanting the Dutchman dead, Torres."

Torres scowled and rubbed a hand over his bare chest. "It is known that he has taken an oath before his God to kill me. I am ready to fight him now."

Nochelte's obsidian eyes glinted in cold amusement. "The Dutchman is a dangerous man, Torres. He is like the cougar that stalks our land and knows many ways to kill."

Torres grimaced. "I am not afraid."

Nochelte nodded. "That is good. An Apache should not be afraid to fight or die. But you must wait. The time is not right." He pointed toward the distant mountains in the north. "Ugashe!"

Torres wheeled his mount and joined the other warriors and they moved off the peak silently as red shadows, Nochelte keeping some distance behind them.

Reaching the very summit of the peak, Nochelte pulled rein and stared back at the willow grove below. The Dutchman was not in sight. His eyes once more swept over the empty land. He was a long time knowing of the way of the horse soldiers. He had worked for the gray fox, General Crook, in his youth. He had made the trip east to the White Chief's home in Washington and received there a silver medal because he was a good Apache and had helped the White Eyes. He had thought that he was helping to bring peace between his people and the White Eyes. Finally he had realized that it was not peace that the Americanos sought, but only Apache land. So long as the Apache held a piece of land that the Americano wanted, there would be no peace. So he had left the Army, feeling deceived and foolish, and he had avoided the White Eyes and his own people as well until the Great God spoke to him. The Great God gave him a plan and the power to carry it out. It had taken years to get his own people to listen to him. But they were beginning to listen now.

The Dutchman had left the Army, also. He had never met the Dutchman, although he knew from stories that the man was scouting for the Gray Fox at least a year or two before Nochelte had left the service. The man had gathered a reputation among the Apaches as a scout and fighter, and then had left the Army to marry a woman and establish a ranch. Torres had killed the woman and taken her scalp when the Dutchman was away from the Ranch. It was a bad thing. It was the kind of senseless thing that gave the White Eyes what little excuse they needed for exterminating the Apache as a people. It was the kind of act that turned a dangerous man into a dangerous enemy.

He turned his horse and watched his warriors disappearing into the scattered clumps of scrub cedar that flanked the north slope of the peak. Tonight there would be a gathering of the chiefs of the Apache tribes on Cibecue Creek. Tonight he would meet with them. He raised his arms to the sky and stared into the blue eternity of the heavens, asking the Great God to give him guidance.

Dutch Schreiber hunched over his saddle staring at the bloating body of young Bill Jackson. The signs were reasonably plain. Jackson had ridden unexpectedly upon the band of squaws and kids along the creek. It was a large band, possibly twenty or more. Bill was new to Arizona. He thought he was surrounded by hostiles and he fired in panic, killing an Apache boy. He never saw the squaw who, concealed by the timber along the creek bank, caved in his head with a large rock. The rock, blood-stained, still lay beside the body.

Dutch reached for tobacco and papers, still studying the ground. This was the beginning of it. This was no food-foraging expedition by reservation Apaches. The group was too large and the tracks showed they were heading south. The reservation was northeast. He lighted his smoke and let his eyes move up the length of the winding creek to where it ran by the log cabin on the south slope of the foothills. It had been his cabin once. He sat quietly a long moment, his mind wandering back to how it had been living in that cabin with Elaine. Finally he pinched out the cigarette and climbed out of the saddle, a sudden washed-out weariness heavy upon him.

He took his rifle from the saddle boot and moved quietly into the dense cover of the willow grove. He squatted on his heels in the grove's heavy shade and built another smoke and let it hang unlighted from his lips. He waited, listening. Overhead a bluejay shrieked its displeasure at his presence. A rabbit moved noisily through a bed of dry leaves and stopped a few feet short of him, nose twitching. Sometimes, he knew, when moving their women and children, the Apaches would send a few warriors along to scout and hunt for them. Finally, satisfied that he was alone, he lighted his smoke and sat awhile longer, then moved back to his horse and stuck the rifle back in the saddle boot.

He moved around the horse toward Bill Jackson's body and dragged it by the ankles to the edge of a dry wash feeding off of the creek. He eased the body over the edge and watched it roll heavily to the bottom. He walked over to the body of the Apache boy and dragged it to the wash and rolled it over so that it rested beside the body of Jackson. He gathered brush, downed by wind and highwater in some remote time, and piled it over the bodies. It was the best he could do for them. The vultures and varmints would work through the brush and reduce the bodies to bones within a few days.

He climbed back into the saddle and removed his hat, running a hand through short blond hair, looking down at the brush pile, lips moving but saying nothing. An Arizona funeral. Finally he rode off, heading toward the log cabin, eyes gray and remote and watchful, sweat beading his bronzed forehead from the exertion and the humidity of the bottomland.

Schreiber crossed the creek again where it made a loop around the base of a timbered hill, and noticed that the spring run-off had washed out the low earthern dam around the impoundment pond he had built three years ago. The bottom of the pond was dry and cracked. Bill Jackson had practically run out of water, because the creek dried up in the summer except for an occasional small pool. He had warned Jackson of this when he had sold him the ranch last year. But Jackson was young and green and his image of an Arizona rancher did not include the dozen menial tasks a man had to do to keep a place together out here.

He dismounted in front of the cabin, moving stiffly, slapping his hat against his dusty pants. He stepped up on the small porch and went inside, fighting against the melancholy that seized him as he looked around the room. The water bucket on the stand by the stove was empty and he picked it up and went back outside. A small spring seeped water from the base of the red rock bluff behind the cabin. He half filled the bucket and went back into the cabin and put coffee on the stove. He was hungry but coffee would do for now because he was short of time. He had been expected to report into Camp Cashe two days ago with military dispatch from Fort Huachucca, but his horse had gone lame a half-day out and he'd walked ten miles to Beezer's ranch for a remount. He killed a half day there at Beezer's, resting, trading gossip, rehashing old times. Next to Pete Kitchen, old Jim Beezer had routed more Apache raiding parties than any man in the territory. His ranch stood like a fortress in the high Sonora country. Dutch had hoped to build this place into a ranch like Beezer's, but things hadn't worked out.

He laid his hat on the table and sat down heavily in a chair made of cedar poles and bottomed with interlaced strips of cowhide. It was a sturdy chair. It would last a long lifetime. He knew, because he had made it. Looking around, he thought of the years he had tied up in this place. Even while he was scouting for the Army he had put all his spare time out here working. Then after he quit the army and went to full time ranching he had done the work of two men day and night and was happy doing it. When he married Elaine and brought her out here, it seemed they owned their own piece of heaven. And in eight short months it became a bloodstained hell.

He shut his eyes against the memories crowding in and sipped at his coffee. Dutch Schreiber had no stomach for ranching now and no time for it. He spent his time stalking the mountains and deserts of the territory like a hungry cat searching for his prey, stopping only when a need for a grubstake brought him to the post for a job riding dispatch.

He reached for the coffee pot and poured another cup, blowing smoke off the top of it. He rolled a cigarette and lighted it and leaned back in the chair and relaxed. There was not much time to relax out there. A man rode trying to figure out what lay ahead and looking behind him at the same time. The Apaches had been quiet now for five or six months, since Victorio got himself trapped by the Mexican troops and fought his last fight in the Tres Castillos mountains. No marauding bands were reported stealing horses or cattle. No wagons had been plundered. But if a man knew Apaches, he worried most when they were quiet. It was not their nature to be peaceful. They were born into a society where status was acquired by killing and raiding and stealing. Before the White Eyes came the Apaches had made war on other Indians and even among themselves. Every Apache child from the day he was born had enemies and was, himself, a potential enemy to others. It was the natural order of things in Apacheria. At one time Dutch had convinced himself that with a little help and understanding the Apache would make a good neighbor. He knew better now.

He warmed up his coffee from the pot on the stove. Bill Jackson killed by a squaw. Wouldn't seem probable to those who didn't know Apaches. Dutch knew how dangerous a squaw could be. One had damned near done him in a few years back. He hadn't seen her. She was crouched against a rock with yucca leaves in her hair and a blanket covered with dust draped around her. She looked like part of the rock. Dutch and the troops were pulling back in a hurry from a raid through an Apache rancheria when he rode past the squaw. She grabbed him and nearly toppled him from the saddle. Her knife grazed his leg and buried itself in the rump of his horse. The horse had squealed and kicked, knocking the squaw flat, and he left her there reviling him in Apache. You didn't think of them as women. They were Apache. And now they were moving off the reservation, heading south toward the border, taking the kids and maybe some of the old men with them. That meant the warriors were getting ready for a fight.

That meant that the Apache shaman, Nochelte, was making his move. He had never seen the medicine man but over the past few years he had heard much about him. He knew that Nochelte had refused to follow Victorio when that bronco made his break with his Mimbreno warriors off of the San Carlos reservation. He knew that with Victorio dead after many bloody battles, some of the survivors of his people had drifted into the Apache camp on Cibecue Creek where Nochelte had his own wickiup. He suspected that Nochelte was about to achieve what no other Apache chief or shaman had ever achieved. If he read the signs right, Nochelte was molding the many splintered bands and tribes into some sort of loose organization, and there could be no doubting the purpose.

Dutch knew that Nochelte claimed that he could bring the great, long dead Apache chiefs back to life, that when the time was ripe they would rise from their graves and lead the Apache against the White Eyes. This was nonsense, of course, for even Dutch Schreiber, not a religious man, knew that only God himself could accomplish a resurrection, and even God had done it only once. That was not important. The important thing was that the Apaches, some of them, were beginning to believe Nochelte. This was the making of trouble. This could be the spark that set hell on fire. Give an Apache a gun, a little food, and a little hope, and you had yourself a war with no winners.

There was the sound of hoofs moving along the trail that stretched from the cabin to the sere basin below. Schreiber moved out of his chair, drawing his gun, listening. Only one horse, coming this way. He waited.

A rider came into view out of a clump of oak that choked the trail. He saw Schreiber's horse and halted and sat motionless a long moment, looking around. Finally he moved on up to the cabin and dismounted, warily, keeping the horse between himself and the cabin. He was a tall man, lean hipped and burned saddle brown by the desert heat.

The man called, "Jackson!"

Schreiber holstered his gun and stepped out. "He's not here, Jesse."

The man showed surprise at seeing Schreiber. Finally he said, "That kid's askin' for trouble with me. His cattle is on my water again. I've warned him twice now." He looked around. "Where is he?"

Schreiber pointed a thumb toward the willow grove over a half-mile away. "Down there. Dead."

The man's dark eyes narrowed suspiciously. "You have trouble with him?"

"No. Got himself killed by a squaw." Dutch studied the man. He had known Jesse Cogar a long time. He hadn't liked him when he first met him and the impression had not improved over the years. Cogar had come up out of Texas with a small herd of longhorns and a few horses and settled ten miles south of Schreiber's ranch. There was plenty of water there because the creek spilled into a natural sink, though the grass was poor quality and hard to find, even for Texas cattle. But Cogar had prospered and was getting a reputation for being a man of some substance.

Jesse Cogar reached for tobacco in his shirt pocket. "You said a squaw?"

Schreiber nodded. "He flushed a covey of them resting in the shade of the willows. Never knew what hit him."

Cogar lighted his smoke. "Goddamn. What are they doing off the reservation?"

"Movin' to the border, from what I see. Headin' for the mother mountains." Schreiber reached for his own tobacco. "That's just the first bunch. More comin', I think."

Cogar's brow wrinkled. He drew smoke deep and let it out. "I've said it before. Been too quiet."

Schreiber shrugged. "Who knows what they're up to. Mostly they move by how they feel. May be different now with Nochelte up there."

The tall man's eyes moved over the cabin, the pole corral off to one side, and the loafing shed inside the

corral. "Nochelte. Heard of him but not much." He
turned and looked down the green, sweeping slope of
the high valley pasture lying between the rolling foothills. "Reckon this place will be on the market." There
was a note of greed in Cogar's voice.

Dutch shrugged. "Could be. Guess the kid had folks
in Missouri where he came from. I'll get into Two
Wells in a couple of days and spread the word. Someone there may know."

Cogar dropped his cigarette and ground it out with a
heel. "About them cattle. I ain't figuring to furnish
them water. They'll be dead in three or four days
without it. Ways things are, they ain't worth five bucks
a head. Tell the marshal I'm takin' them over as abandoned stock and I'll deposit the money with the bank for
the relatives to claim."

Schreiber shook his head. "No."

Cogar's eyes were black stones in his dark face.
"No? What the hell you mean, no?"

Dutch moved out to the edge of the porch, looking
down at the man. "I mean, no. I'll send Max and a
couple of hands out for the cattle. There's not over fifty,
sixty head, as I remember. The Agency will buy them
and deposit the money in the bank for the next of kin."
He looked coldly at Cogar. "You want to make a claim
for furnishing water for three or four days, then turn it in
at the bank. Custom out here is to let a man's cows drink
free if you got more water than you need."

Cogar's face darkened. "To hell with custom. Those
cows are on my place. Nobody takes them unless I say
so."

Dutch felt the dislike for the man spreading within
him. It was like a stench in his nostrils. "Then maybe I
better come out with Max."

"What do you mean by that?"

Dutch smiled without humor. "I've got a mortgage on them cattle, and I aim to get paid. If I have to come out, Jesse, somebody is going to get killed. Maybe me, maybe you. Think on it."

Anger flashed across the man's face but faded quickly and he shrugged. "You're a crazy Dutchman. You'd risk gettin' killed over them mangy cows?"

Dutch nodded. "If I have to. What the hell? I risk gettin' killed every day."

Jesse Cogar turned and walked back to his horse. "Get them off my place and do it quick." He swung up into the saddle, looked at Schreiber and shook his head, then rode off down the trail.

Dutch sighed when the man disappeared into the timber. Some said that Jesse Cogar was quick with a gun. He didn't know about that. But the man was smart. He wouldn't risk a gunfight over fifty-odd starving cows. He didn't have to, because he was well fixed. But all Dutch had was his horse and saddle and a couple of guns and a four-hundred-dollar mortgage on the deceased Bill Jackson's herd.

He turned back into the cabin and cleaned up the coffee pot and his cup and put them away. He straightened the chair by the table. The door to the other room of the cabin, the bedroom, was closed, and he didn't open it. He stared at it a long moment, then turned away and went back outside, pulling the cabin door closed behind him. He walked to his horse and stood by it, looking back at the cabin. There was an uneasiness in him but he couldn't name the reason. Maybe it was old memories, or maybe it was knowing that young Bill Jackson was lying dead in a dry wash below with his head caved in. Or maybe it was knowing that the Apache shaman, Nochelte, was making his move. He got on his horse and rode off.

It was mid-afternoon when Dutch Schreiber rode into Camp Cache, and he and the dun were both feeling the miles they had put behind them. The post was an unseemly collection of pine log barracks with the officers' quarters and headquarters buildings constructed of unseasoned and unpainted wood. It had sprouted practically overnight when the Apaches were on the prowl, and the Army command decided that Fort Apache was too far away to control the western border of the huge White Mountain Reservation. It had been here nearly four years now, and Schreiber had come with the first troops to garrison it.

He rode up to the headquarters building and nodded to First Sergeant Quincy Shannon who was lounging against a pole that supported the wooden awning. The sergeant, a big, redhaired, slow-moving man, straightened slightly, studying Schreiber. Finally he said, "You're late."

Dutch swung out of the saddle and lifted the dispatch pouch from the saddle horn. "I reckon." He jerked a thumb toward the door. "Captain in there?"

Shannon shook his head. "In his quarters. Any trouble?"

Dutch said, "Not for me." He turned toward the captain's quarters.

The sergeant came off of the porch. "I'll walk over with you. Captain stays in his quarters when he can, now that his niece is here."

Dutch looked at him. "Niece?"

Shannon nodded. "Pretty woman. Came out from Pennsylvania. Taking a vacation."

Dutch shook his head. "Helluva place for a vacation."

"Strikes me so," Shannon agreed, "but she claims she loves it out here."

They reached the captain's quarters and Dutch knocked crisply on the door and stood back. The door opened and a middle-aged man with iron-gray hair looked out into the bright sunlight, squinting at the men. He said, "Hello, Dutch. Come inside. You, too, Quincy."

Schreiber moved inside of the shaded coolness of the room, the Sergeant easing in behind him. Schreiber said, "I'm runnin' late and beggin' your pardon, Captain." He handed the leather pouch to the officer. "Dispatch from Huachucca."

Captain Harry Roland had been in the Territory for ten years. Too long now to pay much attention to spit-and-polish discipline. He was in shirt sleeves with collar unbuttoned and the stub of a cigar clenched between his teeth. He motioned toward a couple of chairs across the room. "Have a seat, boys, while I read this."

A woman appeared in the doorway of the room leading into the kitchen. Dutch felt her presence even before he saw her and, looking up, stifled a grunt of surprise. He took off his hat and got up out of his chair.

The captain noticed her, too, and motioned her into the room. She was young and blond and perhaps, Dutch thought, the most beautiful woman he had ever seen. She moved forward gracefully, with no timidity, smiling, a pleasant but impersonal gesture. Dutch looked into the depths of the deep blue eyes, not missing a certain haughtiness in the tilt of her head, not holding it against her, either.

The Captain said, "Catherine, you know the sergeant. Meet Dutch Schreiber." He looked at Dutch. "Miss Catherine Roland, my niece."

The woman's smile warmed, looking at Dutch. "Mr. Schreiber. I've heard many stories about you."

Dutch felt color flooding his face. He looked at her squarely and smiled his own smile. "Believe what you see, ma'am. Out here, anyway."

Catherine Roland laughed softly and the sound was like music to Dutch. It had been a long time since he'd heard a young woman laugh.

"I'll remember that, Mr. Schreiber." She turned back toward the kitchen. "You men will want coffee."

She brought in cups for the three men and left to return with a steaming pot of coffee. She said, "It's noon coffee, but still fresh enough." She poured for each of them, serving Schreiber last, and then standing beside him for a moment. She said quietly, "You have a real friend in Max."

Schreiber jostled the cup in the saucer, spilling some. Carefully he lifted the cup, pouring coffee from the saucer back into the cup. "The Comanche boy?"

She nodded. "You saved his life. He told me about it."

Dutch flushed. "Accident, sort of. Happened by."

Captain Roland laid aside the reports. He was smiling, a relaxed smile, eyes moving over the two men and settling on his niece. "No Indian trouble reported anywhere in the Territory. For the first time since I've been out here the local papers are giving the Army some credit for bringing peace to this country."

Catherine Roland smiled. "I'm glad to hear that. It is

such a beautiful country." She went back into the kitchen.

Schreiber reached for his tobacco. He had known the captain for a long time, worked for him a long time. The captain would like to believe that crap he was reading but he was too smart for that. He had better be too smart to believe it or this country was in for hell, Apache style.

He touched a match to his cigarette. "Bill Jackson was killed by a squaw a few days ago. On his own place."

He heard the sergeant's breath whistle out and saw the captain's mouth pinch in. The sergeant's voice was brittle. "You took your damn sweet time tellin' it."

Dutch saw a hint of anger in the captain's gray eyes. The captain asked brusquely, "Did you see it happen?"

Schreiber shook his head. "Came on it this morning. He shot an Apache boy in a willow grove on his place and a squaw killed him with a rock. Don't figure he ever saw her. Big band of squaws and kids movin' south to the border."

Roland frowned irritably and stood up and stared out the window. "If you didn't see it, how do you know?"

Dutch flushed. "Aw, hell, Captain. You had me on the payroll for three years right here to read sign."

The officer turned from the window. "Dutch, the Apaches have been quiet now for over six months since Victorio was killed. We, the Army, have things under control for the first time. Whether or not an Apache squaw killed Bill Jackson is not the important thing now. If it happened, it's done. If he killed an Apache boy, maybe he had it coming. But if this gets out to the settlers, it will grow in the telling until it's a full fledged outbreak. Then the civilians out here will be shootin' at every Indian they see, and we'll have us another Apache war. I've seen it happen before.''

Quincy looked at Schreiber. ''Anybody else know about this?''

Dutch nodded. ''Jesse Cogar. I came across him at the Jackson place.'' He eyed the captain, feeling a tinge of disappointment. Maybe the captain did believe what he read in the papers. He said, ''I've said my piece a time or two before, Captain, about the medicine man, the Apache called Nochelte. He's pullin' the bands together and it isn't just for a powwow. I said he ought to be picked up by the troops and brought here to the post for questioning and maybe a spell in the guardhouse. Too late, now. From the sign I read, you haven't got enough men to take him.'' He pinched out his smoke. ''Hell, it's not my business. I don't work regular for the Army anymore.''

Roland sat back in his chair and reached for his coffee. ''Dutch, I don't question your idea that Jackson was killed by a squaw. I never questioned your concern over the medicine man. But I don't run this Army exactly like I want to run it. I get orders from Fort Apache and Fort Apache gets order from Willcox and Willcox gets orders from Sherman in Washington. Washington has suddenly decided that it's costing too much to keep an army out here. Every time they read in the paper up there that the Indians are peaceful out here, we lost another company or two of troops. My orders are to keep things quiet, and I usually carry out my orders.''

Schreiber shrugged and smiled and then stood up. ''Your problem, Captain. Thanks for the ridin' job. I won't be around for a while.''

The captain's face relaxed. He stood up and held out his hand. "Good luck, Dutch. I hope you kill the sonofabitch this time out."

Dutch shook hands with Roland, seeing the sympathy in the man's eyes and appreciating it. "Thanks, Captain. I figure to stay out until I do it."

Dutch started toward the door when the captain's voice caught him. "Dutch, one favor. Don't talk it up that the Apaches are leavin' the reservation. We don't know it for sure yet."

Schreiber nodded. "I'll have to tell the marshal about Jackson. He's smart enough to figure out most of it, himself, but he's not a talkin' man."

"What about Cogar?"

Dutch shrugged. "Jesse?" He thought a moment, then said, "I don't think he gives a damn. If the Apaches break out, he'll take care of himself, and maybe find a way to make a profit out of it. He's that kind of man." He moved through the door feeling a little sorry for the captain. Time was when the captain would have mounted a patrol and checked out the reservation and sent a burying detail out for Jackson. The Territory was changing.

An Indian boy dressed in cowboy boots, Levis, and unbuttoned, ragged shirt, leaned on the rail of the porch. "Ho, Dutch." The boy was grinning.

Schreiber scowled. "Goddamn it, Max, button your shirt. That lady in there come out, she'll be staring at your navel."

Still grinning, the boy buttoned his shirt. "Good trip, Dutch?"

Schreiber didn't answer. He reached in his pocket and brought out a thin roll of bills. He peeled off a five and handed it to Max. "Ride over to the Sanchez place and get a couple of hands to help you drive Bill Jackson's cows down to the San Carlos Agency. Only fifty or sixty head. They've strayed over on Cogar's place but he's expectin' you and I'm guessin' he'll have them bunched and waitin'. He ain't the kind of man to let someone ride over his place huntin' strays.''

He pulled tobacco and papers from his pocket and rolled a smoke. ''Tell the agent to put the money to Jackson's account in the Two Wells bank.''

Max looked at the five in his hand and then at Schreiber. ''Hokay with Jackson we take them cows?''

''He don't care,'' Dutch growled. ''He's dead.'' He looked at the boy. ''I'm nightin' with Luis Redoza. He's got an Apache wife. I'll be in Two Wells tomorrow afternoon. When you get your job done, come on into town. If I'm drunk, sober me up.''

Max grinned. ''Been a long time you last drunk.''

Dutch grinned back. ''I'm overdue.'' He watched as the boy moved off across the post toward the stable. He felt a presence behind him and turned to see Quincy Shannon.

The Sergeant said, ''You've got the captain worried.''

Schreiber drew smoke from his cigarette. ''I hope so. What about you?''

Shannon shrugged. ''I don't worry, anymore. I just take orders from the captain.''

Dutch eyed the sergeant narrowly. ''That's what's wrong with the whole damned Army. Everybody passes it on to Sherman to worry about, and he ain't ever been out here.'' He tossed away the stub of his cigarette. ''Can I get twenty round of Spencer cartridges? I'm seeing Luis Redoza and he's always out of ammunition.''

Shannon nodded. "Stop by Ordinance on the way out. Tell Corporal Hayes I said it was okay." He looked at Dutch. "Take care of yourself."

Schreiber nodded. "You do the same." He turned and headed for his horse.

Cathy Roland stood by the window looking out at Dutch Schreiber talking to the Comanche boy, Max. In the week that she had been here, she had talked to Max several times. She had never seen an Indian before, and though he was young and dressed and talked as a white man, she was still intrigued by him.

He had told her that he was captured by the Apaches when he was very young. When he was old enough to take care of himself, he ran away from his Apache captors to rejoin his own people on the Texas plains. Two days out of the Apache camp some cowboys saw him and started chasing him and shooting at him. He was badly wounded but managed to escape. Then he fell off of his horse and knew that he was going to die. He lost consciousness.

When he came to his senses again, Dutch Schreiber was sitting by him. Dutch stayed with him, caring for him, until he could travel again. That had been six years ago and he had been with Dutch ever since. When Dutch rode dispatch, Max stayed at the post and the Army fed him.

She remembered one thing Max had said and she wondered about it because it came out casually and with no elaboration. "When Dutch married that Tucson woman, Elaine, it wasn't the same anymore, and I knew I was going to leave him."

He hadn't said anything else about it. Maybe he felt excluded because of the natural closeness between the man and his wife. Or maybe the woman had resented Max and somehow made it clear that he was not welcome. Cathy wondered about it. And then Elaine was killed and Max said Dutch went crazy. Crazy for a long time, but he was better now. Soon as he killed the Indian who murdered his wife, Max was sure he'd be the same old Dutch again. She wondered.

Cathy thought of Schreiber, stalking the Apache who had killed his wife, surviving in that wild and desolate land that stretched bleak and empty from her window. She thought about her father, now three years dead, and his passion for the Apache and Navajo Indian tribes. He had been an anthropologist and his study of these tribes had been his private hobby. He had hoped to make it a serious project, but there was no financial backing for it.

She could remember him saying, "They are the same people. Somewhere, sometime, they split apart. The Navajos became farmers and shepherds and the Apaches raiders and warriors. The Apache, fighting on his own land, is the best guerilla fighter in the world today." And Schreiber was hunting down one of them, facing all of them. It was a grim prospect.

Cathy was watching Schreiber as he rode out of the post when she heard her uncle say, "What do you think of Dutch Schreiber, Cathy?"

She flushed, turning from the window. "He is not an easy man to know."

The Captain nodded. "He's blazing his own trail. He won't come to the end of it until he finds the Indian." He stuck a fresh cigar in his mouth. "Day after tomorrow we go to Two Wells to spend the night with the Brewers. I hope you enjoy the dance."

Cathy smiled at him. "I will, Uncle Roland. I love

everything about this place, this red country. It's so wild and natural and exciting."

He grunted. "It can be lonely, too."

She nodded. "I know. Like the men who ride it."

CHAPTER TWO

Nochelte stood on the edge of the meadow where the ceremonial dances were held each night. There were many wickiups to be seen. Many others were hidden in the timber of the creek bordering the meadow land. Squaws in brightly colored, ankle-length skirts busied themselves around the evening cooking fires. Children, hungry from playing games, were straggling in bunches toward their lodgings, laughing and yelling at each other, and followed by numerous dogs of various sizes and colors. Warriors in small groups squatted on their heels and talked and smoked tobacco rolled in oak leaves. It was a good thing to look upon and Nochelte was warmed by the peace and tranquility of it. It looked as all Apache camps had looked before the White Eyes came.

His attention was directed now toward another small group of men isolated from the main camp. They were gathered around a small fire on the bare point of land formed by a sharp bend in the creek. These were the chiefs of some of the many bands of Apache. Summoned here by Nochelte they had responded and drifted into the reservation during the past week. Some had brought most of their followers with them, some had brought only a half-dozen or less of their best warriors.

All of them knew of Nochelte but some of them did not believe that he was a great shaman. They had come out of curiosity or boredom to take advantage of a break in the monotony of their lives. Victorio was dead and with his death their hopes for defeating the White Eyes had died also.

Nochelte looked into the setting sun and asked the Great God for guidance and wisdom that he might weld these splintered bands into a great Apache nation. The Apaches had been a great nation once. True, they had always feuded among themselves as separate bands, but, confronted with a common enemy, they had fought together in the past. True, also, that the Comanches had defeated them on the open plains and pushed them into this country, now called Apacheria. That was no discredit to the Apache as a warrior. The Comanches outnumbered them three to one and the Comanches were at their best fighting on horseback.

The Apache could not compete with them on the open plains. The Apache rode horses but merely as a convenience. The horse was a walking commissary, ridden today, eaten tonight, if the Apache belly was empty. But in this country, this ragged, rolling land of mountains and canyons, the Apache was supreme. All that was needed was unity of the bands. Nochelte, with the help of the Great God, could supply the weapons. He moved across the meadow, making his way toward the camp of the chiefs.

He advanced into the camp noiselessly, raising a hand in greeting. He said, "Some of you have been here many nights. You grow impatient to hear from me."

An old, heavy-bellied Apache with skin like wrinkled parchment, puffed on a long-stemmed pipe, looking at Nochelte through slitted lids. "I have known the Prophet a long time now. I have seen him heal the sick. I have seen blood stop running from an open wound at his command. I have sat with him beside a fire such as this on a dark night when he prayed one of our dead chiefs back from the shadow world and caused him to stand before me." He paused and spat and looked at the others around the campfire. "The Prophet will speak when he wishes to speak and I will wait to listen."

A slender, bare-chested Apache, squatting on his heels, gestured impatiently. He stood up and pointed toward the old Apache. "Nana can afford the time to wait. He has lived more than a lifetime already. I have much to do. My people are hungry. I cannot lay around this camp any longer. Six months past, Nochelte send word to me to leave the White Eyes alone, to let their wagons move across our land, to let their cattle eat our grass. He said he had a plan to return our country to us. Many times since then he has sent a messenger to me telling me to be patient, that soon he would call us together for big medicine. Now we are here and he will not speak. I will not be in this camp when the sun rises in the morning."

A stocky, grim-faced Apache, wearing a dirty white tunic and breechclout, paced restlessly around the fire. He looked at Nochelte and shook a finger in his direction. "Geronimo is no fool that he would stop plundering the White Eyes because Nochelte says he has a plan. There have been plans before and they did not work. Each year our land grows smaller and our game more scarce. I have not raided because many of my men have been killed, many have been wounded, and most of us have no rifles that will shoot. I am not here to listen to the Prophet. I am here to invite some of the young men to join me and to buy rifles from anyone who will sell. We cannot fight the White Eyes with rocks and clubs as we do the Mexicans. We must have guns."

Nochelte moved in closer to the fire. He squatted before it and looked around the circle of chiefs. He said quietly, "It is good to know that Nana is with me. The Mimbrenos are brave warriors and not afraid to die if dying is necessary." He looked directly at the slender, bare-chested Apache. "Natchez has a right to be impatient but I ask him for one more day. That is all. It would be a great loss to the Apache if his Chiricahuas were not with me, for they are great fighters, and he is a great chief."

He pointed a finger at the stocky Apache. "I was surprised that Geronimo came to this camp, for I did not expect his help. Even among his own people he is what the White Eyes called a 'bronco'." He fixed a steady stare on the grim-visaged Apache. "Geronimo will take no warriors from this camp until my plan has been heard and a vote taken. After that, he may take any who wish to leave." He paused, and his eyes swept over them. "If any go with him, the plan will not succeed."

Natchez, mellowed by Nochelte's praise of himself and his warriors, shrugged now and nodded. "What is one more day? I will stay."

Nochelte rose. "Enjuh! You are entitled to know why I wait. I wait for Juh."

Geronimo scowled. "Juh? He is across the border. He is in the mother mountains with all of his Nednis around him. I visited him there three moons ago."

Nochelte shook his head. "Juh is a half-day ride from this camp. Before the sun sets tomorrow he will be here. He will be riding a white pony."

Natchez looked doubtful. "How can you know?

What if he is not here tomorrow?''

Nochelte looked at each of them. ''Then I am not your Prophet and my plan is worthless. I will no longer make medicine for the Apache.''

Geronimo laughed. ''Enjuh!'' He looked at Nochelte, a grin making a thin slash across his face. ''If Juh comes in riding a white pony, that will not put food in my belly. We are here to buy or trade for guns.'' He scowled at Nochelte, ''But I will stay another day and listen.''

Nochelte smiled. ''It will be a great day for the Apache if Geronimo listens to anyone other than Geronimo.''

There was laughter around the campfire. Nana pulled a burning stick from the fire and lighted his pipe. ''Remember he is a Bedonkohe, stubborn like the mule, but a good traveler if he is going your way.''

Nochelte looked at them impassively. ''I will leave you now. We will meet here tomorrow when Juh arrives.'' He turned and made his way over the faint trail winding through the timber toward his wickiup.

There was a hunger in him but it was not for food. He hungered for this land, his people's land, and for the welfare of the Apache tribes. They were here to listen to him and he must say the words that would hold them together.

And suppose Juh did not come into the camp tomorrow? He dismissed the thought. Juh had received word of this meeting. Juh was a great chief and a responsible leader. He would be here. Had he not dreamed of Juh only last night? A vision of Juh on a white pony leading a dozen of his finest warriors into the canyons of the Salt River.

He thought about the silver. Two thousand pounds of

it. Twenty large bars of it hidden in a small cave on the south side of the reservation. It represented guns and ammunition for the Apache warriors. Fine guns, repeating rifles, better arms than the horse soldiers carried. He smiled in the darkness. Tomorrow that silver would be on the way to Mexico, if the Apache leaders approved of his plan.

He crawled into his wickiup and sat there in darkness for a moment, thinking, listening for word from the Great God, a God more powerful than Ussen whom the Apaches worshipped. A God who directed all lesser gods and ruled over all of the peoples in the world. A God who spoke to one Apache, Nochelte.

The Great God was angry with the White Eyes, for they had seized the land of the Apache and plundered it, carrying off its precious metals, killing its game, tearing down its forests, and making prisoners of the Apache. Through him, Nochelte, the Great God would work his vengeance on the Americanos and restore this land to his red children. He had given Nochelte the power. Not just Bear power, or Coyote power, or Snake power, like so many lesser shamans had, but All power. He had told Nochelte to take this land from the White Eyes.

He groped in the darkness for his candle and found it. He lighted it and reached for a worn and tattered book beside his blanket. An eagle's feather marked the page he sought, and he opened the book and read:

"This day will I begin to put the dread of thee and the fear of thee upon the nations that are under the whole heaven, who shall hear report of thee, and shall tremble, and be in anguish because of thee."

These were the words of the Great God. But the Great God had not spoken to him in several days. He worried about this.

The sun was low and blood red when Dutch Schreiber came upon the Redoza rancheria. It was a small, patched-up house with a flimsy corral that held a couple of mules. Not far from the house, a half dozen sheep searched for grass. Luis Redoza was Mexican and time-less. He could have been fifty or half again that old. His wife was Apache, Coyotera, and plump and smooth of face. The Mexicans and Apaches had been natural enemies for years before the white man came out here. And yet they often intermarried. Dutch wondered about this as he rode into the yard and reined up.

Redoza was standing in the open door of the house when Dutch dismounted. He smiled, "Salude, amigo. A long time you not visit Luis."

Dutch grinned and led the dun to the corral where there was a stone watering trough filled with clear water. He stripped off the saddle and bridle and slapped the dun on the rump. "Get some rest."

He walked back to the house, fishing in his pocket for the Spencer cartridges. Finding them, he handed them to Luis. "Maybe a young rabbit for supper tonight."

The Mexican's face lighted up. "No rabbit for my friend, Dutch. It will be venison. A young buck has been marauding my garden but he will be on the table tonight." He flashed a smile, and looking back into the house he called, "Senora, we have a guest."

Dutch moved inside the dim light of the house. The woman was seated on a cane chair peeling turnips. She looked up as Dutch entered. Her eyes flashed a friendly recognition but she did not smile or speak. Dutch took off his hat. "It has been a long time, senora."

She nodded silently.

Luis took his rifle off of the wall. "I will fetch the venison." He pointed to a small table on which set a basket made of reeds and straw, coated with resin. "Tiswin, my friend. It will wash the dust from your throat and liven your spirits."

It was a slow thing, getting information from the woman. Dutch knew, like all Apaches living off the reservation by special permission of the Army, Bana went back to it occasionally to visit friends and family. First, he complimented her on her home, then on the fine turnips she had grown, and finally he wondered that she looked younger than when he last saw her. When she began to smile and grunt in response, he brought from his vest pocket a small mirror backed with beaded doeskin. She took it and looked at herself and tilted her head. "Enjuh, Dutch!"

He grinned and walked over to the door. Luis was out of sight. He said, "It was many moons ago that I last visited here, Bana. I was looking for the Apache who killed my wife. The trail has been empty." He turned to face her. "You have visited your people on the reservation many times since then. Is there anything you can tell me?"

He thought that she was not going to answer, but finally she said, "I have heard of it. A man named Torres."

He frowned. "Many Apaches are named Torres."

She gathered the turnip peelings and walked to the back door of the house and threw them out upon the garden. "He is Mimbreno. He was with Victorio. He did not run with Nana when Victorio was killed. He went to the reservation.''

Dutch was quiet a long moment. He could not push her. Finally he asked, ''Is he there now?''

She shrugged, avoiding his eyes. ''I do not know where he is. I hear that he follows Nochelte. I have never seen him.''

That was the end of it. At least it was something. He went outside to the corral and fed the dun. He found an ax and chopped a little kindling for the cook stove. He was putting a new edge on the ax by lantern light when Luis rode up on a mule. Draped over the mule in front of him was the dressed out carcass of a small deer. Luis smiled. ''We eat late tonight, amigo, but we eat well.''

Dutch said solemnly, ''Gracias. I have not eaten well in many days.'' He pointed to the large garden behind the Redoza house. ''The corn is drying. The beans have shriveled. You need rain and the dry season will be around for three or four more weeks. Can you bring water from the creek?''

Luis Redoza shook his head. ''It is too much trouble. It takes too long. We plant much and harvest a little. Enough to get by. Last year, when Nochelte stopped by, he made it rain in the dry season and we had a large harvest.''

Schreiber blinked. ''Nochelte? He was here?''

Luis Redoza nodded. ''He had been on a long ride. Stopped by here for water and we fed him. He is big medicine man, my wife say. I apologized for the poor quality of our vegetables and he walked out and looked at the garden. He said we needed rain and I agreed. That night it rained and it was the dry season. My wife, she say, Nochelte made it rain. Maybe so.''

It was late afternoon when Schreiber rode into Two

Wells. He had spent the night at the Redoza place and much of this day, but he did not pick up any more information. He told them about Bill Jackson being killed. He asked if they knew whether an outbreak was in the planning. They professed to know nothing. Schreiber couldn't really blame them if they withheld information. Luis, with an Apache wife, would be spared any depredation by the Apache. The woman, married to Luis, would not be considered a hostile by the Army. Their life, such as it was, could be lived in peace, unless they took sides. He did not blame them for not wanting to get involved.

Moving the dun slowly down the dusty, rutted street, he saw the man he was looking for standing on the boardwalk in front of the marshal's office. He reined the dun that way and, coming to the boardwalk, he swung out of the saddle, tying the horse's reins loosely to the hitching rail in front of the office.

The tall, sparely built man with the star pinned on his shirt said, "Dutch, you look somewhat used up. Hear you been ridin' dispatch again."

Schreiber stepped up on the walk. "You heard the truth, Marshal." He had a good deal of respect for this lawman, Rusty Welch. Mostly Two Wells was a quiet, almost sleepy little town. But sometimes a tough one would drift in and stir things up. When that happened, the townfolks appreciated Rusty's quiet efficiency.

The lawman turned toward the door of his office. "Come in and sit a spell."

Dutch rolled a smoke and lighted it and followed the marshal inside the small, sparsely furnished room. Two Wells didn't believe in providing for the comfort of the law. An ancient desk, a couple of chairs, an old safe, and a pot-bellied wood stove was all of it. A shotgun and a rifle were racked on the wall but the guns were

Rusty's own property as well as the .44 strapped around his thin waist.

Rusty Welch kicked back a chair and eased into it, motioning Dutch to do likewise. "What's stirring with our red friends?"

Dutch drew on his cigarette. "Nothin', accordin' to the Army."

The lawman eyed Schreiber closely, "Ain't the way I read it."

Dutch shrugged. "Band of squaws and kids left the reservation headin' south. They killed Bill Jackson. His fault. He spooked and shot a kid."

The marshal was silent a moment. Finally he said, "Headin' south, huh? And that don't bother the Army?"

Schreiber shook his head. "Washington wants to believe the Apache trouble is over and the Army big-wigs don't want to upset the powers in Washington. They're pullin' out troops, discharging Apaches who were scoutin' for them, and makin' damn sure the local officers and troops don't do anything to start a ruckus. Roland, the post captain, knows it ain't over yet, but there's not much he can do."

Welch stuffed tobacco in an old briar pipe and laid it on the desk. "Hell, folks ridin' in and out of here every day report seein' hostiles off the reservation. Mimbrenos, Mescaleros, and some Chiricahuas. No raidin' or plunderin' reported but they're movin' and that means something is up. Must be five, six hundred Indians in that Apache camp on the reservation. It ain't a social gatherin' for sure because them different bands don't like each other all that much."

Schreiber rubbed out his cigarette in the tin lid of a coffee can on the desk. "It's the Prophet."

"The what?"

"The medicine man, Nochelte. They call him the Prophet, or maybe he calls himself that, I don't know. You never heard of him?"

The lawman shook his head. "I've heard rumors of some big medicine being made on the Cibecue, lots of dancing and tiswin drinking. Put that together with so many different bands moving in up there and you can figure trouble with or without a Prophet. You know anything about this Nochelte?"

Schreiber nodded. "He's a mission Indian. Went to school in Santa Fe when he as a kid. Scouted for General Crook in the early Seventies. Story has it he told Crook one day that the Great God had spoken to him and told him to go out and help his people, and he just disappeared for a while. Next time I heard of him he had the Cibecue tribes believing in him. Now most of the Mimbrenos are behind him and he's working on the Chiricahuas and Nednis."

Schreiber stood up. "I think he's bad trouble." He turned toward the door. "Be obliged if you'd check on Bill Jackson's next of kin. Maybe get word to them. I got Max out roundin' up his stock. He'll sell them to the agent at San Carlos and put the money to Jackson's credit in the bank."

The marshal finally lighted his pipe, looking at Schreiber over the flame of the match. "You can get in trouble selling another man's cows."

Dutch scowled. "I got a mortgage on them and it says if I believe they are in danger I can take possession. They wouldn't last three days out there with nobody watchin' them."

The marshal grinned. "That's for sure. It's your problem." He drew on his pipe. "Fellow down at the hotel was looking for you. Comes out of Globe working for the smelter company.''

"Say what he wanted?''

"He wants to talk about that missing shipment of silver bars. Near thirty thousand dollars worth, he says.''

Schreiber shrugged. "Hell, I haven't got them.''

The lawman stood up. "He knows that. He wants you to find them.''

Dutch moved out the door. "Not me. I got a job to do.''

He walked the dun across the street to the livery stable and checked in with the hostler, then headed for the saloon. He went inside and moved to the bar, feeling the need for strong drink.

Brownie Malone, proprietor, barkeep and swamper, looked at Schreiber with dark, somber eyes that were like black holes in his gray wizened face. He said, "Long time, Dutch.''

"Too long,'' Schreiber growled. "Give me a bottle of Crow.''

Malone set out a fresh bottle, then reached for a glass. "Drinkin' here?''

Dutch shook his head. "I'm gettin' me a room at the hotel and I'm stayin' in it until I catch up on my sleepin' and my drinkin'.'' He paid for the whiskey and carried the bottle, neck down, as he moved down the boardwalk to the Oasis Hotel.

He went inside the hotel and saw that the desk clerk was a new face to him, a young man with too much flesh on him for his own comfort. Dutch said, "Goddamn, boy, you ought to be ridin' dispatch.''

The young man blinked at Dutch. "Beg pardon, sir?''

Schreiber said, "Nothin'. Not my business. I'm Dutch Schreiber. Be here two or three days."

He signed the register that the clerk shoved at him, picked up his key and, turning toward the stairs, almost collided with the short, heavy-set man in a dark suit. The man said, "You're Dutch Schreiber?"

Schreiber jerked a thumb toward the register. "That's what I wrote down."

The short man flushed. "I am Dawson. Alfred Dawson, with the Globe Smelting Company. I came here to see you, Mr. Schreiber, but was afraid I'd missed you. We heard you stayed around Two Wells."

Dutch looked the man over carefully. This was the man Rusty Welch had mentioned. He said, "Friend, will it keep until morning? I'm tired and I'm thirsty." He held up the bottle.

The short man shook his head, frowning. "I'm on the stage for Globe within the hour, sir. I'd appreciate talking with you before I leave. I—uh, have a proposition that I hope will interest you."

Dutch looked at the bottle. "I know what you want and I'm obliged to you but I have to say that this bottle is more to my liking, Mr. Dawson. I've been ridin' dispatch. Have you ever ridden dispatch?"

Dawson's lips tightened. "No. No, indeed. But there is this silver shipment that was stolen and we need to find it very badly. We will pay you one hundred a month for three months and your expenses. If you find it, there will be a bonus of ten percent of the value, perhaps as much as three thousand dollars."

Dutch looked at the young hotel clerk. "Son, have you got a glass?"

The clerk jerked nervously, startled. "Glass? Why—?" He saw Dutch twisting the cork out of the bottle of Crow whiskey. "Glass?" His round face turned red in anger. "No, sir. No glass. Not here in the lobby."

A pained expression crossed the short man's face. "Mr. Schreiber, if you would just sit down with me for ten minutes. Give me a chance to talk. Then make up your mind."

Dutch shrugged. What was ten minutes? He had the night in front of him. He shoved the cork back into the bottle and set it on the clerk's counter. "You talk. I'll listen."

The short man nodded and motioned to a couple of high-backed cane chairs in the corner of the hotel lobby. Dutch followed the man over to the chairs, wondering why he was taking the time. He had a job that needed doing and nothing else mattered until it was done.

Dawson eased himself into a chair and took cigars from his coat pocket. He handed one to Dutch. He said, "You saw the marshal. That's how you knew I wanted to see you and what I wanted."

Dutch bit off the end of the cigar. He spat it out. "Right."

The room was stuffy. The short man drew a white linen handkerchief from his coat pocket and patted beads of perspiration from his face. "I needn't say that the loss of a wagon load of silver bullion is of major concern to my company. There have been attempted holdups before, but none have succeeded. If this one succeeds it will encourage others to try. So, it's not just the loss of this particular shipment that concerns us so much as what may happen in the future."

Schreiber studied his cigar. "That holdup took place three months ago and the sheriff has had men out tryin' to find the shipment. Your company has had men out lookin' for it. I'd figure it's clean out of the Territory by now.''

Dawson shook his head. ''A ton of pure silver cast in one hundred pound bars is not easy to move, Mr. Schreiber. It's not easy to dispose of, either. As you no doubt heard, the company driver and guard were shot to death and the outlaws took the wagon. But where? A bullion wagon does not move fast. The holdup was discovered within a half-day of its happening. The bandits had three ways to go. They could try to move across open country south to the border and dispose of the bullion in Mexico. We know they did not do that. If they had connections back east they could freight the bars to Silver City and put them on a train. That route has been well covered. That just leaves one alternative.''

Dutch grinned faintly. ''They moved into the canyon country and cached the stuff until things quiet down.''

Dawson nodded. ''Exactly. The bullion is around here somewhere. A bunch of riders scrambling around can destroy more tracks than they can find. One man, a good tracker, might locate it. After we figured that much of it, we decided you were the man. You know the country and you have a reputation for staying on a trail.'' He puffed on his cigar and smiled. ''Besides, we knew you had lost your Army job and weren't working steady.''

Up until then Dutch felt himself getting mildly interested. He could track Torres and maybe track the bullion at the same time. Paths had a way of crossing. But Dawson thought he had him cornered and needed the work, and a cool anger swept over him. He said quietly, ''I'm working on a steady job.''

Dawson's smile faded. "That's too bad. We're offerin' quite a lot of money. We need—"

Schreiber stood up. "Obliged for the offer, but no thanks." He turned back toward the clerk's counter. "Son, you're new around here. Where's Paddy Ryan?"

The young man blinked. "Gone to Illinois. Visitin' his brother. I'm just temporary until he gets back."

Dutch picked up his bottle. "Don't ever let Paddy know you said there would be no drinkin' in the lobby."

He moved toward the stairs when he heard the door open behind him and someone said, "Schreiber, what kind of damn fool do you think I am?"

Dutch turned around. Jesse Cogar moved inside the room, face dark with anger. Dutch studied the man. "I don't know, Jesse. What kind are you?"

Cogar's hands clenched into fists. "You set that little red bastard out to prowl my range. I had them Jackson cows bunched and waitin' for him. Nobody checks my herd without my sayso."

Schreiber moved back toward the clerk's counter and set down his whiskey. "I told him you'd have them bunched. How many head?"

Cogar moved closer toward the counter. "Forty-three by my count. He and the Sanchez brothers moved them out but came sneakin' back and I caught him ten miles inside my boundaries. He said I'd shorted him. He said you told him there would be fifty, sixty head."

Dutch nodded, eyeing the man. "I was guessin'. He knows better than to check another man's herd without permission. I'll get on him."

Cogar grinned tightly. "I done it for you. I whipped hell out of him."

A coldness settled over Schreiber. He moved toward Cogar. "You did what?"

"I fist-whipped him and ran his red ass off my place."

Dutch stepped forward quickly and his right hand whistled upward in a vicious uppercut that caught Cogar on the jaw and rammed him reeling into the wall. Dutch said tightly, "Max is a mite small for you, Jesse. I'm more your size."

Cogar lurched away from the wall and his hand swept down to his forty-five, but Schreiber's voice stopped him. "You put that on the counter and I'll do the same, or you make your draw and I'll gutshoot you. Makes no difference to me."

The clerk waddled out from behind the counter waving pudgy hands. "Gentlemen, please! No fighting in here."

Schreiber said, "Shut up, son. Paddy Ryan would love it."

Jesse Cogar unbuckled his gunbelt and slapped it on the counter. He glared at Schreiber. "You been askin' for this a long time."

Schreiber put his own gun on the counter. "I can usually handle what I ask for, Cogar. Let's try it."

The clerk moved toward the door. "I'll get the law on you."

Rusty Welch appeared in the doorway. "The law is here, boy." He look at Dutch and then at Cogar. "You men pick up your guns and go about your business, if you got any business. Otherwise, get out of town. I don't want any fighting. Fighting leads to killin' and it plumb riles me to have a man killed in my town."

Cogar said thickly, "The sonofabitch sent his Indian out to check my herd."

The marshal shook his head. "I don't give a damn about the particulars. No fighting in Two Wells. You want to fight, get outside the town limits."

Jesse Cogar looked at Schreiber and then at the marshal. "It will keep." He walked over and picked up his gun and strapped it on. He said, "Dutch, you figure Jackson had more than forty-three head, you come out and try to find them."

Schreiber picked up his own gun. He said, "You've given me the invite, Jesse."

Marshal Welch moved inside, out of the doorway. "Dutch, if you all ain't goin' to kill each other right now, there's a lady in my office wants to see you."

Schreiber stared at the lawman. "Lady? To see me? About what?"

Welch raised his hands. "Christ, I don't know. About a lot of things. She's Bill Jackson's sister. Just got off the stage and came straight to my office to get directions to his ranch. I had to tell her. After she got herself in hand, which took a spell, she said she wanted to see you. You found the body."

It didn't seem logical. The next of kin, or part of it, was in town already. Jackson wasn't much over three days dead. And there, setting on the counter, the bottle of Crow whiskey was getting further away from him. He swore silently and looked at the clerk. He said, "Take damned good care of that bottle. I'll be back." He looked at Welch. "Well, hell. Let's get it over with."

Bill Jackson's sister was sitting in the marshal's office when he went inside. She had a heavy leather traveling bag beside her. She was young and dressed in a dark blue traveling dress with a wide-brimmed straw hat practically concealing her dark hair. She was pretty and she was crying.

Dutch pulled off his own battered hat. "Dutch Schreiber, ma'am. You wanted to see me?"

She looked at him through brimming eyes, dabbing them dry with a white handkerchief. "Please sit down."

Schreiber sat down in the only other chair. The marshal lounged against the wall. Dutch was quiet, trying to think of something to say.

The woman said, "You were the one who found him?"

Dutch nodded slightly. "Bad thing to come on. Bad thing for you coming in on it like this. Bill expectin' you?"

She nodded. "I wrote him three weeks ago. I—well, I planned to sell the family farm in Missouri and join him out here if I liked the country."

Dutch studied the brim of his hat. What could you say to a woman who had just lost her brother. "Too bad."

She looked at him. "You tell me how it happened."

He shrugged. "Ma'am, I wasn't there. Came on it a day later, maybe more. I read sign. Well—what I mean is when you been out here as long as I have, you learn to notice things. There was Bill with his head caved in, and there was this Apache boy with his stomach blown out with a rifle shot. There was all those squaw tracks in the willow grove, and you just kind of figure how it happened. Bill rode into them and thought he was surrounded by hostiles. He just naturally started shooting and killed the kid. He never saw the squaw behind him. Squaws are mite near as mean as the bucks. She dropped him with a rock."

Her eyes never wavered. "How can you be sure?

How do you know some rustler didn't kill him? He wrote to me that he was losing cattle.''

Dutch shrugged. ''Ma'am, rustlers don't fight with rocks.''

Ruth Jackson glanced toward the marshal. ''Are you satisfied?''

Welch nodded. ''Ma'am, I never questioned it. If Dutch says it happened that way, then it did. He ain't often wrong about Apaches.''

Her dark eyes looked as though she were still crying, but her chin was firm and her voice steady when Ruth Jackson said, ''I must get out to the ranch. Bill should have a proper funeral.''

Dutch reached for his tobacco. ''You do as you like, ma'am, but it isn't a safe place to be out there. My advice is to put the place on the market and catch the stage back home.''

A hint of anger stirred within the woman's dark eyes, color flushed her cheeks. ''And never see the place that my brother loved, that cost him his life?''

Dutch touched a match to his smoke, looking at her. She was a fine figure of a woman. Not beautiful like Cathy Roland, not even as pretty as Elaine, but a good-looking woman, nevertheless, and she had a temper. He said, ''Bill wasn't the first to die for that ranch. You go out there and get yourself killed and it's a waste of a fine-lookin' woman.''

Ruth looked at the marshal. ''Surely someone here can take me out there. I've traveled nearly fifteen hundred miles to get here. I own the ranch now. I may want to live on it or I may want to sell it. I can't know what to do until I see it. There must be someone—''

Dutch began to squirm a little inside. She was putting the pressure on as only a woman can, and part of what she said made some sense. She ought to see that place, all right, but it was foolish to consider that she might live out there by herself. He looked at Welch who was fishing for his pipe.

The marshal shrugged. "Dutch gave you good advice, ma'am. It's no place for a woman, not with things shaping up for an Apache outbreak. But if you are set on it, I'll find someone to drive you out. It's fifteen miles out there and not much of a road, so it'll be a hard seat on the wagon. You'll have to spend the night because you can't make it there and back in one day and have time to see anything. I'll pick a man you can trust."

Ruth Jackson stood up. "Thank you, Marshal. Unless the man prefers a wagon, we could go horseback. I ride well enough." She looked at Dutch. "I'm sorry you are not taking me. You know where Bill was killed. You know the ranch better than anyone else. Bill mentioned you often in his letters. He was grateful for the help you gave him in getting started. I know he still owes you money."

Dutch ground out his cigarette. "Can't bring myself to take a woman out there, ma'am. Like Rusty said, we may be in for some Indian trouble. I wouldn't want to think of you out there if the Apaches break off of the reservation." He let his eyes move over her slowly, noticing the wealth of dark hair, the fullness of her figure, and the clean lines of her face. He thought of how Elaine had looked when he found what the Apache buck had left of her, and the comparison sickened him.

He said, "You go ahead and do what you think you should do. I wish you good luck."

She reached for her travel bag. "I need a place to stay."

The marshal stood up, kicking back his chair, and

took the bag from her.

"I'll walk you down to the hotel, Miss Ruth. Only one in town. It's all right for a night or two."

Schreiber moved out of his own chair and took the bag from the marshal. "I'm stayin' there myself, remember? I'll walk her down and see she's put up proper.

Ruth said, "I'd appreciate that."

They moved out of the marshal's office and down the boardwalk toward the hotel. Ruth said suddenly, "Your wife was killed at the ranch."

He looked at her sharply and she said, "Bill wrote me about it. That was why you sold the ranch. You couldn't live out there with her memory."

He shook his head, eyes moving along the street. The evening drinkers were drifting into Brownie's Saloon. The smell of frying meat floated from Maude's Restaurant across the street. "It isn't that, exactly. I know she's gone and I can't change that. But I can't spend my days lookin' after a bunch of cows knowing that the Indian who killed her is still walking around."

When she didn't say anything, he added tentatively, "Most folks think I'm wastin' time. I don't see it that way."

It was dark now but he felt her eyes on him. She said, "If what you are doing is right, then I should join you and look for the squaw who killed my brother."

They reached the hotel and went inside. Dutch set Ruth's bag down by the clerk's counter. He looked at the clerk stonily. "Miss Jackson wants the best room you got."

The young man shrugged. "You have the best room available. There's an empty room at the end of the hall but the bed has a leg off and it slants some."

Dutch fished in his pants pocket and brought out his room key. "Put her in my room and give me the other one."

Ruth Jackson tried to protest but Dutch shook his head. "You been ridin' stage as long as you have, you need a good bed. Me, I can sleep anywhere." He took the key to the other room from the clerk and when the young man handed him the bottle of Crow whiskey, he shook his head. "Save it for Paddy Ryan. I'm out of the notion."

He looked at Ruth. "It isn't the same, ma'am."

She looked at him questioningly. "What isn't the same, Mr. Schreiber?"

"My wife gettin' butchered by an Apache buck, Bill gettin' killed by a squaw."

"Tell me the difference."

He smiled slowly. "I will, but I've got to think on it. The boy here will carry your bag up and check you in. After you've rested a spell, there's a good eating place across the street. Good luck to you." He turned and walked out the door. He could have asked her to eat with him but he wanted to be alone. Too much exposure to Ruth Jackson could upset his thinking.

CHAPTER THREE

Cathy Roland dressed carefully for the Brewers' party in Two Wells. She knew that all of the women would be eyeing her critically because she was from the East and could be expected to display fashions not known to Arizona Territory. They would be curious about her and ready to be openly disapproving if she overstepped the acceptable in Two Wells. Nevertheless, she was eager for the coming evening of festivities. It would be fun to dance with Lieutenant Holcomb. He was a handsome young man, too young for her taste, but very attentive and proper.

And Jesse Cogar would be there. She had met Cogar only once when he had visited the post, and she had to admit that he cut a fine figure. Tall and lean and dark and flashing a smile that could light up a dark night. He disturbed her. Or perhaps he only disturbed her own judgment of herself because he was a complete stranger, and she had no right to feel any attraction for him. But he was a handsome man, with a careless, almost reckless way about him, that lent him a certain charm and excited her while still calling up a certain reserve within her.

And there was Dutch Schreiber. Would he be at the dance? She did not know. She could not bring herself to ask her uncle, for, after all, she had seen the man only once and exchanged less than a dozen words with him. Yet she felt that she knew him better than any man she had met out here. This was due undoubtedly to the stories she had heard from Sergeant Shannon, from her uncle, and mostly from the Comanche boy, Max. Perhaps it was also due, in part, to the aura of tragedy that surrounded the man. It seemed to her to establish a certain kinship between them for she still had not recovered from the tragedy of her own broken romance.

Looking at herself in the mirror she saw the flush of color in her cheeks and felt ashamed. Why were her thoughts only on the men she had met out here? The reason was obvious when she gave it an honest answer. She had lost her fiance in Pennsylvania and she was trying to fill the void that suddenly dominated her life. She had lost him to another woman, and with that she had lost stature among her friends.

It made no difference that he had left her purely out of greed for money and social position. In the society in which Cathy moved, a woman fought for love and position as silently and savagely as a jungle cat fighting for survival. But she did it with gloves on her hands and a smile on her lips. If she lost she was lucky if her family name and position kept her afloat socially.

Cathy Roland did not have that kind of luck. There was no prestige surrounding the Roland name in Boston. Her father was a poorly paid professor in a small college. Her widowed aunt had helped her through Boston University. And, she told herself now, if her thoughts were on men, it was because men and not family background were the important things out here in Arizona Territory.

She slipped on a dress of blue watered taffeta with a

white lace collar, low enough to show the swell of her bosom but not low enough to scandalize the local ladies. Around her throat she placed a plain silver chain with a small cameo pendant. Looking at herself in the small mirror, she was not displeased with the image reflected there. The full, gathered skirt of the taffeta gown accented her tiny waist. She knew she was pretty, perhaps even beautiful, but, and this thought sobered her, she was twenty-four. She was getting old as age was judged for unmarried women. And she was living off of relatives.

She took a deep breath and let it out slowly. She did not have to throw herself at just any man. She would not do that, no matter how desperate the circumstances. This was a big country, raw and empty. It needed people who could bring something worthwhile to it. Somewhere out here there was something she could do to make her own way.

Her thoughts were interrupted by the knock on her door and she heard her uncle say, "Cathy, the sergeant is waiting with the Dougherty wagon. Don't forget your duster."

She moved to the closet and took down the ivory linen duster and draped it around her. Cathy looked again into the mirrow and touched up her hair, then carefully put on a blue straw bonnet and adjusted its veil around her face. She called out, "I'm ready," and opened the door.

Captain Roland was in his dress blues. He was smiling and Cathy felt a sudden warmth for him. He had been a bachelor all of his life, following the military action from place to place, responsible for the safety of a hundred men, yet willing to make a place for her when she needed it.

She smiled at him. "You are a handsome man, Captain Roland."

He blushed. "Just an old dog, Cathy. An old dog in a new coat."

She laughed and he took her arm and they went outside into the bright glare of the afternoon. Lieutenant Holcomb was standing beside the wagon. He moved forward toward Cathy, smiling with ill-concealed eagerness, and took her from the captain's grasp. He was a straight-backed, slender man, with sensitive features and mellow brown eyes that moved over Cathy, missing nothing, appreciating everything. He had turned twenty-five the day after Cathy's arrival here.

He squeezed her arm gently. "I have stayed awake nights anticipating this dance."

Cathy smiled. "It is so nice of the Brewers to give this dance, and in my honor! Why, I met them only once."

Holcomb grinned at her. "Once was enough for me. But don't get the big head, young lady. Two Wells thinks a lot of Captain Roland, too."

She laughed, making a face at him. "Is this your kind of flattery, Lieutenant? I was expecting much more from you."

Sergeant Quincy Shannon leaned down from the driver's seat, smiling. "All aboard. Two Wells or bust." The Dougherty wagon moved out, smartly drawn by a team of grays, the canvas roof shading the occupants from the burning heat of the Arizona sun. Behind the wagon rode a detail of six troopers.

As the post faded behind them Cathy saw her uncle searching the distant brown horizon. There was, she thought, an uneasiness growing upon him. He looked at her suddenly. "I can remember the time I wouldn't let a detail through the post gates without Dutch Schreiber riding with them."

Lieutenant Holcomb smiled slightly. "Things have changed, Captain. The Army has brought peace to this country."

Cathy looked at her uncle and then at the lieutenant and finally at the broad back of Quincy Shannon. She felt her own tinge of uneasiness. Her uncle had maintained in his meeting with Schreiber that the Army felt the Apaches were at peace with the whites. Schreiber had said, "No."

Dutch Schreiber felt like a new man. Better still, between the aroma of bay rum and Havana tobacco, he smelled like one. He'd had a shave and a bath, bought new pants and shirt, plus two ten-cent cigars. He'd just finished a couple of drinks at Brownie's but his mind was reasonably clear. He stood under the wooden awning of the saloon and looked out upon the street, figuring his next move.

He was through with the Army. The boys in blue would never head off an Apache outbreak. Once it started they would do their best, but many a grave would be dug between the starting and the stopping of it.

He had thought that working for the Army occasionally would give him access to places he otherwise would have difficulty checking out, and the Army pay would grubstake him while on his hunt. It hadn't worked. Time was running out. He could do better working on his own. He flicked away the white ash of the cigar and squinted into the late afternoon sun. Tomorrow would be a good day to start. He would leave word for Max at Brownie's and the Comanche would find him.

At the far end of the street he saw the Army wagon entering town and he took note of the six man escort behind it. He watched the little procession making its way, wondering at the nature of it. Then the wagon stopped directly in front of him and a beautiful blond woman in a blue dress, partially covered by a duster, rose in her seat and waved at him.

The woman, smiling, called, "Dutch!" and he recognized Cathy Roland and her voice at the same time. He took his hat off with one hand, the cigar out of his mouth with the other, and moved toward the wagon.

He smiled at Cathy, then looked at the men in the wagon. The driver, Shannon, said, "Hello, Dutch," without looking around. The lieutenant nodded curtly, obviously impatient at the delay. Only Cathy and the captain seemed cordial.

Roland said, "No hard feelings, Dutch. You may be giving good advice but I can't take it. Army just doesn't see it like you think it is."

Dutch grinned. "No hard feelings, Captain. No use to say the Army is wrong. I said it before."

Cathy Roland said, "Enough of that. Will you be at the Brewers' party tonight?" She added softly, "Max says my visit here will not be complete until I get to know Dutch Schreiber."

Dutch felt his face heating up. He started to tell her that he had an invitation to the party, that he and Joe Brewer went back to days when each had owed his life to the other several times back in the scouting days. But he said instead, "Ma'am, you can't believe a Comanche. Why—"

A voice cut him off. It came from across the street, from the boardwalk, in front of the Oasis Hotel. It was a feminine voice. "Mr. Schreiber, may I see you?"

He looked through the raised canvas flap of the Dougherty wagon to the opposite side of the street. Ruth Jackson stood in front of the hotel in her dark blue dress and wide-brimmed straw hat. He could see the anxiety in her face. He looked at Cathy Roland.

"Ma'am, I won't be at the Brewers'. It's a dance and I'm an embarrassment to myself on the dance floor." He saw the coolness filter into the blue eyes and he knew he was handling himself badly. He looked at her. "Me and Joe Brewer, we go back a long ways. If I went to the party, me and Joe would get drunk and Mae, his wife, would wind up cussin' us both in front of the guests. Better I stay away."

He saw the tinge of color in Cathy's face, and the faint, impersonal smile on her lips. He saw her look around toward Ruth Jackson and then back at him, and there was complete detachment in her voice when she said, "Sergeant, we should be on our way."

The wagon moved off sharply and he was aware of the sardonic grin on the young lieutenant's face and the stiff-backed posture of Cathy. He waved half-heartedly at the captain but the officer didn't see it, and he watched the Dougherty wagon and the escort move around the bend in the street and disappear.

Dutch stood there in the middle of the street chewing his cigar. Cathy Roland had been affronted by his refusal to go to the dance. The fact that he told her the plain truth was of no moment. He couldn't dance. The only dance he knew was the Apache stomp and the Indians laughed at that. It was true, also, about Mae Brewer. She liked him, he knew, but not too long around her husband, Joe. Joe was settled now and doing well and Dutch had the unhappy faculty of unsettling him.

He slapped on his hat and walked across the street to join Ruth Jackson on the boardwalk. "You wanted to see me?"

Her eyes were on him apprehensively. "Mr. Schreiber, I must see the ranch. The marshal has found only a young Mexican who would lead me out there, and the marshal does not recommend that I go with him. He said the boy might bolt at the slightest provocation and leave me stranded."

He looked at her. "What do you want of me? I made myself clear last night." Looking at her, he began to feel a tinge of admiration at the way she handled herself. She was a long way from home. She had lost an only brother and she was among strangers. But she wasn't crying about it.

She touched his arm. "I know how you feel. I know why. But you are my only hope. I met a man today. A man who calls himself Jesse Cogar. He knew all about me and all about Bill. He said he would take me out to the ranch tomorrow. He is attending a party tonight. I didn't know what to say because he was a stranger, and yet he seemed to know Bill very well. I told him I would let him know in the morning. Then after he left, I remembered Bill mentioning his name. There had been some trouble between them. I, well, I don't trust him. Marshal Welch said he was all right as far as he knew and a man who could take care of himself. I still don't trust him."

Dutch rolled a fresh cigar across his lips. "You got no business ridin' off with Cogar. I figured Rusty to be a better judge of men than that."

She looked at him, her dark eyes lighted up with a sudden lift of spirits. "I don't want to see him in the morning. I have rented a horse and I have a pack animal with some food, and a change of clothes and a few things. It wouldn't take me twenty minutes to be ready. You don't have to really take me out there. You go and I'll follow on my own."

Ruth Jackson was a pretty woman. She was desperate and she was putting on the pressure again. He felt it, together with a reckless stir within him that had been absent since Elaine died. He took the cigar from his mouth. "Why not?" He studied the cigar and tossed it away. "When do we start?"

She looked at him, her face alive with eagerness. "Now. Right now."

He shook his head. "It's fifteen miles out there. Startin' now, we get there one, two hours after dark."

She tilted her head, smiling faintly, returning his look. "What's the matter, Dutch? Can't you find it in the dark?"

He flushed, feeling again the inner stir of excitement. "Miss Ruth, I can find anything I want to find in the dark."

They were two hours out of Two Wells and the sun was down. They had traveled nearly eight miles. Ruth Jackson looked at the dim silhouette of Schreiber's back. He was sitting the dun like he was part of the animal, and the rope on the pack horse was snubbed around the horn of his saddle. It had been a quiet ride. It was not her fault. She had made several tentative attempts at conversation but he was inaccessible and had cut her off, either with silence or abrupt answers. She decided that he felt somehow responsible for her and it bothered him.

She tried to pass the time by taking in the vastness of the country that surrounded her. The high red rough-hewn thrusts of earth reached toward the darkening sky, the yellow floor of the high desert was dotted with gray-green clumps of sage, cacti, and stunted mesquite. It was wild and rugged and frightening, but also fascinating. Nothing like the country in Missouri, and she began to think of her home.

She had, she knew, not been entirely candid with Dutch Schreiber or the marshal. She had not left her farm in Missouri to vist her brother, Bill. She had to leave. The farm had been mortgaged to give Bill a stake out here. It had seemed a simple thing then that the farm would support her and still pay off the mortgage. But it had not been so. She couldn't work the farm by herself, not two hundred and forty acres of heavy dark loam. She needed seasonal help but there was none.

The young people, the ones who could work and who might work for minimal wages, were leaving. They were heading west to homestead their own places. The only help available was from the old men, men who were of no account, else they would have had their own place by now. The kind of men who worked a day and drank a day or more and thought that she must want male company of any kind. She was sick of it. The bank took the farm and left her with two hundred dollars and a ticket to Two Wells.

Bill's letters had been encouraging and yet tainted with a hint of trouble. The ranch was the greatest place in the world. Arizona was the greatest place he had ever seen. But he owed Dutch Schreiber a little money on the spread and he had run out of water. He could restore the

water, given time. But time was running out and he had
not been able to make a deal with his neighbor, a man
named Cogar, for water to tide him over. And he was
losing cattle.

So here she was, out here to give Bill a hand. Out
here because she had no place else to stay. And Bill was
dead. Killed by a squaw.

Up ahead Schreiber had slowed the dun so that she
was only twenty feet or less behind him. He looked at
Ruth over his shoulder. "You say Jesse Cogar was
goin' to a party tonight?"

She nodded. "That's what he told me."

She saw Dutch shake his head slightly. "Wouldn't
think the Brewers would have invited the likes of him.
They were givin' the shindig for the captain's niece."

Ruth smiled in the darkness. "Are you worrying
about that beautiful blond in the Army wagon, Dutch?"

"Not me." He shook his head. "I only met her once
before."

She laughed softly. "That means nothing. You only
met me once before today, and you are worrying about
me."

He looked back at her a long moment but said nothing.

Sergeant Quincy Shannon was heading for the post
when the first drops of rain began to fall. At first he
thought it was his imagination. The moon had been
bright when he left Two Wells shortly after ten o'clock.
And this was the dry season. Still, it was sprinkling
rain. He shrugged. It had been a good night. He had
danced with Cathy Roland once, and he had talked with
some of the men. Men who were busy carving out a life

for themselves in this ragged land. He envied them, and yet felt a gruding admiration for them.

He was going to leave the Army. His time would be up in about three months. Always before, he had signed on again. Not this time. He needed to plant his roots, to grow with the country.

Maybe this was a sorry country for planting roots. It was raw, hardscrabble, too hot or too cold, but it was young and it needed men, and he was here. What would he do? He had saved a little. Maybe try ranching. There was Schreiber's old place and it would make a hardworking man a living. Jackson was dead. Dutch was going to get himself killed. Why not Schreiber's old place? He thought about it, liking the idea.

Shannon moved into the deep darkness between Mule Ear Peaks. The rain was hardly enough to dampen his tunic. Even at night without a moon a man could still see or perhaps feel the bleak silhouettes of the Peaks. He was half way to the post. Another hour. Maybe the rain would hold off. He wondered again about the rain. It was the dry season.

He thought about Cathy Roland, or rather he let her come forward in his thoughts, for she had been in his mind all the time and he had kept pushing her back. She was a beautiful, warm woman, with a way about her that put a man at ease and on edge at the same time.

Jesse Cogar had singled her out at the Brewers' and she hadn't seemed to mind. The lieutenant didn't like it. There could have been trouble but Cathy handled it very well. They were both good-looking men with something to offer a woman.

Yet when he, Quincy Shannon, First Sergeant in the United States Army, had got up the guts to ask her for a dance, she had seemed delighted. During that dance there was no other man on the floor, judging from the way she kept her attention on him.

She was something. She was the captain's niece and it was a damned strange Army that saw a sergeant on the dance floor with a captain and a lieutenant. But that was Roland's way. He held a tight rein but you never felt the bite of the bit in your teeth.

He was nearing the post and the rain was gaining momentum. All of a sudden he realized that he was wet to the skin. He pulled up at the gate and the sentry moved out of the cover of a half shed. The sentry said, "Howdy, Quincy. Where's the detail?"

Shannon looked at him. "Detail? Hell, they came in three or four hours ago under Corporal Dunn." He looked upward. "We're in for a drenchin'." He nudged his horse through the gate.

The sentry called after him. "No detail been through this gate. I been here wide awake since six o'clock."

Quincy Shannon pulled rein. He turned the horse around to face the sentry. "Bob, you tellin' me the detail hasn't checked in?"

The sentry hovered in the shelter of the half shed, barely visible. "Ain't that what I said? I said, where's the detail, didn't I? Then where is it?"

And so there it was. Like that. The captain had let him stay for the dance and he sent the detail in under Corporal Dunn. But it didn't arrive. The rain came at him a little harder. Water streamed down his face. He thought about the captain and the lieutenant spending the night at the Brewers'. He sat there trying to work it out. Should he go back to Two Wells and get the officers out of their beds and tell them the detail was missing? Or should he wait until daylight and try to check it out, himself?

He looked at the blurred figure of the sentry. "You sure that you've been here all the time since six o'clock?"

"That's what I said, Quincy. And what the hell is with this rain? It don't rain out here this time of the year. I been here long enough to know that."

Quincy Shannon felt gutshot. There were things happening that should not be. Six seasoned troopers failed to report into the post. Rain in the dry season. He turned his horse toward the stable. "I'll get the cook up. We'll have some coffee. Come daylight, we'll straighten this out." He was trying to calm the sentry, talking pure bullshit, for he had no confidence in what he said.

CHAPTER FOUR

Cathy Roland had enjoyed the Brewers' party more than any she could remember. Everyone had gone out of their way to be nice to her. She had danced with most of the men in spite of Lieutenant Holcomb's efforts to isolate her. And talking with the women around the punch bowl had been no effort at all. She answered their questions in an honest, straightforward manner, and her own questions were tactfully phrased. When she stated that she thought they were lucky to live in a beautiful, exciting place like Arizona, they actually beamed. They rolled out the red carpet for her and she walked it all night.

This morning she awoke feeling more alive than she had felt for months, perhaps years. She wondered at this and thought about her ex-fiance. Had she really been in love with Streeter Sparkman? Or was he only a symbol of fulfillment? She had landed a good catch that a lot of girls were fishing for, if only temporarily. It had been something to show her aunt that the money spent on her education and social graces had not been wasted. When he broke the engagement in his suave and genteel manner she had been hurt, her confidence shaken, and she had been embarrassed. But had she been heartbroken? She thought not. Looking at herself this morning in a mirror of honesty, she had to admit that she and Streeter had been playing the same game. And she had lost.

Cathy was thinking about all of this while she was seated at the Brewers' breakfast table, having late coffee with Mae Brewer. The dishes were done, the men had gone to town. She liked Mae. The woman was blunt in her talk but there was no malice in it. She was cheerful and friendly and honest. To an admiring Cathy, she typified this country.

She tried to collect her thoughts now so that she could concentrate on what Mae was saying, "Jesse Cogar is a handsome devil and he followed you all night with his eyes. No one knows a whole lot about him, but he seems all right, and he's made some money since he settled here."

Cathy blushed and smiled. "He was very nice. I guess, though, that I'm more interested right now in that talk I heard about the school needing a teacher this coming fall. I think I'm qualified. I have high school behind me and two years of college."

Mae laughed. "Qualified? If anything, you are over-qualified. The school only teaches reading, writing and a little arithmetic. There's about thirty kids attending now. It don't pay much, just a little better than punchin' cows."

Cathy laughed. "Since I can't punch cows, I'll try for the teaching position." She looked at Mae. "Does Max go to the school?"

Mae looked puzzled. "Max? Max who?"

"The Comanche boy. The boy Dutch Schreiber took in."

Mae laughed shortly, shaking her head. "No Indians in that schoolroom. Hard enough to keep the young hellions in their seats, the way it is. You put an Indian in there and you got a war on your hands." She sipped her coffee and Cathy was conscious of Mae's eyes, studying her carefully. Mae said, "Max likes to wild around with Dutch. They're both crazy. Just a matter of time until they both cash in their chips."

For some reason Mae's appraisal of Schreiber struck a spark of resentment in her. She sipped her coffee, trying to think of a discreet way to query Mae on this, when the front door opened. She heard the scraping of men's boots and a terse, low-pitched conversation among them. Mae got up from her chair and walked through the kitchen door into the front parlor.

Cathy heard her say, "What's stirrin'?" She left her own chair and moved in quietly behind Mae.

Captain Roland, the lieutenant, and Joe Brewer were all talking at the same time. In the back of them stood Sergeant Quincy Shannon, hat in hand. Cathy saw Joe Brewer's eyes settle on his wife. He said, "Six-man detail left here yesterday, never made it back to the post."

Mae's eyes narrowed. "Stay out of it, Joe. You got a freight line to run. The Army's got plenty of men to handle it."

Cathy could see Brewer's eyes pleading with Mae, lighted up with momentary excitement. "But, honey, they need a tracker. Rain washed out all the sign. I'm the best tracker around, outside of Dutch, and he's gone to Bill Jackson's ranch with Bill's sister. She just got in town and wanted to see the place."

Mae shook her head. "If there's no sign, then there's no hurry. A man on a good horse can get out to that ranch and have Dutch on the job in eight hours."

Cathy saw her uncle's face redden. He said, "Mae, I'm not sure we can count on Dutch. We sort of parted company a couple of days ago. He doesn't agree with Army policy."

Mae Brewer laughed without humor. "Who does, except those in the Army? Captain, you're after hostiles, aren't you? You figure Apaches are behind it, don't you? Then don't worry about Dutch. He'd leave his own wife a-birthing to go huntin' hostiles. It's in his blood."

Cathy felt her own face flushing and again this resentment of Mae's appraisal of Dutch Schreiber. She didn't know why she cared but it seemed unfair to the man. She said quietly, "If there's no evidence, then why think it was hostile Apaches? Maybe the men just rode off."

Lieutenant Holcomb shook his head grimly. "Not those men. I can think of some in the post who might desert, but not them. They were second enlistments and not troublemakers."

Cathy saw a faint smile around the corners of her uncle's mouth. "Maybe she's right. The official word is that we are looking for six deserters. We don't want to panic the town with rumors of an outbreak with nothing to back it up."

The captain looked at his lieutenant. "We will all ride out to Jackson's ranch. You, me, the sergeant, and his ten-man detail." He smiled at Mae. "I don't balme you, Mae. A man like Joe is hard to come by and easy to lose on an Apache hunt."

Mae smiled back. "When Joe asked me to marry him, I told him I'd work for him, have his kids, help manage his money, but I wouldn't lay awake nights worryin' whether he'd ever come home again. I'm not made to take that because I'd be helpless then, and I don't like bein' helpless.''

The captain nodded. ''I understand.'' He looked at Cathy. ''If we are not back tonight, we'll surely be here tomorrow. Maybe Mae can use your help while we are gone.''

They moved out on to the porch, the men first and the women following. Cathy watched her uncle and the lieutenant and Sergeant Quincy Shannon mount their horses. She watched the ten man detail fall in behind them. Mae and Joe Brewer stood silently as the troops rode out.

When they were out of sight Joe Brewer said shortly, ''I'll be goin' to the freight yard.'' He pulled his hat a little tighter down on his head and walked off the porch. He mounted his own horse and rode off, a square-set, chunky man, whose shoulder slumped just a little.

Mae said, ''He's disappointed. He wanted to go.''

Cathy felt a tinge of sympathy for Joe Brewer. She looked at Mae. ''He got his start scouting. Why are you afraid for him?''

She could see the puzzled look on Mae's face, and then a tightness around the woman's mouth. She thought to herself, I've said the wrong thing. This is between them. Not my business. Then she heard Mae saying, ''It's me I'm afraid for, I reckon. I wasn't anything until I met Joe. I'm a whole woman now. I wouldn't be anything if I lost him.''

They went back into the house. Mae said, ''It's washday for me. Help if you like, or just take it easy. This life is new to you. Break into it gradual.''

Cathy smiled. "I'll help. I can't tolerate a useless woman."

It was hard work. They drew water from the well and carried it in buckets to the black iron pot in the back yard. They stacked kindling around the pot and made a fire, then added heavier wood. The water was steaming when Mae carried out the first basket of clothes.

Cathy was sweating from the heat and exertion, but she liked the feel of it. When the first bubbles appeared on the water, they took long poles and ladled the clothes into it. Cathy ran a hand across her face and, without looking at Mae, she asked, "Why do you say Dutch Schreiber is crazy?"

"That's just my opinion. Most men like him. He made himself a name during the last Apache uprisings. He's a man's man. No good for a woman, to my thinkin'. Married that Tucson filly who he hadn't known over a month. He felt 'like he had to have a woman to put on his ranch. He didn't get much."

Cathy looked at her. "What do you mean?"

Mae stepped back from the fire, wiping sweat from her own forehead. "Well, I never hold much with gossip but that's about all a woman can do out here except work. I know this Elaine that Dutch married was a dressmaker in Tucson. She and her mother both worked at it, but her mother got so crippled up with arthritis that she didn't do much. Rumor has it that some of the town fathers paid for more than just dresses, but that's just rumor, not fact. However, they did buy a fine house and always catered to the wealthy trade. I know for a fact that Dutch told Joe right after they got married that they had to support Elaine's mother. When Elaine was killed by that bronco Apache, after Dutch sold his ranch he gave the money to Elaine's mother.''

Cathy said thoughtfully, ''It's the kind of thing I would expect he would do. I don't know why, but it fits what little I know of him.''

Mae shook her head. ''To me it was a crazy thing to do. Dutch worked hard to get that ranch. Lots of men out here have lost women and children to Apaches. It's part of living in the Territory. But Dutch saw it differently. He couldn't carry on. He felt responsible for Elaine's death, so he sold out and gave everything to her mother and then set himself to finding the Apache who killed Elaine. You asked why I think he's crazy. That's it. He's thrown himself away.''

A man's voice called, ''So that's where you women are! I couldn't raise a soul in the house.''

Cathy looked up to see Jesse Cogar lounging against the back wall of the house. He was dressed in freshly pressed brown pants and tan shirt and a dark brown, wide-brimmed hat, now shoved back rakishly on his head.

He moved toward Cathy and Mae, taking off his hat. ''Mornin', ladies.'' He looked at Cathy. ''Hoped you might be stayin' another day. Got a team around front, if you'd like a little drive.''

Cathy flushed. She looked at Mae and the woman nodded slightly. Cathy smiled. ''That is considerate of you, Mr. Cogar. I would enjoy a little air.'' She touched her hair. ''I'll have to freshen up a little first.''

She went into her bedroom feeling a warm tinge of excitement. Jesse Cogar was interested in her. Mae was right. She wasn't sure that she was the least interested in him. She hardly knew him, but she was flattered. His attention brought out the woman in her. She washed hurriedly in the water basin, brushed her blond hair, then quickly shucked out of the pink calico dress she was wearing in favor of a blue, checked gingham. She moved out on the front porch to see Jesse Cogar standing by the buggy.

He smiled at her. "You don't keep a man waitin' long. I like that."

She laughed as he helped her into the seat. "I didn't have much to work with. Next time it may be longer." She flushed. Next time? That was a badly chosen statement. It was like an invitation. She felt suddenly displeased with herself.

Cogar settled himself beside her and picked up the reins. "Where would you like to go? We got a big stand of saguaro cactus about two miles south, biggest I ever saw, some thirty feet or more. East of here, an hour's drive, is a place called Devil's Lair. It's a big, jumbled mass of rock with rainbow colors in it—red and pink and yellow."

She shook her head. "I can't stay out long. I'd like to see the schoolhouse."

"Schoolhouse?" He grinned at her. "You can learn more outside a schoolhouse than inside. I know, because I did."

She laughed. "I still want to see it. I'm applying for the teacher's position there."

He slapped the reins against the rumps of the dappled grays and the buggy moved out sharply. "Well," he said softly, "I may change my mind about schoolhouses."

They moved down the street in silence and he pulled the team to a stop in front of Brownie's Saloon. "He's got the key," he said, and jumped out of the buggy and disappeared inside. He was back immediately and into the buggy.

Cathy looked at him. "I don't understand. A saloon-keeper with the keys to the schoolhouse?"

Cogar nodded. "Brownie's put out more money on the school than any man in town. Takes the money from the daddys and gives it back to the kids. Never been married, himself. Kind of strange."

He looked at Cathy. "I saw your uncle and the troops, maybe ten, twelve men, headin' west. Anything up?"

She shook her head. "They were going to Bill Jackson's ranch. Dutch Schreiber is out there with Bill's sister. They have a job for him."

Cogar was silent a moment, then laughed shortly. "That Dutchman gets around. Must have taken her out there yesterday evening."

Cathy felt a little coolness stir within her at the tone of his voice. "I'm sure she wanted to see the place where her brother was killed, and see the ranch. I understand it's hers now. Mr. Schreiber is the logical person to show her around."

Cogar shrugged. "All the same, Dutch shouldn't have taken her out overnight. It'll get talked about."

Cathy read the tone of Cogar's voice. She said, "You don't think much of Dutch Schreiber, do you?"

He shrugged. "We've had our disagreements. Figure we'll have more. He's kind of loco."

They were at the schoolhouse now and Cathy liked it instantly. It was larger than she had thought it would be, and painted white. The windows were numerous and large, which would afford good ventilation. Cogar pulled the team to a halt and got out of the buggy. He walked around and helped her from the seat and handed her the key. "Take a look, teacher lady. Hope you get the job."

Nochelte sat around the evening fire with the Apache chiefs. Juh had arrived yesterday. He was on a white mule. That was close enough. The vision had been accurate. He had with him ten of his best warriors and a half-dozen young men to do the camp work.

The chiefs had approved of Nochelte's plan. It was ingenious in its simplicity. Complicated plans did not work well with Apaches. Nochelte explained the plan.

The settlers had to be driven from Apache territory. It was the settlers that brought the horse soldiers out here. Without the settlers, there would be no reason to keep an army in Apacheria.

The Apaches, banded together, could send three hundred or more warriors scattered over the country, but they had no weapons to compare with the horse soldiers. Nochelte had the answer to that. He and his close followers had ambushed a wagon load of silver. They had taken it from bandits who had killed the driver and the guard, and were heading into the canyon country with it. It was on its way to Mexico now. The women and children of the White Mountain and Cibecue tribes were taking it to Mexico. Each mule pulling a travois was pulling also a hundred-pound bar of silver.

Juh had connections with the presidentes of several small villages in Mexico. He could arrange for a trade of the silver for guns and ammunition, blankets and knives. The Mexicans would cheat on the trade. That was expected. But three hundred repeating rifles would take this country away from the White Eyes, and the silver would bring at least that much.

The Apache warriors would wait until the squaws and children and old men were across the border with the silver. Then they would split up in bands of thirty to forty warriors each. They would race for the border, burning and raiding and killing as best they could with their present poor supply of weapons. The Army would take the field after them, but it would be futile because they could not concentrate on any particular place of devastation. They would mill around, chase the Apache to the border, and stop.

And while the Army was returning to their posts, the Apache would be getting new weapons, fresh horses, plenty of bullets, and then charge across the border to finish the slaughter they had started. The Army would not be expecting this. The Army could not cope with it. The white settlers that had not already fled would be killed and their homes burned to the ground.

Nana puffed on his long stemmed pipe, and looked at Nochelte under his wrinkled lids. "I think it is a good plan. But if we take all of this country, we will have more than we need. We are not as many as we were a lifetime ago. Maybe so we can trade part back for lasting peace."

Natchez grimaced. "Who wants lasting peace? The White Eyes do not know the meaning of it. The Apache would find it a dull life."

Nochelte smiled and opened the medicine bag around his neck and took out a pinch of ground herbs. He sprinkled these on the fire and the flame flashed green for a brief moment. He said, "You are both wise men. Your minds are fresh like the green flame. Before we start this war I will make the Great White Chief in Washington a proposal.

"I will tell him we want our mountains and our forests, we want our deserts where the agave and mescal grow. The White Eyes can keep their settlements around the camps where they take out the metal. We have no use for them. They can keep their Army posts around those camps to protect their people from the Mexicans and any bad Apaches who try to molest them. It is a reasonable offer but I do not think they will agree to it."

Nochelte stood up. "It is as Nana says, we do not need as much now as we once did. It is also as Natchez says, the White Eyes will keep the peace only so long as the Apache is strong enough to hold Apache land. We will not fight among ourselves any longer. We will be one people. And we will have access to Mexico where we have always fought with the Mexicans. This is our way of life and we will continue it."

Chavez, a sub chief, half Mexican, half Mimbreno, stood up and walked around the fire. He stopped beside Torres, who was not a Chief, and could not sit at the council fire. He said, "I was with my friend, Torres, two days ago when the Dutchman was within rifle shot. Torres wanted to kill the Dutchman but Nochelte would not permit it." He paused, flexing his arms. "Now I am told our scouts, leading the women and children who are carrying the silver, have captured six horse soldiers. I think the Dutchman will be on their trail, leading an Army patrol after them. I do not think the silver will reach Mexico. I think Torres should have killed the Dutchman."

Nochelte frowned. "Chavez thinks me a fool. There is no trail. The rain washed it away."

Geronimo spat in the fire. "Rain? I felt no rain. There was no rain. Nochelte is dreaming again."

Torres stepped forward, barely into the light of the fire. The flames danced over the silken tresses that he wore around his neck. "Nochelte is right. It rained around Mule Ear Peaks where the six soldiers were taken. It rained hard. There is no sign."

Nana drew on his pipe. He took the stem from his mouth and spat into the flames, looking at Chavez sardonically.

Chavez sat down. "Nochelte is a great shaman. Forget my words."

Nochelte made a chopping motion with a hand. "I blame no one for his concern. It is a good sign. I leave you now." He moved off, motioning for Torres to follow.

At his own wickiup Nochelte built a small fire and Torres gathered wood to replenish it. Nochelte said, "We will talk."

Torres sat across the flame from Nochelte. "Something is wrong."

Nochelte nodded. He had not wanted to kill the Dutchman. His death would sweep over the land like a prairie fire. It would cause much anger and force some action by the Army. The Apache would be the suspect. He had wanted no trouble with the Army until the women and children and the silver were safely across the border.

He said, "The words of Chavez trouble me. The Dutchman will be on the trail of the six horse soldiers. When he sees the sign washed out by the rain, he will ride around the land where the rain fell. It will take much time but he may pick up the sign of the women and children. They are twelve suns away from the border. He could still head them off."

Torres shrugged. "Then make it rain again behind the women and children. He cannot ride circles forever. They will reach the border."

Nochelte shook his head. "You will kill the Dutchman. The scout said he has taken a white woman to the log house where he used to live. Pick six young men. Pick good horses. We will ride out tonight. Maybe we will find him still there.''

Torres stood up. ''If he is there, I will fight him by myself.''

Nochelte nodded. ''That is your right. If he kills you we will hold him prisoner until the silver reaches the border.''

Torres shook his head. ''If he kills me, he is allowed to ride away. That is Apache honor.''

Nochelte smiled thinly. ''Apache honor is between men, Torres. Between two peoples at war, there is no honor. I have learned that without help from the Great God. Ugashe!''

Torres nodded. ''I will have the men here within the hour on good horses.''

Watching Torres leave the light of the fire, Nochelte had his first twinge of uncertainty. It was a good plan. But they should have taken the Dutchman three days ago.

The moon was an hour high when Schreiber abruptly pulled off the wagon road and headed into the sandy bed of a dry arroyo. He could hear the muffled sound of the hoofs of the horse behind him, and he knew that Ruth Jackson must be getting tired. She had finally given up trying to make talk with him and had ridden in silence the last three miles. He rode down the dry stream bed and then cut across toward the dark silhouette of a clump of willows. He said, ''We pick up the trail to the ranch here. Not much farther.''

She said quietly, ''It's a godforsaken country.''

Dutch looked back at her, clearly visible in the moonlight. She was drooping slightly over the saddle horn. He answered, "You have to like bein' alone to live in it."

She reminded him of Elaine. Elaine had fretted occasionally about being lonesome. But she was a city girl, used to lots of people being around. Toward the last she seemed to have gotten used to her new life. She hadn't complained at all the last time he had left her. He closed his mind on his thoughts. That was the past. Elaine was dead. The ranch was gone, belonging now to this woman riding behind him.

They broke through the clump of trees that choked the banks of the creek bed, and moved out into rocky, barren ground. The trail wound around, ascending steeply to the top of a flat mesa. The land was empty except for an occasional agave or ocotillo. Against the hump of the bluff rising to the mesa, a scattered line of large yuccas crowned with masses of white blossoms looked in the moonlight like ghostly figures from the spirit world.

They rode across the top of the mesa to the far edge and he pulled rein there and dismounted. He walked over to Ruth Jackson and helped her from the saddle. "We'll rest the horses. We got a mile of downhill trail with some loose rock, and we don't want to night-ride it with winded horses." He moved back to the edge of the mesa. "That's the ranch down there." He pointed to the valley lying below the upthrust of earth and boulders that rose to the rim of the mesa.

It was quietly beautiful, peacefully bathed in the soft rays of the moon. He said, "I can see the roof of the house. You can't see it because you don't know where to look. If I told you where to look, you still couldn't see it. You have to know it's there."

Ruth Jackson sighed wearily. She looked down the slope of the mesa to the valley and she shivered slightly, although the night was warm. She looked at Schreiber's broad back and forgot the silver-rayed bleakness around her. There was something alive and reassuring about the Dutchman. She smiled faintly.

"You still love it."

He scowled in the darkness, looking at her, lips straight. "I got no use for it, anymore. It's yours. It can be what you make it, if you're able to stay."

He sensed the fatigue that had set upon her: the loneliness of a wild place with no old acquaintances around; the loss of a brother who was her only kin; the ordeal of a ride across half a continent and topped off with four hours in the saddle over rough ground. He felt a sudden tenderness toward her. He dropped an arm over her shoulders, pulling her gently against him. "It's a good place. But not for a woman. Not with Apaches around. Look it over in daylight after a night's rest and breakfast."

It was a natural, unthinking thing, throwing his arm around her. Realizing what he had done, he dropped his arm quickly and moved over to his horse, busying himself with checking the saddle cinches. Satisfied, he walked over and checked her saddle and tightened it a little.

She said, "Dutch, how safe are we? From Indians, I mean."

He thought a moment. "Every country has special problems, I reckon. Out here it's Apaches. It'll get worse before it gets better. It would be sort of happenstance if they bothered us. They're cooking big medicine. We're small game. But you never know what an Apache will do."

Ruth said, "They bothered Elaine."

He rolled a smoke and lighted it, looking at her over the flame of the match. "It was a freak thing. A lone Mimbreno running for the reservation after his leader, Victorio, was killed. Somehow the Mimbreno and Elaine crossed paths. He probably wanted her horse more than he wanted her." His voice trailed off into a husky whisper. "I live for the day I kill the sonofabitch."

He pulled himself up into the saddle and tipped his hat to her. "Excuse my language. Now, let's make tracks."

A half-hour later he was showing her through the house. The kerosene lamps gleamed softly, striking amber rays from the walls of yellow pine logs. He pointed to the floor. "Solid oak. No wearout to it. Roof is heavy pine shakes. Last forever."

She ran a hand over the table and lifted a chair. "You made all this. I know Bill didn't, because he was no good with tools."

He nodded. "You want coffee? I'll build a fire."

She smiled. "I would like that. I'm too tired to sleep."

He hustled kindling and pine chunks from outside and had a fire going in minutes. He got water from the spring seep behind the house and filled the coffee pot. He felt an excitement inside him and wondered about it. Maybe it was talking about the place. God knew how he used to dream about it when it was in the making. Or maybe it was Ruth Jackson. He thought about that as he set the coffee pot on the stove.

He went outside and turned the horses into the corral. He unsaddled them and rubbed them down with loose hay. He had to make three trips to the spring, carrying double buckets of water for the shallow trough inside the corral. He found a half-full sack of oats and put out a generous feeding into two wooden tubs. He slapped the dun on the rump. "Get some rest, boy. Long day tomorrow."

Back inside the house the aroma of strong coffee flooded over him. Ruth had two cups on the table. She smiled at him. "Are you hungry?"

He shrugged. "It will keep 'til mornin'."

She pulled a heavy iron pot off the shelf behind the stove. "I'm hungry, and I hate to waste that fire. I can have biscuits on before you finish your first cup of coffee. And I see a can of honey on the shelf."

They sat there at the table until almost midnight, eating bisuits and honey, drinking black coffee, talking some about little things, occasionally probing into each other's reserve, but gentle and without hurry.

Bill Jackson had come along hunting a ranch to buy right after Elaine's death. Schreiber needed to get rid of the place because he couldn't run it and hunt the Apache. He also needed money for Elaine's mother. She was old and crippled up with rheumatism. He got three thousand for the ranch, all Bill had, and he sold the cows to Bill on credit. Most of the money went to Elaine's mother, all except enough to grubstake him for a while.

Ruth admitted that she hadn't been exactly truthful about coming out here to visit her brother. The family farm had gone to the bank. She needed a home. She had hoped to help Bill out here, to make her way without being a bother. Bill was having some trouble and had run out of water. She had done a man's work on the farm and she hadn't thought ranching would be any different. She planned to settle up with Schreiber on the cows when the money from the agency came in. Still, she was beginning to have some misgivings. She might have to sell the ranch. The vastness of the country frightened her. Missouri was flat and compact with lots of fields and houses and streams. You could ride in any direction and find a neighbor within a half-mile or so.

She watched Dutch Schreiber as he got up from the table and picked up his hat. "I'll sleep outside in the shed. Tomorrow we'll ride over the place. A woman would be foolish to stay out here by herself, but that's your choice, not mine."

After Ruth got into the bed, she had to admit that she was utterly afraid. The wind had risen slightly and made a forlorn, lonely sound through the pines that studded the hills around the cabin. She was in the middle of nowhere. Nothing but timber and rock and cactus and wild things. She recognized the yapping of a coyote on a distant ridge. There were coyotes in Missouri but somehow they sounded different back there. Only the thought that Dutch Schreiber was outside gave her any comfort. She went to sleep thinking about him.

They buried Bill Jackson the next morning. She didn't flinch at the swollen, putrid flesh that had been her brother. She didn't gag at the smell of death three days old under the burning sun. And when he was buried she insisted on burying the Apache boy beside him. Schreiber tried to tell her that no one buries dead Apaches. They buried this one, and she read from a small Bible over the two graves.

An hour short of noon they were on the high point of the ranch, looking down in four directions. He said, "Three hundred and twenty acres of deeded land. The house is on it. It stretches along the creek for a mile.

Two thousand acres, give or take, on government land. It'll run a hundred head.''

She listened to him. She said, ''The watering pond is dry. The damn is broken.''

He fished for his tobacco, nodding. ''Take a man and a team of mules a day or two, but it can be fixed.''

Ruth shook her head. ''No man needed. I'll rent a team of mules and do it myself and do it right.''

He flushed, putting a match to his smoke. ''I did it right, but it takes attention. Nothing lasts forever.''

She looked at him. ''That's right. Nothing lasts forever.'' She turned her horse, looking south. ''A hundred head will make a fair living, not much more.''

Schreiber drew on the cigarette and let the smoke out slowly. ''You're right. Start with beef stock, then breed up. A man could get reasonably rich selling blooded stock to the big ranchers. Takes time to build that kind of herd.''

Ruth Jackson smiled suddenly, looking at him. ''How many women out here run their own ranches?''

He frowned. ''Women? Don't recollect any woman tryin' to ranch out here. Ma Levenson's got a spread northwest of here but she's got two grown boys. It ain't woman country.''

She looked at him. ''It is now. I was afraid last night. The truth is I was scared and I haven't been scared in a long time. But the country looks different under the sun. Can you get me a couple of dogs?''

He took the cigarette from his lips. ''Dogs?''

''A small one for inside the house, a big fellow for outside. I'll need some geese for the pond. No better sentinel than a disturbed goose.''

He pinched out his smoke, grinning. ''After all my advice, you aim to stay.''

She nodded. "More than that, I intend to go to work. This place needs it."

Schreiber flushed. "I ain't owned it for near a year now."

There was movement down below them. A flash of sun on metal. Ruth didn't see it. He said quietly, "We are going to ride slow into that pine grove downhill there. When we get there, we are goin' to run like hell for the house. Stay with me."

She didn't say anything, just looked at his face. He turned the dun slowly and went off at a trot. She stayed close behind him. Once in the pines he said, "Apaches. Let's make a run for it."

Nochelte sat his horse in the fringe of stunted pinyons watching the Dutchman and the woman disappear into the deep shadows of the pines above. He had dreamed last night and the Dutchman had appeared in his dreams. He had dreamed of White Painted Woman and her two sons, Child of the Water and Killer of Enemies. He could recall no form or features of Child of the Water but Killer of Enemies resembled the Dutchman. This could be a bad omen because all Apaches knew that Killer of Enemies had given guns to the White Eyes, while Child of the Water gave bows and arrows to the Apache when the world's goods were divided up in the beginning of time. It was these guns that made it possible for the White Eyes to take much of Apacheria from the Apache.

He looked now at Torres and then at the three other warriors behind him. He said, "They are alone. It is your time, Torres."

There was a flash of movement out of the pines. Two

horses raced toward the ranch house. Torres scowled. "They have seen us."

Nochelte shrugged, eyes black slits in his chiseled face as he squinted into the sun toward the racing horses. "It makes no difference. There are five of us and the Dutchman is burdened by the woman." He jabbed his heels into the flanks of his horse and moved slowly toward the house, the others following.

Getting rid of the Dutchman was a necessary thing. Nochelte had heard much of the man. Apache scouts who had worked with the Dutchman held him in considerable respect. He knew Apache country, he knew Apache habits, and he was tireless like the Apache. It was said he was a fair man and took up for his scouts when the horse soldiers tried to take advantage of them. But Torres had killed his wife and now he was an Apache-hater. He was dangerous and therefore he must be killed or held captive until the Apaches were ready to make war.

He said, "Torres and I will move into the clearing in front of the house. The rest of you conceal yourselves in positions so that they cannot escape. We will call the Dutchman out."

Torres pulled a knife from his breechclout and held it up against the sun. "We will fight with this weapon. I will take his head."

Nochelte's lips stretched in a faint smile. "Perhaps."

He laid a hand on the neck of Torres's horse. "Let us wait until the others have found their places."

Sweat glistened on the bronze face of the Mimbreno warrior. "I am impatient to finish this thing."

Nochelte shrugged. "There is much of the day before us." He looked at Torres. "Why did you pick the Dutchman's wife?"

The warrior stuck his knife back into his breechclout. "I did not know she was his wife. I knew of the Dutchman but she did not come from his house. I found her early in the morning leaving the house of the man called Cogar. I needed her horse."

Nochelte eased his horse forward. "Before you fight the Dutchman, I will tell him of this."

Torres wiped a hand against his long moccasins. "It is done. What difference does it make?"

The shaman smiled. "The difference may be whether you live or die."

CHAPTER FIVE

Cathy Roland sat beside Jesse Cogar in the buggy as it rounded a corner and started down the main street of Two Wells. She was frightened. Somehow a change had come over the man beside her. A change that stripped away the facade of an easy-going, rather gallant, gentle man, and left him intent and brooding and a little sullen. It had started with his comments on Dutch Schreiber, and he had mentioned at least twice since then that Dutch had not seen the last of him. Then when they had come back to the buggy, after looking over the schoolhouse, he tried to kiss her as he was helping her into her seat. She had turned her head and his hands tightened on her arms like twin vises, and she saw the dark color of anger in his face. She was trying now, desperately, to keep a light conversation going between them, but he was working the team hard, paying her little attention.

She said, "I do hope I get the teaching job. I know I would like it."

He grunted, looking at her. "Seems to me a woman like you ought to be lookin' after her own kids."

She forced a laugh. "But I have none, Mr. Cogar."

"Well," he said, "wouldn't take too long to change that."

Cathy felt the blood rushing to her face. If the team had not been moving so fast she would have jumped out of the buggy. She said cooly, "Mr. Cogar—" And then a voice shouted, "Ho! Miss Cathy!" She looked across the street and saw the Indian boy, Max, lounging against the hitching rail in front of the bank.

She waved at the boy, then said, "Please stop. I need to ask Max about something."

Cogar slowed the team to a walk. "Schreiber's Comanche brat? He's a thief. No account, just like the Dutchman. Why would you want to see him?" He pulled the team to a halt. "Why?"

Cathy fumbled for an answer. "Why, he's been staying at the post. My uncle, Captain Roland, asked me if I saw him to tell him to come back to the post. There is something he wants the boy to do. I don't know what." She jumped out of the buggy, not waiting for Cogar to come around to help her down. She ran over to Max.

Max waited for her, grinning, tucking in his shirttail. He was dusty and grimy and looked a little used up, she thought. There was a bad bruise under one eye and his lower lip was puffed and split. She looked at him. "What in the world happened to you?"

The boy reached inside his shirt and pulled out the biggest knife Cathy had ever seen. He pointed it at Cogar, now standing beside the buggy. "He knows."

A bead of perspiration trickled from under her bonnet and down her cheek. She wiped it away, feeling suddenly cold inside. "Knows what, Max?"

"Dutch sent me out to get Bill Jackson's cattle. We got the herd and I went back to look for strays because the count was low. Dutch say maybe fifty-sixty head. We short many head." He jabbed the knife toward

Cogar. "He beat me up. I on his range without permission, he say. He beat me up good. But I no have my knife then. I loan it the Sanchez kid to cut poles to prod the cattle." He looked across the street at Jesse Cogar. "He no be here if I had knife then."

Cathy's chin firmed. "Wait here a minute, Max." She turned back across the street toward the buggy and Cogar. She stopped a few feet from the man.

"Mr. Cogar, you may have had good intentions when you asked me to take a ride with you. I don't know. Perhaps you don't know, either. I can say that neither of us will ever have a chance to find out because I promise you, there will not be another time."

Cogar's lips twisted in a smirking smile. "There's plenty of time, Cathy. Don't pay no attention to that kid's lies. I was takin' care of what was mine when I roughed him up. When I settle on a woman, I'll take care of her, too. After you've been here a spell, you'll see there ain't too many men out here that can take care of a woman." He laughed at the shocked look on her face.

He tipped his hat. "I'll see you again and I think I'll have better luck the next time." He moved around the buggy and climbed back into the seat. He smiled down at her. "Good day, Miss Roland. It's a quarter mile walk to the Brewer house." He flipped the reins and drove off.

Max was standing behind her when she turned. She flushed. "Did you hear what he said?"

The boy nodded. "Sure."

She said quietly, "Don't ever repeat it. I don't want to cause any trouble."

Max shrugged. "No make much sense to me, what he say."

She smiled. "Good." She took the boy's arm. "We're going to the Brewers' house. Mae Brewer is washing and that shirt of yours needs it. Your face needs some attention, too."

Max scowled. He took off a weather-stained hat and ran a hand through his crow-black hair. "I got to get out to Dutch. He at the Jackson place with a woman. He told me catch up soon I could." He jerked a thumb at the bank. "I just stop off to leave cattle papers with banker and feed horse."

The mention of Dutch Schreiber being out there somewhere with another woman caused her a moment of concern, and she wondered why. The man was nothing to her. True, she had resented Mae Brewer's remarks about him, but that was only because they seemed unfair and contrary to her Uncle's estimate of the man.

Cathy shook her head. "You don't need to ride after Mr. Schreiber. He will be coming back here with Captain Roland and the soldiers. They went out this morning to get him. Besides, if he sees your face like that, he'll certainly have some words with Mr. Cogar."

Max grinned. "No words. Dutch already punch him. Banker say Marshal broke up good fight."

So. Jesse Cogar said there had been trouble between him and Dutch Schreiber. And he implied it wasn't over. She hoped that Cogar left town before Dutch Schreiber arrived. Cathy said to Max, "Come with me," and she started down the boardwalk with the Indian boy behind her. The boardwalk would end in a hundred yards or so, and she'd be ankle deep in dust the rest of the way. It didn't bother her. It was better than riding with Jesse Cogar.

An hour later Cathy was helping Mae Brewer with

the last of the washing. Max sat in the shade of a cottonwood holding a wet cloth to his bad eye and waiting for his shirt to dry. Mae took the last load of clothes out of the boiling pot with a sawed-off broom handle, wiped a strand of hair out of her eyes and looked at Cathy.

"So you walked home with the Comanche kid and left Jess Cogar sittin' in his buggy by his lonesome?"

Cathy shrugged. "What else could I do? Max needed attention and he surely couldn't ride to the house in the buggy with us. Not after the trouble he'd had with Jesse Cogar."

Mae smiled. "Well, now, a girl out with a man and enjoying it would have thought of something. Like telling Max to get his horse out of the livery and ride on down here. He knows the way." When Cathy didn't answer, Mae Brewer said, "Did Jesse try to kiss you?"

Cathy felt a little anger at Mae's prying but passed it off, telling herself again that the woman was not malicious, just curious and blunt. Cathy looked at her. "I would say that he was a little too forward for my taste."

Mae Brewer chuckled. "I figured it. That's the way with men out here. Good part of the women, too. Not much time for courtin' when you're hardscrabblin' around to make a livin' and tryin' to keep things together. Folks go at it kinda sudden when they do get together. Should have warned you, I guess."

Cathy dried her hands on a cloth hanging on the clothes line. "I really couldn't have any use for a man who would beat a boy like he did Max."

Mae leaned on her broomstick, eyeing Cathy. "Remember, you're in Arizona and Max is an Indian. Some men out here just naturally don't think of Indians as kids, even when they're young. Many a good man has died with an arrow in his gut, shot by an Apache no older than Max. Makes no difference that he ain't Apache. He's still red."

Cathy thought that Mae was probably right. Just because Dutch Schreiber had taken up with the Indian boy didn't mean that others would view the young Comanche any differently than they would any other Indian. And there had been terrible wars between the two races. She said, "I'll get used to it out here, Mae. It will take some time but I know I will. I love the country and that's a big part of it."

Mae nodded. "I ain't criticizing you, girl, nor sayin' you shouldn't have done what you did, walking home and leavin' Jesse. That's your business. I'm just tryin' to educate you a little along so you'll see both sides of things." She slapped at a fly buzzing her face. "I don't hold no brief for Jesse Cogar. Don't know him that well. But he's here and you aim to stay here, you say, if you can. And he's young enough, not bad lookin', and he's got a home and ranch and a little money. Not many men out here who can take care of a woman."

A sudden feeling of despair seized Cathy. She thought, dear God in heaven, she talks just like Jesse Cogar. She said quietly, "Mae, if we're finished with the washing, I think I'll go in and freshen up." She turned toward the house and for the first time since she'd been in this country, she wondered if she was up to it.

They made it to the ranch house. Schreiber had been worried that Ruth Jackson would panic at the word, "Apache." She hadn't. She galloped stirrup to stirrup with him through the pines and they slid out of their saddles and dashed inside the house, leaving their horses windblown and heaving by the porch.

Dutch ran to the back window in the room and looked out. It was a small window, made so purposely so that no man could crawl through it, but it afforded a good view of the cedar-choked slope where he had first seen the Apaches. Nothing moved out there. He walked over to the door and edged his head out beside the frame, squinting into the strong rays of the sun. They were out there. He could feel them.

Behind him Ruth said quietly, "I never saw a thing. Are you sure?"

Dutch nodded. "You see Apaches mostly when they want you to see them. I was lucky. Hope the luck holds."

"Are there many?"

He shrugged. "I saw one. They seldom travel alone. We'll know soon enough."

Looking out the door at the green timbered slope, it seemed a tranquil land out there. Dutch rolled a smoke and lighted it, drinking in the wild beauty of the country, thinking back to better times. A gentle breeze drifted in the back window and brushed by Schreiber as it went out the door, carrying the small fragrance of Ruth Jackson with it. He flinched. He was a damned fool. He had brought a woman here once before and she had died at the hands of the red devils out there. He had known better, so that made him stupid. He drew on the cigarette, waiting. They would not get this woman alive.

A jay shrieked and fluttered from a lone oak. He dropped his cigarette and stepped on it, feeling the hairs on the back of his neck rising in anticipation. He eared back the hammer on the rifle. He said quietly, "Check the back window again." He heard her footsteps over the plank floor. He felt the sweat suddenly on his forehead. It was a hell of a way to die, particularly for a woman.

Her voice came to him softly. "There is nothing I can see out there."

Two riders suddenly appeared in the clearing in front of the house. One moment the land was empty and now here they were. He said, "Can you use a rifle?"

Her voice carried soft and clear across the room. "Very well."

"Then come get this one. There's two out there in six-gun range. You stay with the window."

She was beside him instantly, taking the rifle. She saw the two horsemen, and he saw the sudden fear in her eyes. She looked as if she wanted to scream. Instead she said, "Don't worry about me, Dutch."

One of the Apaches was a small man, wearing a high-crowned black hat and white tunic over his breechclout. The other was large for an Apache, broad-shouldered and naked except for breechclout and deerskin moccasins that reached above his knees. They seemed to be waiting for him to come out, but he was not about to expose himself to some hidden Apache's rifle. He stood against the wall, just beside the door, with his sixgun in hand and waiting for their move. He had outwaited Apaches before.

Finally the small Apache raised a hand. "We would talk with you, Dutchman."

Dutch called, "I can hear you. Say your piece."

The small Apache moved his horse closer. "I am Nochelte. You have heard of me?"

"I've heard of you," Dutch answered bleakly. "Nothing much good."

A faint smile crossed the little Apache's lips. "We are at peace now, Americano. Why do you hold a gun in your hand? We have not come to shoot."

Dutch looked at the gun in his hand, feeling somehow embarrassed. How did the shaman know he held a gun? He couldn't see it. Dutch said, "Ride up closer."

Nochelte touched a foot to his horse's flank and the animal moved a dozen steps and stopped a few feet from the porch. Dutch came out the door, still holding his gun. He said, "This thing has a hair trigger and it's right on your gut. If I catch a bullet, you'll never live to see me die."

The little Apache shrugged. "It does not matter whether I see you die, Americano. I have seen many White Eyes die and many Apaches, also. We have fought the horse soldiers until our guns burned out and our bows broke and we have no weapons. We are at peace with the White Eyes now but you still hunt one of my brothers. You cover ground like a hungry dog trailing a wounded deer.

"My brother cannot sleep for fear you will come upon his wickiup and plant your knife in his heart. He cannot hunt for fear it will be you that comes out of the brush, and not the buck deer that he trails. This thing must be settled. That is why we have come." He looked over his shoulder toward the big Apache. "Ride up, Torres, and let the Dutchman see you so that he may know the look of the man he has hunted these many moons."

Torres! The name scalded Schreiber's brain like a hot iron. Torres, the Apache! The red savage who violated and then destroyed the only woman Schreiber had ever wanted. He was riding up now beside the shaman called Nochelte.

Nochelte's voice came at him from the red haze of hate and fury that rocked his mind. "If you kill Torres with that gun, you will be killed, also. There are others watching this thing, but you cannot see them. Torres has no gun. Torres had a bow and arrows but you have none. You both have knives. So you will fight with knives and this trouble will be settled. If Torres is a better fighter, he can hunt in peace. If he is not, then he can sleep forever."

Schreiber was conscious of Ruth beside him. He heard her say, "Dutch," and he glanced at her. There was no color in her face. Her eyes were dark and haggard and there was a wildness in them.

She moaned softly, "For God's sake, Dutch. Don't do it. Don't go out there. It's a trick. I feel it. I know it."

Some men who set themselves upon a hard and solitary trail to a certain goal have second thoughts when the trail ends and the moment of accomplishment is at hand. Dutch was not one of them. The suddenness of it had him momentarily off balance, but the desire burned as deep as it had the day he found Elaine's body.

He said, "Then it will be knives." He holstered his gun and unstrapped the weight of it from his waist. He walked out on the porch and sat down on the edge of it and pulled off his boots. Stiff leather soles have a way of sliding out from under a man who moves quickly. Finally he stood up and motioned to Torres.

"Let's get at it, Apache."

Nochelte raised a hand. "A moment longer, Americano. Torres wishes you to know that he did not realize it was your squaw that he killed. He would not have bothered the Dutchman's woman. Torres was passing the house of the man called Cogar one morning when the sun was not yet up. He was tired and without a horse and without a gun, when this woman came out of Cogar's house and saddled up a fine horse. The horse also carried a rifle. The woman was nothing to Torres. Just a brief moment of pleasure. But the horse and rifle meant that he could live and perhaps reach the reservation.''

The shaman smiled slightly. ''If you think perhaps you are facing the wrong man, that it was some other woman Torres killed, then look.'' Nochelte reached over to Torres and spun the rawhide thong around his neck so that the raven tresses of the scalp with its streak of snow white hair covered the chest of Torres.

Schreiber never knew that he moved off the porch. He didn't know that the wild, screaming voice was his own. A red haze blurred his vision and he was swinging his knife wildly even before he reached the big Apache. He felt, rather than saw, the Apache's horse lunging into him. He found himself rolling on the ground and the face of Torres, like some demonic death mask, leered down at him.

A sharp, stinging flash of pain in his left arm brought some reason back to his clouded mind. Instinctively he rolled into the standing Apache and grasped at his legs. Torres stumbled back. Schreiber lunged as best he could from his prone position, bringing the weight of his shoulders on the Indian's legs. Torres toppled across Schreiber's back and again Dutch felt the red-hot sting of steel as Torres's knife made a shallow furrow across his back.

The two fighters were on their feet in unison, facing

each other, arms outspread, crouching slightly. Dutch felt the crimson stream gushing from his slashed left arm and he knew he would not last long. Already he felt the weakness from loss of blood. But nothing mattered now. Torres stood before him. If he should come this far and fail, then at least Dutch felt he had been given his chance. Out here a man never expected a guarantee. He circled Torres slowly, dodging a feint from Torres's blade, moving in and slashing at the Indian's belly, barely missing.

Schreiber stepped in again and jabbed quickly with his knife like a boxer. The blade sliced across the shoulder of Torres, opening the skin, and the sight of the Apache's blood brought momentary strength to Schreiber's body. He pressed in on the warrior, slashing, fending off the Apache's counter thrusts with his injured arm. Again he brought blood from Torres, this time a deep gash across the chest. Again he felt the bite of the knife of Torres, high in his shoulder. He was losing his ability to focus on the Apache. He felt himself swaying, weaving, from a great weakness within him, and he tried to cover it by moving in again, on the attack, probing, slashing with the blade.

He sensed that Torres knew his condition. There was no emotion on the bronzed face. No hint of triumph in the obsidian eyes. The Apache watched him as a snake might watch a bird. Waiting, biding his time.

A shadow moved out of the dense foliage down the trail leading to the house. The shadow became an Apache. An Apache yelling, pointing behind him, jabbering in his strange tongue.

Nochelte moved his horse between Schreiber and Torres. A rifle was in his hands. He said, "*Silaada'*," and motioned to Torres who ran for his horse. The shaman looked at Schreiber impassively. "You are a fortunate man. In another five minutes, Torres would have taken your head." He motioned over his shoulder. "Army patrol. We must go. We are off the reservation." He smiled thinly. "That gives the horse soldiers the right to shoot. It is our land but we are captives in it." He looked steadily at Schreiber, who was still fighting to keep on his legs. "This will change."

The Apaches were gone. Dutch still stood where he had last faced Torres, mind numbed and body weakened from loss of blood. He watched them leave and cursed them as they faded from sight. And then he fell forward, with no instinctive reaction to abate the force of the landing. Just a dead, sodden weight hitting the baked earth face first.

Captain Harry Roland led his patrol out of the timbered trail into the clearing around the ranch house. He was a naturally observant man, and ten years in Indian country had whetted the edge of this trait. They had picked up a horse, saddled and still wearing a bridle, three hundred yards down the trail. Standing impatiently by the porch of the ranch house, the captain recognized Schreiber's dun, saddled and bridled and coated with drying flecks of foam. And there was the feeling of violence and death spread on an empty landscape.

He looked at young Lieutenant Holcomb. "Stay with the men." He nodded toward Sergeant Quincy Shannon. "Let's go inside."

Captain Roland was not prepared for the situation inside the house. He had never seen Dutch Schreiber helpless. But there he was, face down on the table, arm wrapped in a blood-soaked bandage, crimson seeping out of the back of his shirt. And there was the woman working over him.

He asked, "Miss Jackson?" He instantly regretted the aloofness of his voice. He was a man in his mid-fifties and had seen a lot of women, some good, some not so good. But he had not seen one like her. He asked again, with a warmer note, "Ruth Jackson, I believe?"

She nodded, eyeing him quickly, still working on Schreiber. "I believe so, too, but right now I'm not sure." She straightened up. "Thank God for the Army."

He smiled. Sergeant Quincy Shannon smiled, too.

She said, "I've done all I can for him. His arm has a six-inch slice, pretty deep. He has an eight-inch gash across his back just breaking the skin, and he's been cut a couple of other places, but not bad. He's alive, but he's lost blood and he is weak." Roland saw her eyes move from the sergeant and settle on his own. She said, "Captain, I'll make some coffee."

Roland took a chair beside Dutch Schreiber. The man seemed unconscious but he said, "Dutch, what the hell?"

Schreiber's head raised slightly. "I found the sonofabitch. I found Torres." There was a long silence. Schreiber added, "Goddammit, Captain, I would've had his scalp in another five minutes."

The captain left his chair and moved over to Ruth who was setting the coffee pot on the stove. He asked quietly, "Tell me about it."

She shook her head. "It was sudden. We were on the mesa, Dutch and I, checking out the range. We were on the far side of the pine thicket. I don't know how, but Dutch saw them. We made it to the house. Then this—

this man, Nochelte, called Dutch outside. He said the Apache who killed Dutch's wife was ready to fight. He said it was all a mistake, that this Apache, Torres, caught Dutch's wife early one morning leaving Jesse Cogar's house. He didn't know she was Dutch's wife.''

Roland's face turned gray. "Good God!''

Ruth ran a hand through her dark hair. "Schreiber went crazy. He was a madman!''

He nodded. He turned and walked off a few steps, looking at the room. Sure, Dutch went crazy. What man wouldn't? He thought of the time Dutch had put in building this place. He remembered the first time Dutch had ever mentioned Elaine. He remembered the wedding and how the men had hurrahed Dutch and got him drunk. He looked over at the man slumped across the table, carved like a Christmas turkey. Dutch Schreiber? He found it hard to believe.

He looked over at Ruth Jackson pouring coffee for the sergeant. Two days in Arizona. Walked into a funeral the minute she stepped off the stage. Watched a man being carved up by an Apache on her second day. He thought about her. What kind of woman was she? One thing for sure, she didn't panic easily.

He thought about his niece, Cathy, a beautiful girl without a place of her own in this world. She wanted so desperately to find her place out here. She loved this country, she said, but did she really? Or was she talking herself into it because she was here and there was really no place else to go?

He thought briefly about himself. He had been a captain a long time. Many of his contemporaries had surpassed him in rank. He was getting along in years. He could retire any time, but the Army was his life. Could he make a different life for himself and be happy? He didn't like these thoughts and moved over to the stove for a cup of coffee.

He took the steaming cup from Ruth Jackson. He smiled. "We will have to get you and Dutch back to Two Wells. Never can tell when those red devils will strike again."

She looked at him somberly. "If they had wanted to kill us, I think they might have done it. I'm new out here, but I know some things. This was not a war party. This was just a fight between two men. One of them red."

Roland sipped at the hot brew. She was a perceptive woman. He smiled slightly. "Probably. But after Dutch had been looking for six months for this Apache who killed his wife, why does the medicine man suddenly produce him?"

He sighed faintly, "I have six good men missing without a trace, and I need Dutch Schreiber." He looked over at Schreiber, still face down on the table. "I have been in Arizona a long time. I've fought Apaches a long time. This did not just happen. There's got to be a reason behind it. Not so important I know what it is right now, but it's important that I realize it was planned."

He saw her glance over at Schreiber and then her eyes, darkened with anxiety, finally settled on him. "I'm ready to go back when he is, Captain Roland."

He smiled. "Dutch is rawhide and steel. I'll get him on his feet and he'll be ready to ride."

She shrugged. "I don't think so."

Her answer nettled him. "He's not bad hurt. Lost a lot of blood. Needs a few stitches."

"He'll get up pretty soon and go after that Apache, Torres. That's my thinking, Captain. If he does that,

I'll be waiting here for him when he comes back."

Roland set down his cup. "You wouldn't stay out here alone?"

She smiled. It was the first time he had seen her smile and he felt suddenly that he may have been missing something in his life. She said, "He didn't want to bring me out here. I coaxed him into it." She sipped at her own coffee. "Back in Missouri a woman believes in going back with the man who brought her."

Roland set down his cup. "I'll be damned." He felt his face grow hot. "Beg your pardon, Miss Jackson, for my language." He got up and walked over to Schreiber who had lifted his head and was staring around the room.

Dutch managed a grin. Without moving he said, "Howdy, Captain."

Roland lifted the cup in his hand and motioned to Ruth. He looked at Schreiber. "I thought you were too savvy for this, Dutch."

Schreiber adjusted the bandage around his arm. "I thought so, too, Captain. Funny thing, a man never knows all there is to know about himself."

Ruth Jackson brought over coffee for Dutch and smiled at him.

Dutch said, "Thanks. Sorry to be a bother."

She put a hand on top of his head. "Dutch, it's me that's the bother." She looked at Roland. "I'll invite the men in or serve coffee outside, whichever you say."

Roland looked at her. Why did she have to be so goddamned young? He said quietly, "Let them in. They're people just like us."

He looked at Schreiber. "You were right the other day. Something coming off here that we haven't seen before. This medicine man, he was raised with Americans. He caught you with the oldest white man's trick there is in the fight business, no matter how you fight. He got your goat with this rubbish about Elaine.''

Schreiber studied his cup. ''That came to me, Captain, but about thirty seconds too late.'' He smiled faintly, ''I left her alone a lot. I reckon it was my own conscience turning on me. If it was true, what he said, I couldn't blame her.''

''It wasn't true.''

Schreiber sipped the hot coffee. ''No. But it was said and I got to live with it or make it out the lie it was.''

Roland reached for cigars and laid one in front of Dutch. ''I came out here on business. Your kind. I got six soldiers missing. Started in from the party at Two Wells a little after dark. Never made it. Two of them, Scott and Adams, are good friends of yours.'' He looked around the room. ''Helped you build this place on their time off, as I remember.''

Dutch leaned back in his chair, fighting off the dizziness that seized him. He took the cigar in front of him and clipped it with his teeth, then leaned over to the captain's match. He said, ''You know what I got to do.''

The captain let smoke out through his nose, studying his cigar. ''Time and place for everything, Dutch. These men are missing. I'll let it out that they may have deserted, but we both know better.'' He paused and studied the gray ash on his cigar. ''The woman, here, needs to be in Two Wells, but she won't leave without you. You need stitching up. Let's go in to the post and talk.''

Dutch Schreiber shook his head. ''No. I know where my Indian is, Captain. I'll be going after him.''

Dutch Schreiber was five miles inside the Apache Reservation when he cut the trail of the southbound Apaches. Squaws and kids, mostly, with a few old men and all undoubtedly headed for the border two hundred miles away. It was bigger than the band that Bill Jackson flushed.

He pulled the dun to a halt and dismounted, building a cigarette. His left arm ached, his back was stiff and sore, and his estimation of himself had dropped considerably. He had let the sonofabitch, Torres, outfox him and outfight him.

He walked around, studying the tracks, loosening his muscles from nearly ten hours in the saddle. It was a big band, maybe seventy to eighty in all, and lots of horse or mule drawn travois, heavily laden, making deep scratches in the ground except across the rock outcroppings. This was the second band to leave the reservation. There could have been others whose trails he hadn't crossed. It confirmed his opinion that a big outbreak was due. He sat down under the shade of a pine grove and finished his cigarette, thinking about the ranch.

Captain Roland had decided to stay at the ranch for three days, along with most of the troopers. Lieutenant Holcomb and the Sergeant, with a couple of soldiers, would go back to the post and send back a detail with enough food to hold them over. If Dutch didn't show back at the ranch at the end of the third day, Ruth would go to Two Wells escorted by Roland and his troopers. If Dutch made it back to the ranch, if he killed Torres and got out of the Apache camp alive, he would sign on to try and find the six missing troopers.

Rested a little, he climbed back into the saddle and began crisscrossing the Apaches' trail, studying the sign. The travois were really heavily loaded, more than seemed ordinary. They would have taken everything they owned. Could be some guns and ammunition loaded on, too, he thought, although he figured they were short on guns. Then, moving across the stream of the trail nearly a quarter of a mile, he picked up sign of mounted horses. Apache warriors, maybe ten or twelve, moving with the squaws and kids, moving ahead of the fleeing band, he figured. These were the scouts and hunters.

They would range a mile or two ahead of the squaws and kids. If they ran into an Army patrol, they could stir up enough of a ruckus to divert the patrol's attention from the fleeing Indians, giving them a chance to take cover and wait it out while the warriors drew the patrol further away. The warriors would also supply fresh meat for the foot-weary band. Nearly two hundred miles to go, heavily laden, probably holing up during the heat of the day, the band would take twelve to fifteen days to cross the border. These tracks were maybe two or three days old.

He moved the dun against the grain of the trail, heading north, wondering if it would take him directly into Nochelte's camp. Probably not, he reasoned, because the Apaches were a clannish people, and each clan would ready its own squaws and children and old men for the long journey. Each would have one or two of its young braves riding herd on their own folks. Somewhere they would converge into a central group.

He crossed a deep, dry wash and noticed a wide area where the grass and small brush had been trampled. There were the remains of several small campfires. They had met here, then, to assemble themselves for the trip. He rode along the north bank of the wash, following a well-marked trail recently made. When the trail appeared to stop abruptly, he saw that it really headed straight down the bank of the wash. The ground was torn and raw earth exposed, forming a kind of slide, breaking obliquely across the bank into the bed of the wash. He moved the dun down the slide, picking his way carefully, wondering why the Apaches had chosen such a laborious route. Then he saw the wagon.

It lay on its side with one rear wheel broken, but the lettering on the upside was still clear enough and it spelled *GLOBE FREIGHTING COMPANY*. Off to one side, lying against the bank of the wash, was the skeleton remains of two men, some of their clothing still partially covering the bones.

Dutch rolled a smoke and stepped out of the saddle. So this was what happened to the silver shipment. The robbers drove the freight wagon into the canyon country, looking for a hideout, and found Apaches instead. Nochelte's work, most likely. Taking the men by surprise, they forced them to drive the wagon onto the reservation, then killed them.

And now it was pretty plain how the Apaches were going to arm themselves for another war. And it was very clear why the travois of the southward bound band of squaws and kids were so heavily loaded. They were taking the silver across the border. Once safely across, they could trade the white metal for guns and ammunition. Old Juh and his Nednis had lived in Mexico all their lives. They would have many contacts for working out a trade.

Thinking about it made Dutch's scalp crawl, and he took off his hat and ran a hand through his short, blond hair. Once the silver was in Mexico, Nochelte would lead his three or four hundred Apache warriors in a wild dash off the reservation. They would break up in small bands and run and fight their way to the border. Once in Mexico, they would re-arm with the best guns money could buy, remount on fresh horses, and be ready to plunder the country and fight the Army. There would be more hell raised than this country had yet seen, and it had seen plenty over the years.

He squinted through some low-hanging branches into the sun, sliding down the western horizon. It had been his plan to make the Apache camp on Cibecue Creek before noon tomorrow. He could still do that, in spite of the time he had killed following the Apaches' trail, but it came to him suddenly that if he should be seen by a prowling Apache near this wagon, he wouldn't live to fight Torres. The silver was Nochelte's big medicine. With it the Apaches might actually retake a part of Apacheria from the White Eyes. Without it, Nochelte was just another shaman, holding dances and making empty promises. A chill settled over Dutch as he mounted and reined the dun around and moved back up the bank of the wash.

He decided that the best thing he could do was cache himself and the dun in the thickest stand of timber he could find close by, and then wait for darkness. Once night fell, he would ride two or three miles due east, well away from the Apaches' trail. The main camp was north and east of here, anyway. In the morning, when he resumed his ride to the camp, he would be seen, for Nochelte was expecting him, but perhaps not so soon. But with any luck they would not suspect that he had seen the wagon.

He found a thick stand of scrub pinyon to his liking and moved the dun into it. He climbed out of the saddle and sat down on an outcropping of red rock. It was a time now for just waiting.

He removed his hat and wiped a sleeve across his face, mopping up rivulets of sweat. There was no movement of air in the dense stand of trees, and the earth threw back the baked-in heat of the afternoon sun. He rolled a smoke and lighted it, and thought about Ruth Jackson. She had insisted on staying there at the ranch at least three days. He might come back badly wounded, she had said, and the ranch was fifteen miles closer than Two Wells or the post. It might make the difference in his surviving.

Besides, she felt guilty because she had gotten him out here. She should know that it wasn't her fault. He was coming after Torres, anyway. She had liked the ranch. That was obvious and it pleased him, probably because it was mostly of his making.

His thoughts switched to Cathy Roland. The captain's beautiful niece seemed out of place in this raw land, but she said she loved it out here. He wondered if she really did, and why she had chosen such a godforsaken place as Camp Cache for a summer vacation? He was curious about her, but he'd gotten off to a bad start as far as she was concerned.

And what would happen to these two women if Nochelte managed to get the silver across the border? What would happen to the Brewers and the captain and all of the settlers? All of them were out here, for one reason or another, trying to make a life for themselves, trying to live in a place that was never meant to be the white man's home.

This was Apache land. The rugged wildness of the terrain was created by nature to fit the unfettered,

nomadic life of the earth's toughest race. Yet, and he
smiled faintly at the thought, he, himself, had sought to
tame it, to build a home in it, and even though he had
failed he was not ready to leave it. Was it just Torres
that kept him here? He had no answer for that. The
answer would come, perhaps, with his knife buried in
the Apache's gut.

The sun was down now and the timber was black
against the red hills. Another hour and he could move.
He got to his feet and stood in the fringe of the timber,
looking toward the trail of the moving band of Apaches,
trying to guess at the direction they would take. South,
of course, but likely a little east because the country was
more mountainous in that direction.

The Apaches needed to move across the desert floor
with their heavily laden travois, but they would want
mountains close by. His eyes swept the horizon, settling in the direction of the post. Had the six missing
soldiers run into this moving band of squaws and children and warrior scouts? It seemed to him likely that
they had. Cutting a trail south by east, they would have
skirted the rough range of the Mule Ear Peaks. The road
from Two Wells to the post ran between the peaks.

The captain had said a rain came up and washed out
all sign of tracks between the town and the post. It was a
freak rain here in the dry season and covered only a
small area, for it had not rained on Ruth and him on
their trip to the ranch that evening. He had known it to
happen before, the little freak rains, but not often.
Damned convenient for the Apaches. Either the
Apaches had killed the six troopers and carried off the
bodies, or they had somehow captured them and taken
them along toward the border. If they were alive, they
were badly in need of help before the Apaches settled in

permanent camp where they could torture them at their leisure.

Schreiber rolled another smoke and when he had finished it the trees were dark silhouettes against the sky. He mounted the dun and headed east. Tonight he would make a small fire and boil coffee and eat the three biscuits soaked in sorghum that Ruth had fixed for him early this morning. It did not matter if an Apache saw the light of his fire.

It occurred to him that he should turn back now, that he should ride to the ranch and tell Captain Roland about the fleeing band of Apaches and the silver. He dismissed the thought. He had to live with himself and he could not do this if he turned away now, knowing that Torres awaited him. Besides, it would take another two weeks, maybe longer, for the squaws and children to make the border. Plenty of time to head them off, if he got out of the Apache camp alive.

CHAPTER SIX

Jesse Cogar turned in the buggy at the livery stable in Two Wells, and pulled his own horse out of its stall. Anger colored his face and he was rough with the horse when he pushed the bit of the bridle between its teeth. The animal shied and Cogar cursed and slung the saddle blanket and then the saddle upon the horse's back.

The hostler, a young, stoop-shouldered man, shook his head. "He's a good animal, Jesse. Take care of him."

Cogar didn't answer. He was mad and the worst part was that he was mad at himself. He didn't give a damn about Cathy Roland, he told himself. He just wanted her to warm up to him enough that he would have an excuse to hang around the post a little more. A man could pick up worthwhile information hanging around with the officers and troopers, things like when the next herd of agency beef was expected and where it was coming from. Or maybe a remark dropped in idle conversation about the next supply train coming into the post with guns and ammunition and other supplies.

He had a few friends among the reservation Apaches, derelicts mostly, that looked to him for the rotgut whiskey that let them exist in a drunken stupor, that kept them from realizing what they had become. A word to one of them and a raiding party could make off with a few head of cattle or a wagonload of supplies. Then Jesse could pick up the plunder for two bits on the dollar and a little whiskey thrown in.

Now he had messed himself up with Cathy Roland and it might be a hard thing to straighten out. He didn't quite know what had come over him. She was a damned pretty woman, all right, but he had gone to bed with lots of pretty women. What made her different?

He rode the sorrel gelding out of the barn and down the dusty, wheel-rutted street, heading for his ranch. Things had been quiet with the Apaches. He hadn't had any worthwhile traffic with them for near six months. But they were moving into the reservation from all over the country. A man could hear of a small band coming up from the Chiricahuas or a party of warriors seen between here and the Warm Springs country, and nothing happened. They were just moving.

And these stories about this shaman, Nochelte. He didn't know anything about the medicine man. Just fragments of talk here and there, but Dutch Schreiber seemed worried. He hated the Dutchman's guts but he would rely on the man's intuition about Apaches.

It was near sundown when he rode into the ranch yard. He didn't like this place. The house was in the middle of the big, sandy sink that spread itself over a two-mile area. It had water but not much grass. The shallow basin held the afternoon heat, and the grass was so thin that the slightest wind kicked up yellow clouds of dust. He thought about the Jackson ranch, Schreiber's old place, and wondered about the woman there now. Would she try to stay or would she sell? He aimed to find out.

As he pulled up by the corral, two men sauntered out

of the weathered adobe shack that served as a bunkhouse. In season there might be as many as five or six
temporary hands quartering there. Now, with the spring
calf crop branded, his foreman and all-around handy-
man, Whitey Doaks, was the only permanent occupant.
Whitey stood outside the door of the bunkhouse and
waved casually to Cogar, then turned and said something to the man beside him.

Cogar recognized the man as Chastino, a halfbreed
Apache, who stayed drunk most of the time on Cogar's
corn whiskey and occasionally turned up with a little
useful information in return. He lived sometimes with
the reservation Apaches, and sometimes in an abandoned shack outside of Two Wells. Cogar wondered
now at his presence here.

He climbed out of the saddle and motioned to Whitey
to take his horse. He slapped dust from his shirt with his
hat and walked toward the bunkhouse, eyeing the
halfbreed.

"You run out of drinking whiskey again, I reckon."

Chastino grinned. He was a small man, almost as
brown as a full blood, wiry and mean-eyed, with long
black hair held close to his head with a band of woven
hemp. "Maybe big news. Maybe trade big news for
bullets and whiskey. We see."

Cogar eyed the man coldly, reaching for tobacco and
papers. "We see, hell. Your credit's gettin' damned
thin with me. You ain't turned anything my way since
that little herd of mother cows last fall."

Chastino shrugged. "No rustling now by Apaches.
No raiding. All quiet. Nochelte making big medicine.
All tribes listen to Nochelte."

Cogar touched a match to his cigarette and slapped
his hat back on his head. "What are they hearing?"

Chastino reached out a hand. "Tobacco." Cogar handed him the sack. Chastino rolled a cigarette with great deliberation and stood there while Cogar lighted it for him. He handed back the sack of Durham. "I do not know all of it. I do not sit at the council fires." He looked directly at Cogar and his voice was bitter. "I am halfbreed."

Cogar scowled. "You hear some of it. You get the young bucks drunk on my whiskey."

The halfbreed nodded. "I hear big fight coming. Nochelte say the Apache take this land back from the Americanos before the first snow falls in the mountains."

Cogar tossed his smoke in the sand and ground it with a heel. "Bullshit! You believe that crap?"

Chastino shrugged. "I do not know. Nochelte can make it rain. I have seen this. I have seen the dust storm rise off the desert floor at his command. Nana says that Nochelte brought Cochise from the grave to stand before him." He was silent a long moment, then shrugged again. "So, I do not know."

Cogar squatted on his heels and the halfbreed sat down beside him, crosslegged, Indian style. Cogar said finally, "They're restless and maybe hungry. They been quiet too long. Not their nature. They'll believe anything because they're spoiling for a fight. But, hell, they got nothin' to fight with. They lost most of their guns and best horses in the last big ruckus near a year ago."

Chastino asked for the tobacco again. He rolled another smoke and Cogar lighted it. Chastino said, "That is the big news."

Cogar frowned. "What big news?"

"The Apache will get many guns. Repeating rifles,

better guns than the horse soldiers have now. They will get good horses and every warrior will have a new blanket.''

Cogar grinned derisively. Whitey Doaks walked up from the corral and sat down with them. Cogar said, ''Listen to this wind, Whitey. The Apache medicine man, this Nochelte, is going to manufacture guns and horses out of thin air and turn his warriors loose on us. Maybe we ought to be huntin' ourselves a hidin' place.''

Chastino's face was impassive. ''The Mexicans have many new rifles for sale, and good horses.'' He blew smoke into the air and looked at Cogar. ''Nochelte has the white metal. A wagon load of pure silver.''

Pieces of fact and rumor began to fit together in Jesse Cogar's mind: the stolen silver shipment that was never found, the infiltration of the huge White Mountain Reservation with bands of Apaches who normally preferred to live elsewhere, and Schreiber's statement that the squaws and children were heading for the border.

He pulled at an ear. ''You tellin' me that there's a bunch of Mexican smugglers loco enough to cross the length of the Territory with guns and horses to swap for that silver? Hell, they won't get north of Tombstone before the Army picks them up.''

Chastino rubbed out his cigarette in the dirt. He sliced the air with the edge of his hand in a sharp, cutting gesture. ''Dah! Nochelte is not stupid. He is sending the white metal to Mexico. The squaws are taking it on travois.''

Cogar took a long breath and let it whistle out between his teeth. ''For Christ's sake! Thirty thousand dollars wandering around out there just waitin' for a man to come get it.'' He looked at Whitey Doaks.

"You and me are goin' to gather up some old boys and take a ride."

Chastino grimaced and shook his head vigorously. "You cannot take the silver. The squaws are three days gone. They will rest in the Dragoons a day and cut new travois poles. Nochelte is watching over them. I tell you this big news so that you will have time to sell your cattle and ride to Tucson where there are many Americanos and Mexicans. When the squaws have crossed the border, Nochelte will send many war parties across the land. They will wipe out the small settlements and ranches, but they will not bother Tucson on the way to the border." He smiled thinly, "When they come back across the border with their guns and fresh horses, they will destroy everything. Perhaps even Tucson."

Jesse Cogar stood up. He said, "Get him a pocket full of bullets for his rifle, Whitey, and give him a jug of whiskey." He looked at Chastino. "You best get back to the reservation. If this medicine man is as sharp as you say, he'll be keeping an eye on you. Even he will know that a drinking man talks too much."

Chastino nodded. "He is angry with me now. Two of his young warriors were drunk on my whiskey this morning." He looked out across the yellowish-brown expanse of the sink. "I think I will go to Tucson, myself."

Nochelte was seated in front of his wickiup eating an evening meal of venison and hominy stew, when he suddenly sensed that the Dutchman was coming. It was simply a brief sensation that sent a little shiver down his spine. He set down the gourd shell that served as his bowl and remained still a moment, eyes looking into the flickering campfires of the numerous small bands of Apaches having their evening meal or taking their rest afterward.

He had hoped that the Dutchman would come for Torres but he did not know that he would do so. It would take a very brave man or a crazy one to come alone into the heart of the Apache camp.

The squaws and children and the mules and horses pulling the travois would now be east of the settlement the White Eyes called Globe. They would be following the western flank of the Gila Mountains where they could scatter and hide, should they encounter the horse soldiers. But there had been no sign of the soldiers, according to word brought back by a scout. No search party had ventured out for the six missing troopers. The Great God was with the Apache now. It was a good thought.

He had heard good advice from old Nana, spoken casually around the council fire. The Apaches did not need as much land now as they had once dominated. There were fewer Apaches. If he, Nochelte, could impress upon the White Chief the strength of the Apache position, there could be bargaining.

There were only the two alternatives: reach an agreement or kill. He was confident that the Apaches could route the White Eyes, but killing not only struck terror in the enemy, it also compounded the hatred between the races. He picked up the gourd shell and began to eat again, thinking on this.

When he had finished, it was dark. He rose and left his wickiup and found Torres with a small band of Mimbrenos. He said, "We have some things to talk on."

Torres left the group and followed Nochelte into the darker shadows of the timber. He asked, "What is it?"

Nochelte laid a hand across the warrior's shoulder. "The Dutchman is coming. He will be here tomorrow."

Torres was silent a long moment. "How is it you know this?"

Nochelte shrugged. "I know only that it is so."

Torres nodded. "I am ready. He has a bad arm."

Nochelte looked at him somberly. "He carries the reputation of a great fighter. If you kill him, you may become a chief."

"And if I don't?" There was a hollowness in the voice of Torres.

"You will have died a brave warrior. But I think we can use this man if he lives. He may save many lives, Apaches as well as White Eyes."

Torres grunted. "I think the Prophet wishes me to lose the fight."

Nochelte chuckled. "That is wrong. I would like to think that, man to man, the Apache is a better fighter. But it will comfort you to know that if you lose, you have still helped the Apache people."

A lone horseman pulled rein by the campfire, and Nochelte left Torres and walked into the light of the fire. He recognized the squat, heavy-bellied figure of Chapparo, leader of the scouts sent to protect and forage for the squaws and children.

Nochelte asked quietly, "Why have you left the band? The signal smokes this evening said all was well."

Chapparo grunted assent. "We will pass the fort of the White Eyes called Thomas in two suns. Beyond that we are not likely to see horse soldiers by chance."

Nochelte nodded. "Not by chance. But if the Americanos learn of the silver, they will send the soldiers for you. Why are you here?"

The fat Apache gestured impatiently. "We want to kill the six soldiers we captured at Mule Ear Peaks. They are a bother. They slow us down. Besides, if one escapes he will lead the Army to us."

Nochelte sliced the air with the edge of his hand. "Dah. That is foolish. They are walking with the squaws. You have taken their horses. Their hands are tied behind their backs. This has been reported to me. How can they escape?"

Chapparo punched a finger in the direction of Nochelte. "I have long respected the wisdom of the Prophet, Nochelte. But what good are the soldiers to us? They slow us down."

Nochelte sat down on a large stump and motioned Chapparo to dismount. Chapparo slid off his horse and stood before the shaman. Nochelte said, "The White Eyes are not like our people, Chapparo. If you were leading a war party and came upon a patrol of horse soldiers who had some of our people captive, what would you do?"

Chapparo blinked. "We would kill the horse soldiers, of course."

"But what about the captive Apaches? Suppose the horse soldiers threatened to kill them if you attacked?"

Chapparo shrugged. "That would be a bad thing. It would make us very angry. Some of the horse soldiers would die very slowly, I think."

Nochelte smiled. "But you would still attack?"

"Ha'aa! That is the reason for a war party."

Nochelte nodded. "But it would not be so with the horse soldiers. If they come upon you, you will hold knives to the throats of the captives. You will threaten to kill them unless the soldiers allow the women and children to retreat into the mountains. You will promise to release the captives when the women and children are safe. They will not attack. They will wait.''

He raised his arms and lifted his face toward the star studded sky. ''The Great God sent us the captives, Chapparo. Do not let anything happen to them until you have crossed the border.''

Chapparo dropped his head. ''I am not wise like the Prophet. I can make no medicine for my people. But I can follow the Prophet. I will return to the band tomorrow. I will protect the captives. I will explain to the others why this must be done.''

Nochelte smiled. ''That is good. You do not realize it, perhaps, but you are becoming a wise man, yourself.''

The shaman looked toward the great meadow where the ceremonial fires were now burning. The Apaches were gathering there, waiting for him to start the dancing. There was strength to be had from the dancing. Strength of Apache purpose, strength of body, and spirit. The dance had come to him in a vision sent by the Great God, a rhythmic, undulating ring, formed by the Apache warriors, moving to drums beaten by old men whose warrior days were over.

He, Nochelte, was the hub of the circle, talking to the Great God in the beginning, and then to the warriors. He exhorted them, praised their strength, then moved around them sprinkling them with hoddentin, the yellow pollen of *nada,* the native corn.

He started toward the meadow. After the dancing he would counsel with Nana and Natchez and Juh and some of the others. There was much to decide, much to

talk upon, much to do within the twelve suns it would
take the silver to reach the border.

Lieutenant Holcomb pulled the detail to a halt in Brewer's front yard. Sergeant Quincy Shannon was embarrassed at having only two troopers under his command.
He said, "Hit the ground. Take care of your horses.
Coffee will be comin' up."

The lieutenant dismounted leisurely. He said, "I'll
get Cathy ready for the ride to the post." He strode
upon the porch and knocked on the door. The door
opened quickly and he said, "Hello, Mrs. Brewer."

Mae Brewer knew trouble when she saw it. She said,
"What's the matter, Lieutenant? Where is the captain?"

Holcomb wiped sweat off his forehead with a sleeve.
"He's at the Jackson Ranch. We've got some trouble
out there. I'm taking out a food detail from the post. I'm
supposed to pick up Cathy on the way." He looked
beyond the door, beyond Mae Brewer. "Where is
she?"

Mrs. Brewer looked over her shoulder. She called,
"Cathy," and there was a rustle of skirts, a murmur of
voices. Cathy was at the door with Max, who grinned
when he saw the lieutenant. "You bring Dutch?"

Holcomb scowled. "No. I didn't bring the Dutchman. He's off on the reservation with a bad arm, looking for the man who killed his wife. I have orders to take
Miss Roland to the post."

Cathy looked at him, unsmiling. "Where is my uncle?"

The lieutenant straightened. "At the Jackson ranch.

We're takin' food out. Could be there two, three days, waiting on Schreiber.''

Cathy looked at him. "We will go with you, Max and I."

The young officer frowned, then flushed. "Look, my orders are to take you to the post and then lead out a food detail." He smiled. "No real worry. The captain is stayin' because the woman won't come in without Schreiber. He's got three days. If he doesn't show at the ranch, they'll all come into the post."

Cathy smiled back, a faint gesture. She said, "Max and I will go out with the food detail. He wants to find Dutch. I want to be with my uncle."

Holcomb shook his head. "My orders are to take you to the post."

Cathy's smile faded. Her blue eyes met his own. "Lieutenant, I'm not in the military. Neither is Max. We will go with you or without you." She smiled suddenly. "I think the captain would prefer that we go with you."

The lieutenant waved his arms; he started to bluster, but, looking at her, he decided she was right. She was not in the military. Besides, it was a five-hour ride from the post to the ranch and he would have her company. He grinned, "I'd admire to have you along. This is not Apache trouble. It's safe enough." He looked at her levelly, "But protect me from the captain. He'll be angry."

Max eased out around Cathy, looking at the officer. "Dutch hokay?"

Holcomb squinted at the slight, brown-faced boy. "No. Dutch is cut up pretty bad. He tangled with the Indian called Torres and we came up just in time to keep him alive. Torres is the Apache he is after. He's on the trail of Torres now, somewhere on the reservation, and he should be in bed."

Max blinked. "Dutch take a lot of killin'."

Mae Brewer came back to the door. "Coffee and cake for the Army. Seein' as there's only four of you, come on in." She looked at Sergeant Quincy Shannon. "But get out of here before Joe comes home. I don't want to fight him again today. Never saw a man so set on huntin' Apaches unless it is Dutch."

It was nearly noon the next day when the food detail reached the Jackson ranch. Lieutenant Holcomb brought the riders to the porch of the ranch house. There was the sergeant, three troopers, the lieutenant, and Cathy and Max. They sat their horses while the lieutenant dismounted and walked up on the porch. He didn't get a chance to knock. Captain Harry Roland opened the door and looked out. Anger colored his face.

He said, "For Christ's sake, Lieutenant. Why isn't Cathy at the post?"

Holcomb flushed. "Because she does not take Army orders, sir. Ask her, yourself."

Max slipped off his horse and helped Cathy dismount. They moved around the troopers' horses and walked up to the porch. Cathy smiled at her Uncle. "I wanted to see this country. It was a great ride. I'd like to meet Ruth Jackson."

Roland scowled, not hiding his displeasure. "Army or not, it's smart to take orders from those who know." He stood aside. "Come on in."

Cathy had a feeling about the place when she first stepped inside. The table and chairs were heavy and hand-hewn. The place was solid. Like the Dutchman.

A woman was working over the wood cookstove. Ruth Jackson wiped a hand across her forehead, looking over her shoulder. "Well, you'd be Cathy Roland, I guess. The captain has told me about you."

Cathy extended a hand. "I am so glad to meet you. It was a terrible experience, coming in as you did without knowing."

"You mean learning that Bill was dead?"

Cathy nodded gravely. "Yes, of course. It was such a dreadful way to end such a trip." She was studying Ruth Jackson, trying to calculate the measure of the woman. She looked young, not much older than Cathy, herself. She was a wholesome-looking woman, not pretty, but with a certain carriage and air about her that made her seem more attractive, perhaps, than she was. She was in control of herself, Cathy was certain about that, and she fought down an instinctive envy.

Ruth Jackson lifted a steaming pot of coffee off the stove with a dish towel wrapped around the handle. "It was a shock to find Bill dead. Even when Dutch Schreiber explained how it happened, I still couldn't accept it." She looked solemnly at Cathy. "I accept it now. But it may be too late. I coaxed Dutch into bringing me out here, to let me see this place for myself. And now he's in trouble because of me."

Cathy felt the color leaving her face. She was fighting the agitation inside her. She said, with a calmness she did not feel, "I hear Dutch has been around here a long time. He can take care of himself."

Ruth shook her head. "You didn't hear what the medicine man said about the Apache, Torres, finding Dutch's wife at Cogar's house. It was early morning and she was just leaving. Dutch went crazy when he

heard that. He would have been a dead man if your
uncle hadn't appeared with the soldiers. He's out there
now, somewhere, still hunting for Torres.''

Cathy felt a wave of fear sweep over her, fear for the
man called Dutch. She forced down the emotion inside
her. She said quietly, ''Don't blame yourself. He was
hunting Torres before you came.'' She turned toward
the door to speak to Max, still struggling to keep her
voice calm.

She said, ''Can you find him?''

Max grinned. ''That why I came. To find Dutch.
Maybeso I find.''

Cathy looked at Ruth. ''Can you put him up a little
food? He'll be riding off very soon.''

Ruth Jackson nodded. ''He can have the best we
have. I don't know what it is, however, until the Army
unpacks.''

Max smiled broadly and flashed his black eyes at
Cathy. ''No worry. Dutch tough.''

It was the next morning while Cathy was helping Ruth
fix breakfast for all of the men when she noticed her
uncle on the porch. His hands were shoved deep inside
his pockets and he stood, slightly hunched, staring out
into the empty land, a cold cigar stub clenched between
his jaws. She felt a sudden compassion for him
and left the stove and walked out to him.

She said, ''You're worrying about your missing soldiers.''

He looked at her. ''I'm worryin' about a lot of things.
When you've been out here as long as I have, you begin
to feel things are goin' to happen before they do. I got
that feeling now.''

He tossed the cigar stub away. "Sure, I'm worryin' about my men. I feel like I ought to be leading a patrol lookin' for them instead of waiting on that Dutchman." He looked at Cathy directly. "I worry about you, too. You're goin' back this morning with the food detail."

Cathy sensed the concern in his voice and felt a moment of guilt for adding to his troubles. "All right," she said softly. She started to turn away, then added, "Will you and Dutch Schreiber be coming to the post before starting your search?"

The captain shrugged. "I don't know. I don't know if he'll come back here. If he does, I don't know what shape he'll be in. If he's able to track, I don't know where he'll want to start."

He sighed heavily. "That's what's wrong. I'm supposed to be in charge, making the decisions and, instead, I'm dependin' on him. Have to, because he's the only man who's got a chance of doin' the job, and the only man I'd trust to lead me and my men, if I have a choice."

A horseman rode out of the timber-choked trail into the ranch yard, and Cathy felt a swift apprehension as she recognized Jesse Cogar. The rancher pulled rein at the porch, tipping his hat, then stepped out of the saddle, smiling at her.

He said lightly, "I do get to see you again." His face sobered as he looked at the captain. "Is Schreiber here?"

Roland shook his head. "Out huntin' his Indian." He looked at Cogar. "Why?"

The rancher moved up on the porch. "Had a matter to settle with him. I'm goin' to be out of the country a good spell. Fellow I grubstaked in Mexico has made a good strike, but if I don't get down there and grease a few palms, them Mexican politicians will take it over.''

Cathy moved back into the house, wondering what it was that Cogar wanted to settle with Dutch Schreiber. As much as she wanted to see Dutch, she was somehow glad now that he was not here. Jesse Cogar had suddenly become a sinister and threatening image to her. She had really never been afraid of anything before. But now she was afraid of Jesse Cogar.

CHAPTER SEVEN

Schreiber rode into the fringe of the Apache camp a little after noon. He had, he knew, been under Apaches' eyes most of the day. Not that he had seen them. He didn't have to see them to know they were there. A birdcall here or there when there were no birds flitting between the trees; a squirrel chattering in a cedar grove where there was no food. A man learned to know what to look for, what to listen for, and to never expect to see the Apache until he was ready to be seen.

He pulled rein when the timber thinned and exposed several wickiups in a large meadow. Cibecue Creek made a bend around the meadow, throwing up a thin stand of willows and sycamores. A large grove of stunt oak flanked the east side of the meadow, and other wickiups were visible among the trees.

A few Apaches were lounging in the shade of the oaks and a couple of young squaws were working over a deer carcass. There was a kind of unreal quality over the place. It was too quiet. Even as he thought about it, he missed the clamor of Apache children and the usual pack of barking dogs.

He sat there in the saddle and rolled a cigarette and lighted it. He took off his hat and ran a hand over a sweaty forehead. He had come to the end of his trail.

Somewhere in this camp was Torres. The Apache
might be expecting him.

What would happen if he killed the Indian? Would
the others let him ride off? They were an unpredictable
people. Twenty years ago there would have been no
cause for concern. They had a strict code of honor then,
and lived up to it. Time and the white man had changed
them. They had been lied to, cheated, brutalized, until
they had become brutes, themselves. He flipped the
cigarette into a green clump of yucca. It was chancy.

He spoke to the dun and the horse moved forward
toward the wickiups. Apaches began to appear out of
the dwellings, out of the oaks, and out of the trees along
the creek. They moved out into the meadow, looking at
him. There was no yelling, no chanting, no menacing
gestures, and yet somehow their very silence seemed
ominous.

A small Apache wearing a high-crowned black hat
moved out of the screen of oaks and toward Schreiber.
Dutch recognized the man as Nochelte and he reined the
dun toward him, pausing twenty feet away. Nochelte
raised a palm, smiling slightly.

He said, "The Dutchman has come to die."

Schreiber shrugged. "No. But there's that chance.
Where's Torres?"

Nochelte pointed toward the oaks. "He will be here
soon. He is making his peace with his god, Yusn." He
looked at Schreiber. "You did not believe what I said
about your squaw being with the man, Cogar."

Dutch felt cold anger tighten his stomach. He said
bleakly, "Hell, no."

Nochelte shrugged. "That is your choice. You
would not have come, had you believed it. An unfaith-

ful Apache squaw has her nose cut off and is not considered of any value." He smiled again. "I am glad you came."

Schreiber swung out of the saddle and moved toward the Apache. His left arm was stiff but not throbbing, and he hoped the bandage would keep the cut from breaking open. He was not worried about the cut on his back, for it was too shallow to bleed seriously.

He asked, "Where does this fracas take place?"

Nochelte nodded toward the meadow, now half-circled with Apaches. "Out there. There are three hundred warriors waiting to see the white man fall under the blade of Torres."

Schreiber drew his knife and walked out in the open patch of ground. There was a tenseness in him and he kept moving, walking back and forth, working it off. A kind of sighing sound broke from the Apaches ringed around him, and he looked over his shoulder to see Torres moving toward him. He pulled off his boots.

The big Apache's face was a stone mask, his black eyes boring into Schreiber. His knife hung from a hand at his side. When he was a dozen paces away from Dutch, he stopped, then twisted the rawhide thong around his neck so that the scalp hung down his chest.

He touched the scalp. "This is what you have come for, Americano. See if you can take it."

Dutch moved into the Apache slowly, warily, taking his time. He had pushed anger out of his mind and his eyes were coldly calculating. This was a job he needed to do, a man he needed to kill, and there was no rage or passion in him. Nothing but purpose.

Torres blinked, then rushed suddenly and swung his knife up in a flashing arc. Schreiber moved to one side and watched the blade miss his stomach by nearly a foot. He smiled thinly. "Take your time, Indian. We got all day."

Torres pressed in, holding his knife at waist level. Schreiber circled him, staying barely out of reach. Torres jumped toward him, jabbing the point of his blade at Schreiber's chest. Dutch caught the steel on his own blade, then stepped inside the Apache's outthrust arm and ripped his knife across the Apache's stomach. Torres gasped and blood seeped, then flowed freely from the gash.

Schreiber said, "This is different than butchering women, Indian. You're goin' to get butchered up some yourself."

Schreiber could see fear and uncertainty in the Apache's eyes. He stepped in quickly, feinting a slash at the Indian's throat, then dropping the blade and ripping steel again into the man's stomach. Torres stumbled back, mouth sagging open, pain etched on his face.

Schreiber moved slowly toward him. "You got about ten minutes, Apache, before you get so weak you can't hold the knife." He pointed toward the crimson flow from the man's stomach that had stained his breechclout and was trickling down both legs.

Torres grimaced. His hand tightened on his knife. He crouched low and ran at Schreiber, knife poised for a finishing blow. With his left hand Dutch caught the wrist of the Apache's knife hand just as the knife was striking toward him. Dutch pulled forward and Torres teetered off balance. Quickly Dutch whirled behind the man and thrust his blade into the Apache's neck. Torres went to his knees, blood pouring from the neck wound.

Dutch stood back while Torres struggled to his feet.

He felt no excitement within him, he wasn't even breathing hard. The big Apache was swaying unsteadily but he kept coming forward, the look of death upon his face. He hooked his knife in a savage, desperate swing at Dutch's throat but Dutch pulled back, the blade flashing by him.

Dutch stepped in and buried his knife between the Apache's ribs, puncturing his liver. Torres fell to his hands and knees, dropping his knife, face contorted. He was scrambling frantically for his knife when Dutch grabbed him by the hair and yanked up his head, slashing his blade across the Apache's throat. Torres made a strangling noise, tried to rise, and pitched forward on his face.

There was a moaning sound swelling from the Apaches, growing louder, becoming angry. Dutch saw the medicine man raise a hand. He heard Nochelte say, "Torres is gone. He did a bad thing and he has paid for it. We pay for it, also, for we have one less warrior."

Dutch felt the hold that the shaman had over these people. The noise stopped. They were silent, listening to Nochelte, the Prophet.

Nochelte looked at Dutch and then at the closing ring of warriors. He said quietly, "This is a small thing. The woman was of no value. But she belonged to the Dutchman and he had the right to fight Torres. The Dutchman will stay with us awhile and we will say no more about it."

Schreiber's knife was still in his hand, hung loosely at his side. He said, "You red heathen, she was my wife." He moved toward Nochelte, a cold, bitter anger within him. "She was a good woman. She was good for me. Your people destroyed her."

He spat near Nochelte's moccasins. "I will spend no

time in this camp. Once I worked with the Apaches. They were my scouts. They were honorable people. Now they are less than dogs."

He felt the bleak eyes of the shaman upon him. He turned and knelt beside the dead body of Torres, and with his knife he cut the thong that held Elaine's scalp. He took the scalp and walked away and made a small fire. When the flames were surging through the dried twigs, he placed the scalp on the fire and watched the hair singe and curl and puff into flame.

When it was done he stood up and looked upward into the sky. He struggled for words to fill a silent prayer, but none came to him. He had never been a praying man, but he had been in love with her. She was gone, of course, and so now was the quest that had kept him going. The future seemed as empty as the space into which he stared.

Nochelte's voice came to him. "You will stay awhile, Dutchman. We have many things to talk upon." He motioned toward a young squaw cooking over an open fire near a cluster of wickiups. "Go fill your stomach with hominy and stewed rabbit. A full belly lends itself to deliberate counseling."

It was a half-hour later that Schreiber sat down opposite the shaman in the shade of a flimsy ramada. His arm was hurting him some now, and there was a great weariness spreading over his body. He reached for tobacco and papers and fashioned a smoke. He said, "I see lots of warriors in this camp, but no children, not many squaws."

Nochelte nodded. "Enough young squaws to cook for the men. Most of them with the children and old men are traveling to the border. You know this. You saw the tracks when you found the young rancher and Apache boy.''

Schreiber touched a match to his cigarette and drew the smoke deep, letting it out slowly. ''That's true. I told the Captain at the post that it shaped up to be an outbreak soon. You've been pullin' the different Apache tribes together near a year now. You've been holdin' your dances and making your speeches and getting your people to believing they can whip the horse soldiers and retake this country.

''But you're smart enough to know it can't be done. You'll get your followers butchered.'' He drew on the cigarette and looked at the medicine man through the wisp of smoke. ''What in hell will you fight with? I don't see many guns in this camp.''

Nochelte smiled faintly. ''I am a shaman, Americano. I have much power. The Great God has told me that when the time arrives to fight the White Eyes, I will be able to call up the great dead chiefs. Warriors, such as Cochise and Mangus and Delshay. I will have their counseling. They know much of fighting the White Eyes.''

He paused and looked around the camp. ''My people believe in me. They had lost hope. They believed in nothing. Now they have faith again and hope. Do not be deceived into thinking we will fight with arrows and rocks. There was a great Comanche medicine man who it was said could belch up stacks of guns and bullets. Perhaps I have this power.''

Schreiber studied the medicine man through slitted lids. The Apaches were, he knew, steeped in the supernatural. They had many deities. Child of the Water, perhaps the greatest warrior of all time, and White

Painted Woman, who saw after the needs of the Apache. Did Nochelte really believe in these spirits? Did he really believe in the one he called the Great God? Or was Nochelte simply educated enough by the white man to make these primitive tribes believe in him and his power?

Looking now at the little Indian, pale, slight of stature, with a chiseled face and eyes like gleaming pebbles of coal, Dutch knew he did not have the answer. Too many times he had tried to think like the Apache, react like the Apache. Too many times he had been wrong.

Dutch said quietly, "I know nothing of your powers. If you have these great gifts, why are your people still on the reservation? If you can produce guns and bullets for your warriors, then why do I see bows and lances around the wickiups? If you arouse your people to an outbreak, armed as I see them armed, you will destroy the Apache as a people. If you are gifted with wisdom from your God, then you should now know a better way than war."

Nochelte nodded, smiling. He held up both hands, fingers outspread. "Before your time, Americano, and before my time, the Apache owned this land, from the mountains where we now sit down to the border where the Mexicans live. In the summer, when the sun was hot, we lived in these mountains. In the winter, when the snows came and covered this place, we moved to the desert and slept warm.

"Now we are prisoners in our own land. The mountains are empty of animals to eat because they have been hunted out. In the summer, we are hungry. In the time of the snow we are hungry and cold, and our warriors die like old men from empty bellies and disease. Our children die, also, because the milk of their mothers has no nourishment. We cannot stay in these mountains any longer. If our leaving brings war between us, then we will have war."

The shaman folded his arms in front of his narrow chest and threw back his shoulders. "I want to speak to you of another plan. I want you to consider my words and carry them back to the chief of the horse soldiers. We, you and I, Americano, could save many lives, both Americanos and Apache."

Schreiber reached for tobacco and rolled a cigarette. He said, "Torres killed my wife. I have killed Torres. I think the killing will go on until there are no more Apaches."

The little Apache shook his head. "There is another way, if the chief of the horse soldiers will listen." He stood up and swept a hand across the meadow. "There are three hundred warriors here. They will fight if I say so. They will keep peace if I say so. This you must understand before we can talk."

Dutch lighted his smoke and drew deeply on it. He looked up at the shaman. "I think you are in charge. I never doubted it."

Nochelte sat down, crosslegged. "That is good. What I say I can do, I will do. You cannot say what the White Eyes will do. That is bad. But we have no choice."

Schreiber flicked an ash from his cigarette, studying the shaman, then looking out upon the camp. He could not rid himself of the emptiness inside him. Elaine was gone. The ranch was gone. In payment of these losses, an Apache lay dead. What did it matter that he was dead? He was still without a wife and without his ranch. He was without purpose. He sat there and smoked and looked at the medicine man. Everything he had cherished was gone and he was a prisoner of the Apaches. A cool anger swept him and suddenly he just didn't give a damn.

Finally he said, "You may get guns. You may get bullets and horses. I know that. I know how you figure to get them. I know where you'll get them. With guns and bullets and good horses, you can raise a lot of hell. You can kill a lot of people. But you can't win a war. So what do you have to bargain with and what is the deal?"

He could see a little doubt in the shaman's eyes, an uncertainty that was not there before. Nochelte said, "The Dutchman reads sign like an Apache."

Schreiber grinned. "The silver? Hell, I didn't figure your squaws were haulin' rocks. But you are still over a hundred miles from the border with it. A lot can happen in a hundred miles. There's Fort Thomas and Camp Huachucca. There's three to four big ranches to cross, with cowhands ridin' boundaries lookin' for something to shoot. You make it through all that and you still got to deal with the Mexicans, and they don't love Apaches. So tell me now about this plan to save the lives of Americanos."

Schreiber could see the Apache's face tighten. He could see the chilling cold of the Indian's eyes. He could hear the words, "You are a fool, Dutchman. The Great God is with the Apache. When we need rain, the rain comes. When we need wind, the wind blows. If the squaws and children and old men encounter the horse soldiers, they will have their knives against the throats of six soldiers to hold the others off. I have seen to that. The Great God has done it through me."

And now Schreiber knew where the six missing soldiers were, and Captain Roland and his horse soldiers were staring into a cold deck. Try to stop the squaws with their travois and you get six soldiers with their throats cut. Don't stop them and you get hell all over.

Dutch pinched out his smoke. He said, "You can't make it. The squaws have at least twelve more days on the trail. Something will happen. Maybe six horse soldiers will get killed. But I doubt the silver will reach the border. So what is this plan you have?"

Nochelte stood up again. He motioned to Schreiber to follow him. They walked up a steep hill where they could look down on forty miles of territory in any direction. Nochelte said, "With my three hundred warriors, I can make of them fifteen or so bands of raiders. Send them out into that country to burn and kill and drive off stock. What can the horse soldier do?"

Dutch grinned coldly. "You want to know? The Army can have two thousand men on the Apaches within twenty-four hours. You seem to have the idea that the Army has pulled out."

Nochelte looked at Dutch. "No. I know the Army is here, what is left of it. It is half as large as it was during the last big war. The scouts have gone. Who is to lead the horse soldiers? Will they chase one band of Apaches or another? It cannot chase them all. Who makes the decision? Perhaps they will simply mill about in the desert and choke on their own dust." He smiled at Schreiber. "I doubt this Army will see many Apaches."

The man was near the truth. It took Apaches to find Apaches, and it took white men that knew Apaches to work with them and keep them part of the Army unit. Dutch knew this. This had been his life before he married Elaine. He shrugged. "You start something and we'll find out."

Nochelte nodded. "We will find out if that is what is

to be. Eventually your soldiers will chase the Apache to
the border and the soldiers will have to stop there. They
will return to their forts, used up, hungry, horses worn
out. These same Apaches will come at them again from
across the border with good horses, repeating rifles,
and food and blankets for a long war. Many White Eyes
will fall before these warriors.''

He looked at Schreiber. ''This need not be, Dutchman. The Apache people are not so many now as they
were when they held all this land from these mountains
to the border, from the western part of what is called
New Mexico Territory, throughout what you now call
Arizona. We do not need so much land now. But we
need mountains and desert and the right to cross into
Mexico and make war with the Mexicans, which we
have always done. We can give up land to the White
Eyes if the White Eyes will give up land to the
Apache.''

The shaman made a sweeping gesture with his arm.
''From here to the border, give us a hundred miles east
to west. We can live in that country as we have always
lived. We will permit the White Eyes to cross it, but we
will decide where and how many at one time.''

Dutch shook his head. ''You're loco. To give up that
country would be wiping out half a dozen settlements,
more than that many ranches, thirty—forty farms.''

Nochelte nodded. ''One way or the other, they will
be wiped out, Dutchman.''

Schreiber took off his hat and wiped a sleeve across
his forehead. The little medicine man was crazy. You
couldn't move people out of a land that they had spent
years working for, settling on, fighting to hold. To an
Apache, moving was a simple thing. Simply pack a
handful of belongings on a travois and take out. It was

different with white men. They did not move easily. Their roots grew deep and memories held them to the place called "home."

He said, "So this is the message I'm supposed to take to the chief of the horse soldiers? Nochelte, the medicine man, says move the settlers off of this land you speak of, move out the soldiers, and there will be peace. Otherwise, it is war again." He looked hard at the Indian. "Hell, Apache, I can give you his answer now."

Nochelte smiled faintly, "Do not be too sure, Dutchman. It is not a bad bargain. There are some large towns such as Globe and the place called Tombstone, where many are gathered to dig the white metal. These will not be disturbed. The boundaries are not inflexible. The White Eyes will still have twice as much Apache land as the Apache will have. It is better for the White Eyes this way instead of having three hundred warriors with repeating rifles empty the land with bullets."

Dutch shrugged. "It's not me you have to convince. My answer would be no, but it's not my decision. I'll take the message." He turned to leave but Nochelte raised a hand.

"Not now, Dutchman. You will stay with us until the silver is across the border. Then you will take the message and you will know that the Apache has the guns to make war."

CHAPTER EIGHT

The food detail was halfway back to the post with the two o'clock sun pulling water out of their bodies, while a searing wind flung dust and grit into their faces. Lieutenant Holcomb led the detail, with Cathy riding beside him. The three troopers kept a respectful distance in the rear so as not to overhear the officer's banter with the woman.

The lieutenant was not displeased with himself. He was a good soldier and he knew it. The captain knew it, too, and had no orders to give him about handling the post in the captain's absence. He was young but he was remedying that as fast as nature allowed. He wanted to see action but that would have to come. It could not be forced, and he was patient enough to realize that. In the meantime, he fought against boredom. Having Cathy Roland with him lightened his spirits considerably.

He said now, "Perhaps after the search for the troopers is over, the captain will send a supply detail into Tucson. It is quite a place. Dances, dinners, even stage shows. Would you like to see it?"

Cathy nodded. "Yes, that would be fun." She said this, remembering Dutch Schreiber's dead wife had lived in Tucson. She would like to know more about her.

The lieutenant looked at her. "You're in a pensive mood. Something troubling you?"

Cathy forced a smile, looking back at him. "Not really. My uncle is worried. He says he has a feeling that something is about to happen. I guess knowing he is worried also worries me. That's all."

She knew she was lying but the lie hurt no one, and it would deflate the young lieutenant if she said she was worried about Dutch Schreiber. And why should she worry about that man? She had no answer. She hardly knew him.

The lieutenant said, "Pull up," and he laid a hand on her horse's neck. There was a lone horseman sitting his mount across the trail in front of them, perhaps fifty yards away. He was a strange-looking man, with long black hair drooping down to his shoulders. He was bare-chested above his faded Levi's. A jug, setting on his horse's back, was held close to his crotch. He was motionless, waiting for them.

The lieutenant spoke to the troopers and two of them pulled their mounts beside Cathy's horse. The third rode up to the lieutenant and together they moved up the trail toward the horseman.

Cathy asked apprehensively, "Who is that?"

One of the troopers spat tobacco juice on a cholla cactus and wiped a hand across his mouth. "That's Chastino. Half Apache, half white, and all bad."

She saw the three men up the trail in what appeared to be a heated discussion. Chastino, the halfbreed, waved an arm toward the south. The lieutenant was jabbing a finger at him. Presently they all rode back toward Cathy.

The lieutenant's face was flushed with excitement. "We've got to get back to the ranch. We've got something big here, if the man's not lying. He says that stolen silver shipment we heard so much about is being taken to Mexico by a bunch of Apache squaws. They're dragging the stuff across country on travois. Our six missing troopers are with them. Captives."

Cathy felt a tremor run through her. Her uncle had been right. Something was about to happen. She couldn't put a name on it, but it was, she knew instinctively, something bad.

They wheeled around toward the ranch. Holcomb said, "They'll trade the silver for guns in Mexico. That's what that bunch of heathens on the reservation are waiting on. They need guns and ammunition. If they get them, we'll have us a war on our hands."

Cathy looked at the halfbreed riding silently beside the troopers. "Why did he tell you this? Which side is he on? I heard he is half Apache."

The young officer smiled thinly. "Chastino has no side. He's as alone as a lobo wolf. He wants bullets and money. Says he's going to Tucson and stay until the trouble is over."

"Will the Army pay him for this information?"

Holcomb nodded. "I promised him thirty dollars. "He wouldn't talk unless I promised. If the captain doesn't back me up, there goes my savings."

Cathy shook her head, looking out upon the dry, desolate land shimmering in the heat-laden air. "How can you find anything out there? How can you stop them from crossing the border?"

The lieutenant looked at her. "Dutch Schreiber. If he's alive and if he will work."

An odd thought came to Cathy. For a man some said was crazy, a man Mae Brewer didn't trust, and a man Jesse Cogar didn't like, it still always came back to

Dutch Schreiber when there was trouble with the Apaches. But what would become of a man like that when there were no Apaches to hunt?

Jesse Cogar had not been looking for Dutch Schreiber when he dropped by the Jackson ranch this morning. He had a score to settle with the Dutchman, all right, but it would keep. He had been looking for the halfbreed, Chastino. He had gone to sleep on the job when he hadn't put a bullet in the halfbreed yesterday evening. He was so accustomed to the halfbreed selling him information that only he could use, he forgot that this time Chastino had information he could sell in several places. And he was just the man to do it.

Cogar thought perhaps the halfbreed knew that Captain Roland was at the Jackson ranch, and had gone there to make himself another deal, this time with the Army. But he wasn't there.

So Cogar was having coffee with the captain and Ruth Jackson when his man, Whitey Doaks, rode up and called him outside. He told him that he had picked up sight of Chastino just as the halfbreed entered the post. There the halfbreed would find out where he could see the captain, and now Cogar knew where to find Chastino. On the trail to the ranch.

He and Whitey were making good time down the trail about an hour behind the food detail when Cogar spotted riders in the distance. They pulled into some boulders and waited for the figures to take recognizable shape. In about fifteen minutes Cogar made out Cathy Roland riding beside the lieutenant. Behind them was Chastino and three troopers.

Jesse Cogar looked at Whitey. "We got to get five

men in five shots. If we don't we'll have a fight on our hands.''

Whitey looked at him. ''What about the woman?''

''We won't kill her but we can't let her go. We'll take her. Just figured out how I can use her.''

Whitey shook his head. ''I done a lot of things wrong, but I don't hold with abusing a woman.''

Jesse Cogar scowled. ''Goddammit, I didn't say abuse her. I said I can use her. She'll help get us to the silver. I got no time to explain now. Get these horses around that hill and let's get in shooting position.''

Whitey Doaks looked doubtful. Finally he said, ''What's in this for me?''

Jesse could have shot him. But, hell, he did need the man, and if Whitey was driving a hard bargain now, bargains had a way of being renegotiated. He said, ''If we get twenty-five to thirty thousand for the silver, you'll get two thousand. If we get less, you get less. I've got to hire on six or seven gun hands at Benson and they won't come cheap. I got to buy some gear and grub and ammunition. Hell, I won't clear much more than half.''

Whitey nodded. ''I'll shoot with you.'' He took the reins of Cogar's horse while Cogar dismounted, then he took the animals around the base of a red sand hill and tied them to a pinyon tree.

They were settled in among the huge, misshapen boulders, out of sight of the approaching riders. Cogar said, ''Not until they're in front of us. If the woman's horse starts to run, shoot it. We got no time to chase her all over the country.''

It seemed to Jesse Cogar that the food detail would never arrive in front of the red boulders. Lieutenant Holcomb was moving the group at a steady but slow pace. Time was becoming important. The squaws were moving the silver south while he sat here. When he finished this business he had cattle to sell before he could leave. He fidgeted with his rifle, checking the lever action, wiping off the sight with his fingers.

Suddenly the detail was in front of him. He said, "Start shooting."

Hell can come to life and play out its hand in twenty seconds. It did that now, using the bleak and unrelenting terrain in front of the boulders as its stage. With the first crack of rifle fire, men were screaming and shouting. Horses were squealing and bucking and reaching for the sky with their front legs. Blood spilled from lifeless bodies and men writhed out their final agony on the desert floor. It took ten shots.

Cathy Roland heard the first blast of gunfire. She remembered the startled shout of Lieutenant Holcomb and then her horse reared and came down hard, jarring her out of the saddle. For a moment she did not see the men dying. Her brain was stunned by the fall and she did not hear the screaming.

But when she opened her eyes, lying on her side, she saw the bleeding corpses stretched out on the burning sand. And then a shrill, piercing sound filled the air and she fought to shut it out but could not. She shut her eyes, not realizing that she was hearing her own wild screams.

Later she opened her eyes again. She did not know how long she had lain there with her eyes closed. She looked up at the tanned, smiling face of Jesse Cogar. This was a dream, she was sure. She closed her eyes again, deliberately, and lay there a few seconds longer.

When she opened them again, he was still there.

Cathy said, "Dear God in heaven, it was you who did this!"

He reached down and pulled her to a sitting position. "Take a good look, woman, and remember—it don't pay to cross Jesse Cogar. The halfbreed found that out. Too bad about the soldier boys. They just got caught in something that wasn't their business."

She said faintly, "You'll have to kill me, too."

He shook his head. "You're going to Mexico. I can probably sell you there to some rich politician who likes his women's skin a little whiter than they grow it down there."

She shook her head, fighting off the unreality of it, trying to understand it. She said, "You are a monster."

He flashed a smile. "No. I'm a businessman. And I mean business now. Get on your feet. We're pullin' out."

Chapparo, the Apache and head scout for the squaws with the silver, left the reservation after the knife duel between Schreiber and Torres. Nochelte had permitted him to stay for the fight, and now it would take two days of hard riding to catch up with his charges. The fight had been short and brutal and somehow it brought to Chapparo certain misgivings. The Apache had lost the fight. Too many times the Apache had lost the fight to the Americanos. Nochelte said it would be different next time.

He was thinking on this when he heard the shots. The noise was perhaps a half-mile away on the desert floor, and the shots came so fast he could not even guess at the number of them. And then it was quiet again.

He was a curious man and, since he had to descend to the desert floor anyway, he reined his horse a little west to about where the shots had come from. He eased his way down the timbered slope. He was also a cautious man and he took a full half-hour covering the distance, staying in the timber, stopping to listen.

When he reached the trail that led to the Jackson ranch, he stopped and looked for some sign of the target of those shots. A riderless horse, carrying an Army saddle, scrambled out of a draw and ran past him. The draw paralleled the trail and he rode into it and turned north, for it appeared that the horse had come from that direction.

Ten minutes later he dismounted and eased his way up the bank. He could see the bodies strewn around the trail a hundred yards away. He waited awhile.

When nothing moved, he got back on his horse and rode out of the draw and toward the bodies. Four of them were horse soldiers. Then there was Chastino. He knew well the halfbreed and despised him thoroughly. He wondered about this. Nobody shot horse soldiers except Apaches. He knew that Nochelte would not permit this thing to happen and stir up trouble before the Apaches were ready. But the Apaches would probably be blamed.

This was a bad thing. He wondered if he should go back and report this to Nochelte. He sat there deliberating on it. The squaws and silver were his responsibility. Nochelte might be angry with him if he turned back to the reservation.

Still, this was a thing that could cause much trouble, and if Nochelte knew of it the trouble might be avoided. If he failed to report this, Nochelte might be angry with him. He did not like to make decisions. He reached into

the cowhide bag slung across his horse's back and
pulled out a thin strip of venison jerky. He chewed on
this, mulling the situation over.

Many young soldiers, some of them lieutenants, died
for their country fighting the Apache in Arizona. Death
was a possibility every man faced who donned the
uniform out there. Yet very few ever really thought it
could happen to them. It was always the other man who
got killed, burned to death, or shot full of arrows like a
pin cushion and left to scream himself to death.

Lieutenant Holcomb was no exception. He could see
himself fighting gallantly, killing the enemy, leading
the charge that would rout the Apache for all time. He
never thought of being wounded, much less of being
killed. But lying there with the sun scorching his face
and lips crusted with sand, he realized now that he was
dying. And he never saw the enemy.

Pain seared his stomach and the taste of his own
blood sickened him. But for the moment his mind was
clear. He felt something in his hand and he opened his
eyes and looked at it. It was his Army Colt. Somehow,
he had found time to draw the gun, but he did not
remember firing it. He lay motionless, only his eyes
moving. And then he saw the Apache.

The red man was big-bellied and he sat there in the
middle of the trail eating on something. The sight
sickened the lieutenant. How could the red bastard gun
down a whole detail without mercy and then sit there
and eat while he surveyed the carnage? A terrible rage
filled the young officer. Slowly he raised the gun and
leveled on the Apache's fat belly. He pulled the trigger.

The Apache's mouth flew open. He toppled off his

horse and rolled around in the dust. He sat up, grabbing at his stomach. Lieutenant Holcomb smiled. He rolled to his hands and knees, still holding on to the gun. He crawled toward the Apache. The Indian was moaning, rocking back and forth, arms pressed against his stomach. He paid no attention to Holcomb, who kept crawling toward him.

When the lieutenant was barely six feet away from the Apache, he stopped and fought against the sickness that swept over him. Something was choking him, nauseating him, filling his throat. He dropped his head and vomited and looked at his own blood rapidly sinking into the thirsty sand.

He moved again toward the Apache. Three feet away he raised the gun again and shot the warrior squarely between the eyes. The man fell over on his back. His legs thrashed briefly, then only his feet twitched for a second or so.

Lieutenant Holcomb lunged forward, sprawling across the Apache's body. He lay there, wondering vaguely what happened to the girl, Cathy Roland, and what the captain would think about this. He died with this on his mind.

In the brassy Arizona sky dark wings began to gather as the buzzards looked down on this great supply of food that some nameless bounty had bestowed upon them. The desert has a purpose for every living thing it permits to exist within it. From the beginning of time the buzzard had been its grounds keeper, cleaning up the debris of human conflict and natural tragedy, leaving only the bones of the victims to fertilize the barren soil.

It made no difference to the buzzards that one of the

victims was a young lieutenant with the promise of a good life awaiting him, nor that another was an innocent Apache whose curiosity brought him to this place at the wrong time.

CHAPTER NINE

It was evening of the second day since Schreiber had started after the Apache, Torres, and Captain Harry Roland was feeling the raw edges of his patience. Seated at the table, he looked at Ruth Jackson over a late cup of coffee.

He said, "If he isn't here by four o'clock tomorrow, we are starting for the post. I've got to get a patrol out for those missing troopers, whether I have a scout or not." He paused as an idea came to him. "I might get Joe Brewer to scout for us."

Ruth sipped at the strong coffee. "And who is Joe Brewer?"

Roland smiled slightly, "He was a damned good Apache tracker until he got married. Used to work with Dutch. Now he's running a freight line and missing the excitement of the hunt some." He rubbed a hand over his chin. "I'll have a fight with his wife, Mae, but maybe she'll come around. My judgment is she's keeping too tight a rein on her man."

Ruth left the table and came back with the coffee pot. She filled the captain's cup. "Maybe some men need that." She looked at him. "Are you married, Captain?"

"Me?" Roland looked mildly startled. "Not me. Never have been. When I decided on an Army career, I also decided to remain a bachelor. Army life isn't much of a life for a woman, particularly out here. If you're in Washington, or one of the big forts back East, it isn't so bad. But out here?'' He shook his head.

Ruth filled her own cup. ''Perhaps that's just your judgment of it, Captain. There are women living out here, married to men working at all sorts of jobs.''

He shook his head. ''Army work is different. Woman sees her man go out after hostiles and never knows for sure if he'll be one of those coming back. Hell of a thing to live with.''

She smiled at him. ''Then you can't really blame Mae Brewer for keeping a tight rein on her husband, can you? Aren't you asking her to go through the same agony of uncertainty that you just said a woman shouldn't have to bear?''

She was right, of course. His mild criticism of Mae Brewer stemmed from his own need of her husband's services, and the opposition he knew he would get from Mae. He studied Ruth Jackson over his coffee cup. She was a smart woman, direct and to the point. And, he thought, a fine-looking woman, too.

He said, ''You're right, but I need a scout and she needs a husband. That puts us in opposition but I admit I can't blame her.'' He sighed and set down his coffee. ''One of these days, not too long now, I'll be out of the Army. I think I'll enjoy a different kind of life. Been at this, one way or another, over thirty years.''

She smiled. ''You seem young for retirement. I think you'll be bored with it.''

He clasped his hands on the table, studying them. She was wrong. He had thought a little about retirement for the last three years. He had thought about it a lot these past few days. Sometimes, when the going was rough, like during the last outbreak, he told himself he was simply trying to find a way out. He wondered if it was the pressure of responsibility that he sought relief from, rather than any burning desire to have a new career.

But he knew now that this was not so. He could handle the pressure as long as he held his command. He could do his job. But there was another life waiting for him. He could have his own ranch and raise fine horses. He would have time to write of the things he had seen and learned in this country. He would have time to travel over it, not as a horse soldier, but as a student seeking to learn even more about it.

Captain Roland shook his head. "I don't think so, Miss Jackson. I am fifty-three years old and if I have learned anything as a horse soldier, it is how to judge good horseflesh and how to raise and train them. I like to work with them. I have also discovered some little ability and a great desire to write.

"I sold an article on the Apache chief, Alchesay, to the *New York Sun*. There are many things to write about out here, and I want to write them. Not just for the money, which will amount to very little, but because I feel the need to do it." He looked at her directly, "A man does not get bored when there are many things he likes to do and has the opportunity to try to do them."

He could see her interest in what he was saying. She was looking at him intently while he talked, as if she was thinking beyond his words and studying the man who spoke them. Suddenly, seeming to realize that she was staring at him, she flushed and dropped her eyes to her cup. She picked it up, shifting from side to side the dregs of cold coffee inside it.

Finally she said, "I believe you. You are one of the

few men I have known who knew what he wanted to do.
You are a lucky man, Captain.'' She smiled slightly,
"Even if you are not married.''

He grinned. He liked this woman. He said, "Drop
the Captain business. You're not in my Army. Call me
Harry.''

She got up from her chair and took the cups. She
asked, "More coffee, Harry?''

Before he could answer the heavy voice of Sergeant
Quincy Shannon came at him from the open door.
"Captain, sir, begging your pardon. Can you come
outside, sir?''

There was a strained, urgent note in the sergeant's
voice that caught Roland's attention, sent a little chill
up his spine. He got up from his chair, moving toward
the door. "What is it?''

The sergeant stood stiff backed beside the door, then
saluted the captain when he walked outside. Something
was about to happen or had happened. Quincy Shannon
had worked under him too long to put on Army airs if
the situation was casual.

He said again, "What's up, Sergeant?''

Shannon pointed to the group of troopers in the yard.
"There's a boy down there, sir. The sentry caught him
running down the road. He has something to say to
you.'' The sergeant's face contorted in a passion of pain
and agony. "It's a terrible thing, sir.''

Captain Roland walked past the sergeant, out into the
ranch yard. He looked at the men clustered around. He
said, "Where is the boy?''

There was a movement within the group of troopers.
A small boy appeared. He stood before Roland, body
trembling, a well of tears showing in his eyes by lantern

light. The boy said tremulously, "I am Jesus Garcia. I have seen many dead soldiers."

Roland motioned the troopers back. He knelt down on a knee before the youngster. "Where, son? Where did you see them?"

The boy stood silent, clasping his hands in front of him. He said, "I was going home, down the road. I work late at the Whitaker's place."

The captain nodded. "Get it out, boy. You can tell me."

The boy sucked in his breath. "Sir, there are four dead horse soldiers six miles down the road. Shot all to pieces, sir. And two dead Apaches." His mouth twitched, he rubbed his eyes. "It was an awful thing to look upon."

And there it was. He had felt it for days now. Something was going to happen. Hell was breaking loose. The Apaches had struck. Lieutenant Holcomb was dead, along with three good troopers. Then he remembered Cathy and a vise tightened around his gut. He could barely get the words out, "What about the woman, boy? Was there a woman?"

The youngster shook his head. "No woman. Four dead horse soldiers, two dead Apaches."

Ruth Jackson had moved in behind the captain. She saw Roland stiffen, saw his head drop slightly. She felt the muscles in her throat constrict as she put her hand on her throat. She said, "Oh, my God!"

Slowly the captain got to his feet. He said, "We thank you, son. I will see that you are rewarded for this." He looked around for Shannon and found him. He said, "Sergeant, get the men in the saddle. We will pick up the bodies and head for the post." He paused, then said flatly, "This is war, men. You know what we have to do."

It was a different Captain Harry Roland that looked now at Ruth Jackson. His face was hard-planed in the lantern light. He said, "Miss Jackson, get yourself together. We are pulling out."

Ruth Jackson suddenly found a new respect for Harry Roland. A moment ago he had been a man, talking of a man's dreams, gentle, soft spoken. He was a different man now, hard-faced, stiff-backed, sharp of voice. He was a commander in the United States Army and he was in charge.

She turned toward the house, frightened at the boy's story, yet secure in the presence of the captain. She said, "Have my horse saddled. I won't be a minute."

It was a grim and silent procession that made its way in the dark down the trail. Some of the men realized that, except by circumstance, it could be them lying dead on the trail. Others, less imaginative, figured it was one of those things you come to expect in this man's Army. Harry Roland was trying to keep his mind on his duties as commander of the post, and trying hard not to think of his niece, Cathy, and what was happening to her in the hands of the red devils.

Ruth Jackson had her mind on Harry Roland, Captain in the U.S. Army. He was a man who could be as gentle or as tough as the situation required. He was a good man to ride with, wherever he went.

Dutch Schreiber was sitting up in a ramada on the flank of the Cibecue village, as helpless as a hog-tied calf waiting to be branded. He was propped against a big pine pole and his hands were tied behind the pole. He couldn't roll a cigarette, which he desperately wanted, and he couldn't get the Apache guarding him to do it for him.

He sat there and stared out into the night and listened to the Apache drums. The drums were talking of war, of vengeance. Occasionally the wind would carry to him the low chanting of the dancing warriors. The grassy meadow was Nochelte's stage and there each night he whipped his followers into a mounting frenzy.

The shaman was smart. You didn't have to talk with him very long to know this. War now, without guns, meant another defeat for the Apache, and even harder times than they presently endured. With guns he had leverage. Maybe work out a peace that meant a better deal for the Indian. If not, then war—but with the means to carry it on.

But Apaches were an unpredictable people. Whipping up their emotions every night like this could be dangerous. Dangerous for the whites and for the Apaches alike, and also for Nochelte. For if he lost control, they would sweep him along with them into destruction.

Schreiber found himself suddenly thinking of Cathy Roland, a proud woman whom he had offended by not going to the Brewers' dance. He grinned in the darkness. She would have been embarrassed if he had attended. He had none of the social graces. He was raw and rough and blunt-spoken, with a tendency to overdo it, on the seldom occasions when he had access to a bottle.

The few women he knew didn't trust him. A lot of the men he knew didn't like him, but at least they all respected his singular ability as an Apache hunter. Brewer liked him, but Brewer was cowed now by his wife. The captain liked him. Thinking about that, he felt better. If Roland liked him, he must be all right, because Roland was a good judge of men.

He looked at the broad back of the Apache guard. He yelled, "Nat'oh!" The guard didn't move. Schreiber said, "You red bastard, roll me a smoke."

The guard remained silent, not turning his head. Schreiber said bleakly, "If I ever get my knife back, I'll send you off to join Torres."

The guard turned his head; "Dant'ehe."

Dutch grinned. "You make me shut up. Come on in here. I'll kick you to death with my hands tied."

He sat there in silence awhile. It came to him that he had not thought of Elaine since he had burned her scalp. He wondered about this. Always before she had been with him, her face in front of him, urging him on to kill the Apache who had destroyed her. He didn't see her face now.

He shifted himself against the pole, easing the ache of his back. The captain had said that Nochelte's story about Elaine being at Cogar's house was a trick to destroy his reason, make him blind-mad so he would be easy prey for the blade of Torres.

He didn't think so. Roland knew Apaches some, but not like Schreiber knew them. This was not their way. They fought with no sophistication. Just their natural agility and strength and deep hatred for the white man. They were deadly only as a cougar is deadly when treed and forced to fight. But maybe Nochelte was different. He had a white man's education.

A half-hour passed. The drums continued to send out their throbbing message. He tried to sleep but it wouldn't come. He saw the guard stand up and look around. The Apache stood there, looking, then moved hesitantly around the ramada. There was a dull thud as something hit the ground. Schreiber straightened his back, peering out into the darkness.

A voice said, "Ho, Dutch. You hokay?"

He said, "Goddamn. Max, are you all right?"

A grinning copper face split with white teeth peered at him from the far corner of the open ramada. "Comanche always whip Apache."

Dutch grinned. "Not in this country, you damned heathen. You're fightin' on their ground." He jerked his head. "Cut me loose, you lucky bastard."

Max was beside him as silently as a brown shadow. The big blade of his knife slashed the rawhide thongs that held his arms. Max said, "We get to hell out."

Dutch nodded. The drums had stopped. The dance was over. The Apaches would be seeking out their wickiups. He said, "Right. We get to hell out. We ain't got much time, kid."

They slipped out of the ramada and hugged the dark shadows. Dutch led the way to a grove of pinyons near the edge of the camp. He asked flatly, "You got any horses?"

The little Comanche nodded. "One. Maybe a mile south of here. I came in on belly."

"Damned good thing." Dutch was silent a moment, thinking it over. He said finally, "The horse is mine. Take me to it. I got to get to the post by tomorrow. That's a thirty-five mile ride. I'll probably kill the horse."

He looked at Max. "There's a spring fifteen miles south under that big peak. You've been there. You head for it and hole up. I'll send a patrol out to bring you in. Don't let the Apaches see you. They know you ride with me and they are after me. If they can't get me, they'll take you as bait."

Max nodded. "You boss now."

Dutch scowled at him. "What do you mean, now?"
He saw the bulge in the boy's shirt pocket. "What the
hell?" He reached over and fished out a sack of Durham
tobacco. "You light a cigarette and you're sending a
flare up for some Apache to take your scalp."

He hefted the sack in his hand. "Besides, I'm short
on tobacco and you are too young to smoke."

Max grimaced. He said plaintively, "Hell, Dutch."

Schreiber grinned. "Ain't it? Now take me to that
horse."

He was ten miles from the post and it was high noon. He
had chosen the longer ride to the post instead of heading
for the ranch and the Captain, because Nochelte would
likely expect him to head for the ranch. Dutch and the
horse were both needing water, but there was no time to
search it out.

Nochelte would have discovered his absence in the
ramada within an hour from the time he left. The
shaman would have a dozen of his best trackers fanning
out over the country to bring him in. His one shot was to
ride and ride hard, and to hell with trying to cover his
tracks. The horse was feeling the pace and so was he.

He pulled rein on top of a mesa and looked around.
There was nothing moving. He didn't expect to see
anything. You saw the Apache when he was looking
down the barrel of his rifle or over the tip of an arrow.
The horse was heaving and he let him blow a few
minutes. He hated to kill a good horse. He hooked a leg
over the saddle horn and rolled a smoke and rested,
watching the land.

It was an empty land. A vast expanse of brown and red with little clumps of green. The green was not grass but cactus, cholla, pear, agave, with barbs and thorns and leaves like bayonets. A mean, uncompromising land.

He finished his smoke and spoke to the horse. The drooping head lifted. The horse shifted his weight in anticipation. Dutch said, "Let's make tracks." He nudged the animal's flanks with the heels of his boots and the horse responded, starting at a trot, then slowing to a walk. Dutch thought, ten miles, three hours. I could run him and make it in two. He knew he wouldn't.

He pulled up to the post a little after three o'clock. The sentry knew him and waved him in. He rode up to the corral and dismounted, handing the reins to a red-faced trooper. "Give him a little water. Later give him some grain. I'll be out to check him over."

The trooper was new. He eyed Dutch coldly. "Who the hell are you to give me orders?"

Dutch said quietly, "I'm Schreiber. Dutch Schreiber. I'm giving the orders."

The trooper flushed. "Well, hell, Dutch. I've heard of you." He took the horse into the corral.

Dutch walked up to headquarters and shook hands with the orderly. He said, "Don't reckon the captain's here yet?"

The orderly nodded. "Yes, sir. Arrived about an hour ago. He's in his quarters."

Dutch looked toward the captain's quarters. "He's early. He said he would wait."

The orderly looked at him uncertainly. "Sir?"

"Nothin'." Dutch walked away, moving toward the captain's lodgings.

A corporal walked by him, talking with a couple of

privates. He heard the trooper say, "This is it. Them Apaches will catch hell now."

Schreiber wheeled and laid a hand on the corporal's shoulder. "What's going on, Corporal?"

The trooper scowled. "Who wants to know?"

"Me," Dutch stood back a step. "Dutch Schreiber."

The corporal's frown faded. He grinned. "You're the man we're waitin' for. Captain will be glad to see you. We got us an Apache hunt."

"Why?"

The frown appeared again. The corporal said, "You ain't heard? The Apaches ambushed Holcomb and three troopers. Got off with the captain's niece."

Schreiber felt his stomach knot up. His mouth was suddenly dry. He turned and ran toward Captain Roland's quarters.

It was a half hour later. They were grouped around the captain's dining table in Roland's quarters. There was the sergeant, big, bleak-eyed, face glistening with perspiration, mouth tight, looking at Schreiber. There was the captain, agony in his eyes, grim-faced, hunched over, staring at Schreiber. There was Ruth Jackson, pale, wide-eyed, staying away from the men, finding things to do, but listening to Schreiber.

He felt the intensity of the emotion in these people. He was trying to explain why he doubted Apaches were involved in the attack on Holcomb's detail. He had told them about the squaws hauling the silver south. He told them the six missing troopers were with the squaws. He wasn't getting through. He said again, "That fat-gutted Apache you found under Holcomb has to be Chapparo.

He was head scout for the squaws. I saw him ride off the reservation alone yesterday." He looked at Quincy Shannon. "You remember him. He was with Victorio in the last outbreak."

Shannon said grimly, "So what?"

"Well, hell, he left alone. Nochelte doesn't want any trouble until he's sure he's got guns. He wouldn't pull a thing like this now. With guns, he can maybe work out a deal. If he can't, he'll fight, that's for sure. But not now."

Roland said, "Maybe he's losing control. Maybe a bunch of bucks decided to break out. Maybe Chaparro decided to join them."

Schreiber shrugged. "Give me some time. I can look over the ground where it happened and be back tomorrow. You can't get a company on the road to the reservation before late morning, anyway."

The captain stood up. "I can get a company on the trail in two hours, Schreiber. Don't tell me my business."

Schreiber picked up a coffee cup. "Well, you won't need a scout going to the reservation. You been there before and Nochelte and his warriors won't be hard to find. I still think you ought to wait until I check out the ambush."

Shannon pounded a fist on the table. "If those red bastards have Miss Cathy up there, no tellin' what she's going through. I say mount up now and make this medicine man do some talking."

Schreiber shook his head. "I was saying that six months ago. Too late now." He looked at the captain. "More advice. Take it or leave it. Don't take so many men up there. They see a hundred soldiers, they'll figure you're attacking. A dozen troopers can check out the camp for Miss Cathy, if Nochelte will permit it. If he won't, you couldn't do it with a hundred."

Roland nodded slowly. "I'll think it over, Schreiber."

Dutch stood up. "I need a detail. The boy, Max, is hiding out at the spring below Castle Peak without a horse. He needs to be brought in."

Roland nodded again. "It will be done." He looked at Schreiber. "I'll send a dispatch to Camp Huachucca and alert them about the squaws with the silver. After I check the Cibecue camp for Cathy I'll get a patrol after the squaws. Maybe between the troops from Huachucca and my men, we can box them in."

Dutch shrugged. "Maybe. Time you get started, they'll be eight days away from Mexico. It'll take you five days to catch up with them, even if you knew where to find them. It'll be close."

Roland took a cigar from his shirt pocket and lighted it. Dutch noticed a slight shaking of the hand that held the match. Roland said, "What are you going to do?"

Dutch picked up his hat and moved toward the door. "Check the ambush. After that, whatever seems likely. Tell Max to meet me in Two Wells tomorrow morning."

Ruth Jackson felt a sudden compassion for the captain. She knew the conflicts that were tearing him apart. His niece vanished, probably in the hands of Apaches, six troopers of his command held hostage by a fleeing band of Apaches, and the silver. As he had said, when talking to Schreiber, the silver came off that part of the reservation for which he was responsible. It was his job to keep it from reaching the border.

She said, "You men haven't eaten since early morning. I can stir something up."

Roland shook his head. He stood up and walked to the window, looking out upon the grounds. He said, "Quincy, pick twelve of your best men. Get them in the saddle. We are heading for the Apache camp. We still have four hours of riding time before dark."

The sergeant stood up. He saluted. "Yes, sir. My pleasure, sir. Only twelve?"

Roland nodded. "Schreiber's advice makes sense."

Ruth watched the sergeant stride out of the room. She sensed he didn't agree with Dutch Schreiber but he would not question the captain's judgment. He and the captain knew each other well, had gone through many hard times together. The captain made the decisions, gave the orders, and Quincy Shannon saw that they were carried out.

She walked over to Roland. "Harry, I think I should go into Two Wells. I can get a room there for a night or two. I know now that I can't hold the ranch together. No woman could out here, alone. I'll put it on the market and take a stage back to Missouri."

He turned, frowning, looking at her. "No. I want you here when I get back."

Something changed between them at that moment. She could not say what it was, simply a feeling. She asked, "Why?"

He shook his head. "I'm not sure. For the first time in my life, I want somebody waiting for me to come back."

She smiled, then turned away toward the kitchen. "All right, Harry. I'll be here."

It was near dark when Captain Harry Roland gave the orders to Shannon to bivouac. They had covered fifteen miles. The Apache camp lay north another twenty. They would be there before noon.

Fires were made and the smell of coffee and frying side meat filled the coolness of the evening air. Sergeant Quincy Shannon took a seat on the ground beside the captain.

Shannon said, "I get the feeling you believe Dutch was right about the ambush, that it wasn't Apaches who wiped out the detail and took Miss Cathy."

Roland studied the steaming hot coffee in his cup. "More I think on it, more I think he is. But we can't take that chance. We have to check it out."

Quincy chewed on a piece of side meat. "Suppose the Apaches won't let us?"

Roland's mouth thinned. "Then we come back with a hundred troopers. If they don't let us search, that means they're guilty, as I see it. We'll be at war again."

Shannon shook his head. "Always hoped I'd have sense enough to get out of this man's Army before the next big fight."

Roland nodded. "Me, too, Sergeant. But here we are."

It was Cathy that worried Roland, gnawed at his guts. A young woman, a good woman, coming out here to heal the scars of her life back East. Perhaps even now she was being tortured, raped, God only knew what was happening to her. And whatever he did, even if he got her out alive, it would be too late.

He had known women to lose their minds under the savage treatment of Apaches. And if it was not Apaches, would she fare any better with renegade white men? These thoughts crowded in on him and he could not sit still. He got up and walked around the camp.

Roland knew he faced a probable court-martial for this time spent looking for his niece instead of trying to stop the silver from reaching the border. His superior would say that stopping the silver was more important to the safety of the Territory and that would be true.

It made no difference. It was his command, his responsibility—and he would handle it his way. With him, Cathy came first.

He didn't minimize the necessity of stopping the silver from crossing the border. If it was turned into guns by the Apache, this country would once again face the awful terror of an Apache uprising. But he had sent two riders to Huachucca, one leaving three hours behind the other. One ought to get through even though, knowing Apaches, he knew the post was under surveillance by the Indians.

Huachucca had the best chance of stopping the fleeing band with the silver, because they were already south of the band and would be working north. Once he got his own men on the trail they would be as Schreiber pointed out, five days ride north of the approximate position of the squaws and old men hauling the silver bars.

The big question was whether any Army patrol could locate the band in that Godforsaken expanse of mountains and burning desert. That could not be answered. It simply had to be tried.

The sharp voice of a sentry on the outskirts of the camp jerked his mind away from his troubling thoughts. Pulling his Army Colt, he walked up to the sentry. Shannon was there, also. He asked, "What is it, trooper?"

The sentry, a youngster, pointed up the sloping rise toward a stand of oak trees. "Riders, sir. I saw them." He paused. "I think I saw them."

There was no need to tell the sergeant to alert the

patrol. Every man had left his meal and grabbed a rifle. They were spread out in a long, thin line, facing the slope ahead of them.

It was a long moment before three riders emerged from the stand of oaks. They moved slowly toward the camp, barely discernible in the deepening shadows of late twilight. When they took form, Roland could make out the leader as a small man in a high-crowned black hat.

When the riders were a hundred feet away Roland said, "That's far enough. What do you want?"

The rider in the black hat raised a hand. "I am Nochelte."

Roland moved forward a dozen steps, then stopped. "What are you doing here?"

The Apache dismounted and stood by his horse. "I am on my reservation, Captain. Perhaps the day will come when I can ask what you are doing here."

Roland spat in the dust. "This is not the day, Apache." He motioned with a hand, "Come on in, but leave your guns on the horses."

Nochelte turned toward the other two riders and made a quick gesture with his hand, "Naghaa." The riders dismounted and the three of them moved into the troopers' camp.

Nochelte said, "We were coming to the post for a talk with the captain."

Roland looked closely at the shaman. The flickering light of the camp played across the thin-lipped, finely chiseled face. He did not, Roland thought, have the harsh, often cruel features of the usual Apache. He did not look like a war chief. He was actually a small, unimpressive, rather mild-mannered man. And that, Roland decided, made him more dangerous, for he knew the reputation of the shaman called Nochelte.

Roland motioned for the Apaches to sit down. He offered coffee and they refused it. He waved a hand at Quincy Shannon, beckoning the sergeant to join in the discussion. He said, "Talk is not enough, shaman. We have come to search your camp. There is a young woman missing. My niece. There was a detail of three troopers and my first lieutenant ambushed and killed. There were two Apaches lying beside them."

Nochelte nodded. "I know of this. This is why we wanted the talk with you. This was not the work of the Apaches. It is not exactly as you say. There was only one dead Apache in the ambush. My best scout, Chapparo. The other was Chastino. He is not Apache."

Roland grunted. "Schreiber says he is a halfbreed. Hangs around your camp a lot."

Nochelte folded his arms around his knees. "He was a mongrel. A dog living by scavenging. I have ordered him out of the Apache camp many times. Like a dog he always came back. Always he had white man's whiskey and he would get my young warriors drunk with it."

Roland squinted across the flame of the dying campfire. "Maybe that's what happened. Maybe he got Chapparo and some of your men drunk and they pulled this ambush."

Nochelte shook his head. "Chastino was ordered from camp three days ago. He would have been killed if he returned. He did not return. My warriors are still in camp. They have not left it. Only Chapparo. He left alone to join the squaws."

Roland feigned ignorance. "The squaws? What squaws?"

Nochelte smiled. "You have talked with the Dutchman. You know of what I speak."

Roland nodded. "You stole a shipment of silver bullion and you're dragging it across Arizona to Mexico to trade for guns. Isn't that it?"

Nochelte shrugged. "My squaws and old men and the children are homesick for the mother mountain. They have gone to them. I will not admit to stealing the silver. You cannot arrest me for that without proof. Do you have proof, Captain?"

Roland said, "I got Schreiber's word on it."

The shaman's lips curled. "The Dutchman? He hates the Apache. He would say anything to hurt the Apache. He came to my camp two days ago and killed one of my warriors. We held him captive. We were going to turn him over to the Army for killing the Apache. He escaped."

Roland tossed cold coffee from his cup. "You're lying, medicine man."

Nochelte smiled thinly. "I will say this, Captain. I do not lie to the white man so much as the white man lies to the Apache. In the old days when the white man wanted the land of the Apache, he could not take it by force because the Apache was strong. Then the Big White Chief promised much to the Apache for part of his land.

"When the Apache made treaties and put up their weapons and became children of the White Chief, the White Chief treated them like slaves and took the rest of the land. Now we, the Coyoteras, the Tontos, and the White Mountain Apaches have a small piece of land that is hunted out and cold in the winter. If we leave it, we will be shot on sight by the horse soldier. The Chiricahuas will not live here, and they live like outlaws wherever they can find food."

Roland took a cigar from his pocket. "Is this what you have come to talk about, shaman?"

Nochelte sliced the air with the edge of his small hand. "No. You are the captain of a small post. You cannot make agreements with the Apache. You cannot do anything to help the Apache. Someday I will talk again to the Big White Chief in the place called Washington. I talked to him once before. I was scouting for the Army then. The Big Chief gave me a medal and I was proud to wear it. I was very young. I was a fool."

He looked directly at Roland. "I came to talk of the ambush where you lost four troopers, where you lost your woman relative. I say again, we did not do it. We would be fools to kill for nothing. What did they have that we want? The woman? We have plenty of squaws."

Roland studied the little Apache. He was somehow convincing. He made sense, like Schreiber made sense. But he had to be sure. He said, "I cannot prove you killed my men and took my niece, but you can't prove you didn't. It is well known that only Apaches kill horse soldiers. Who else would kill them? I will search your camp."

Nochelte nodded. He rose quickly to his feet. "We will expect you tomorrow. Some of my warriors speak Americano. Talk to them. Search every wickiup for the white squaw. Take plenty time. We do not want any trouble with you."

Roland thought, the more time I take, the farther away the silver gets. If he thought I'd find anything, he wouldn't let me near the camp without a fight.

Quincy Shannon put Roland's thoughts into words, "We got to do it, Captain. Maybe it's a waste of time, but we got to do it. Even then we won't be sure. The girl could be hidden anywhere.''

Roland nodded. ''We'll never be sure. Not until we find her.''

Cathy Roland remembered little of the long ride under the furnace heat of the afternoon sun. She remembered being dragged to her horse and forcibly put into the saddle. She remembered the terrible sight of the bodies strewn along the trail. And then, by some protective mechanism of nature, her mind simply ceased to function. She had no thoughts, no fears, no sense of impending disaster. She rode and her body took the physical punishment of five hours in the saddle and she endured it.

It was when they stopped at a weathered, flimsily built shack in a rough canyon country that she looked at Jesse Cogar and recognized him, and bit her lips to keep from screaming.

Cogar dismounted and pushed open the door of the shack with a boot. He said, ''Get her in here, Whitey,'' and went inside.

His lanky, stoop-shouldered companion ran a hand over his thin, whiskered face. She saw his pale eyes looking her over. He walked over to her and touched her arm. ''Get down, miss. We'll be here a spell.''

She sat frozen to the saddle. The man put an arm around her waist and pulled her off the leather, swinging her to her feet. ''You'll be all right, ma'am.''

All right? Dear God in heaven! How could she ever be a whole person again? After what she had seen? She stood there, not moving, and he took her arm. ''Inside with you.'' She went through the door.

Jesse Cogar was grinning at her. ''We took another

ride, didn't we? You said there wouldn't be another time. Don't count on nothin' as being for sure out here, woman.''

Cogar looked at Whitey Doaks. ''You stay with her. Don't let her out of sight. I got to go to Two Wells and make a deal on them cows. Can't go off for two months or more and leave cows running loose.''

Whitey scratched his chin. ''Two months? That long?''

''Hell, yes.'' Cogar reached for tobacco. ''We got to find the Indians and get the silver. Then we got to get it across the border and hide it out until we can figure a way to make a deal on it. After we get the money, we'll want to live it up a little down there. Them Mex gals ain't bad and tequila is cheap.''

Cathy felt a wave of indignation sweep away her numbness. How could these men talk about cheap women and cheap liquor after killing five men? Slaughtering them like pigs! She whirled on Cogar and hit him across the face with the flat of her hand, knocking the cigarette from his mouth.

The blow surprised him, staggered him, so that he almost fell over a chair. Fury contorted his face into a mottled red mask of rage. He hit her in the face with his fist, knocking her sprawling across a filthy pile of blankets that served occasionally as a bed. She lay there, stunned, yet conscious.

She heard Doaks say, ''I told you once, Jesse. I don't like to see a woman abused. I just can't stand it.''

Cogar swore. ''Abused? Goddammit, she had it coming, didn't she? Teach her who's boss around here. Teach her to keep her damned hands to herself and her mouth shut.'' He looked at Whitey. ''Why're you so touchy about women?''

Through half-opened eyes Cathy saw Doaks pacing

the floor, running a hand through stringy, blonde hair. "Brought up on it, I reckon. Pa hit my ma once too often."

"What do you mean, once too often?"

"I killed him. Shot his guts out with his own bird-huntin' gun. Long time ago, down in Texas. I left then, knowin' the law would be on me. About fourteen then, I think. Never did know what happened to ma after that."

Cogar looked at him. "Hell of a thing, killin' your own pa."

"Didn't bother me none. I killed a lot of men since then. Killin' men don't lose me no sleep. But I can't put up with hurtin' a woman. Remember it."

She heard Cogar say, "Well, for Christ's sake. I'm goin' to town. I'll bring you back a bottle."

Cathy heard the door slam and later the sound of hoofbeats fading away into the distance. She lay there, not wanting to move. She closed her eyes and thought about her uncle. What would he do? What would he think when he found out about the lieutenant and the troopers? How would he ever know who the murderers were?

She found herself thinking of Dutch Schreiber. She didn't even know if he was alive. If he was, what could he do? He was a tracker, they said. The best in the country. But how could he find these killers?

She drifted into unconsciousness, a merciful black void where nothing threatened her.

CHAPTER TEN

Dutch Schreiber didn't get into Two Wells the next morning. He didn't get there until mid-afternoon. He was tired and wolf-hungry and out of sorts. He needed a bath and a shave. Checking out sign on the ranch road where the ambush occurred had been a slow job. By dark yesterday he hadn't found enough to know what to make of it, so he spent the night in a cold camp without supper.

For one thing, there had been too much horse traffic over the road. There was the lieutenant's detail, and then those that carried out the ambush. There was Captain Roland's troops who gathered up the bodies, and God knows who else had come by. It was a maze of hoof prints and boot prints and the sand was beginning to blow and it all sort of ran together. So he stayed until morning.

It was better in the early light of the desert. The wind hadn't come up. He told himself he had all the time he needed to do it right, and he took that time. Finally he had it figured that of all the horses that had been over that ground, only two were unshod. He was reasonably sure they belonged to the Apache, Chapparo, and to the halfbreed, Chastino.

Scrambling around on foot in the big boulders that edged up on the trail, he finally found the shells of spent cartridges: .44-40, repeating rifle ammunition, Winchester. Not many of those around except among white civilians. The Army didn't use it. Damn few Apaches could afford one, unless he stole it.

Then an hour later he was circling wide, still on foot, and he picked out the fragments of the tracks of two shod horses going around the big red hill behind the boulders. Still looking, he picked out a few tracks of the same horses coming back from around the hill.

After leaving the hill he had gone down into the draw that flanked the road. Snooping around there, he had picked up the tracks of one unshod horse. Chapparo's. He was sure of it.

Going back in front of the boulders, he ranged a little wider and found one print of a woman's shoe in some deep sand. It was smeared and stretched out like she had stumbled or been dragged.

Finally he headed for town and rode in, convinced he was right. It wasn't Apaches that slaughtered the detail and made off with Cathy Roland. But knowing who didn't do it wasn't enough.

The men he wanted were the ones who took those two shod horses around the hill in back of the boulders. But he couldn't pick up their tracks leaving the scene. The ground got rocky and what soil was there, was thin and blew badly in the wind. One thing he would remember—the left front hoof of one of the horses toed out a mite.

Another thing puzzling him some was the broken whiskey jug on the trail in front of the boulders. Fresh broken, not drifted over much with sand, it had to be dropped on that rock outcropping about the time of the ambush. The detail of troopers sure weren't carrying it, and Chapparo wasn't carrying it, either, for Nochelte would have skinned him alive if he got into the bottle now.

That left the halfbreed, Chastino. He was a drunk. But if he had whiskey, why wasn't he laid up somewhere drinking it, instead of being out on the trail? Dutch sighed. Lots of questions, no answers.

He pulled his horse over to the marshal's office, ground-reined him, then moved upon the boardwalk. The office door was open and he went inside. Rusty Welch looked up from a pile of papers on his desk. He said, "Howdy, Dutch." He motioned to a chair. "Rest yourself."

Schreiber sat down and took off his hat and laid it on the floor. "You seen Max? I was supposed to meet him here this morning."

The marshal nodded, shoving the papers aside. "He came by. Said he'd be in the hayloft at the livery. Kind of tuckered, he was." He fished a pipe out of the desk drawer and filled it from a leather pouch. "Glad you're late. Cogar came in last night, left early this morning. Wouldn't want you two meeting up again in Two Wells. Plumb riles me to stop a good fight but that's my job."

Dutch shrugged. "He'll keep. I got other fish to fry."

Welch touched a match to the pipe, sucking on it, blowing smoke. "Like the ambush on the ranch road and somebody getting off with the captain's niece?"

Schreiber nodded. "Like that. Wasn't Apaches. But who the hell? I can't figure it."

"You check it out?"

Dutch nodded. "That's why I'm late. Checked it damned good and don't know nothing except it was a couple of men on shod horses.'' He paused, then added, ''Headin' south.''

Welch studied his pipe. ''You picked up their tracks?''

Dutch shook his head. ''No. Goddamn wind drifted them over. But where else except south? West, they head into the ranch, and Roland was there with a bunch of troopers. East, they're headin' for the post. North, they get into the reservation. They got any sense at all, they headed south.''

The marshal nodded. ''Seems logical. Takes them over Cogar's range, don't it?''

Schreiber pulled a sack of tobacco out of his shirt pocket. ''East flank of it. Rough canyon country. Doubt Cogar ever sees it except at spring roundup.'' He touched a match to his smoke. ''You seen Chastino lately?''

Welch shook his head. ''Been a spell. Doesn't come into town unless he has money to spend. That ain't often.''

Schreiber blew smoke through his nose. ''He had whiskey. Dropped a half gallon jug when he got hit. Like to know where he got it.'' He picked up his hat. ''I'm goin' to get barbered up. Smell like a wet javelina. Max comes by, tell him I'm here.''

The marshal nodded. ''You figure on riding over Cogar's ranch, don't worry about it. He won't be there.''

Schreiber put on his hat and stood up. ''Wouldn't make a damn to me if he was, but where is he?''

Welch looked at a cold pipe and stuck it back in the drawer. ''Waldo Andrews got a power of attorney from Cogar to sell Cogar's cows. Says Cogar grubstaked a fellow in Mexico who's struck it rich. Cogar aims to see he gets his share. Be gone a couple of months, accordin' to Waldo.''

Dutch pulled his hat a little tighter on his head. "Cogar's had too much luck already."

Welch grinned. "You never liked him. Me, I never heard much bad about him."

Schreiber moved toward the door. "I don't pay much attention to what I hear. It's what I know that counts."

"You know something on Cogar?"

Dutch paused, turning around, facing the marshal. "I know he trades with the Apaches. Little stuff, a few head of stolen cows now and then. He's built a herd off it."

Welch looked at Schreiber. "You got any proof?"

Dutch moved toward the door again. "Aw, hell, Rusty. I know it. That's all that counts with me. Ain't my job to jail a small-time thief."

He was out the door when the thought struck him that maybe Chastino got that jug of whiskey from Cogar. In return for what? The Apaches hadn't pulled any raids or stolen any cows that had come to his notice.

He was sure there had been times when the half breed had put Cogar in touch with Apache raiders holding a few head of rustled cows, and got paid off in cash, whiskey, or whatever for the information. But none of that was going on now. Why would Cogar give Chastino a jug of whiskey? He had no answer and he dismissed the thought.

An hour later he stood under the wooden awning of the barber shop, looking out at the street shimmering in the heat waves of a five o'clock sun. He'd had a bath and shave and his hair trimmed a little. The woman in the laundry next door had washed his shirt and sundried it, while he was getting bathed and barbered.

He thought about a drink at Brownie's Saloon and decided against it. He needed to round up some grub and ammunition and a new water bag for a long trip through hot country. He needed to rent or buy a pack mule. And he needed to go get Max.

Dutch was turning this over in his mind, looking down off the edge of the boardwalk at the hitching rail, when he saw the tracks of a horse whose left front foot toed out a little. It was like a cold splash of water in his face. He sucked in his gut, blew air through his nose, and walked back inside the barber shop.

The barber, a small, paunchy, bald-headed man, was reading a newspaper between customers. He looked up, "Forget something, Dutch?"

Dutch nodded. "Forgot to ask who has been here today?"

The barber blinked. "You checkin' up on my trade?"

"Just today's trade. Got a reason."

The barber scratched his chin. "Well, hell, I ain't got no secrets. The marshal was first in this morning for a shave. Doc Siler came by for a beard trimming. Then there was Jesse Cogar in a hell of a hurry, wanting a fast shave. Said he was lighting out for Mexico. Got a partner struck it rich down there." He paused. "Wednesdays are slow. After lunch—"

Dutch waved a hand. "I was just checkin' on the morning trade, Gus." He turned and walked out, heading for the livery stable.

Marshal Welch didn't ride a horse down to the barber shop for a shave. Neither did Doc Siler. But Jesse Cogar came in on a horse and left on a horse and Dutch knew without seeing it that the horse with the toed-out left front foot was Jesse Cogar's horse.

He found the hostler shoveling horse droppings out

of a stall. The young, stoop-shouldered man looked up as he sensed Schreiber standing beside him. The hostler said, "Howdy, Dutch. Max is still up in the loft. Kid must have seen hard times."

Dutch said, "I'll blast him out of the hay, Bill." He looked around. "Jesse Cogar stable his horse here last night?"

The hostler nodded. "Came in late. Left early."

"You notice whether he rode him over to the barber shop? He stopped for a shave on his way out."

The man thought about it, then nodded. "Fact is, he did. I didn't see him ride over, but I went outside the barn to help unload a wagon of hay, and I seen his horse tied over there. Why?"

Dutch shrugged. "Nothin'. I'll go up and get Max." He started off, then turned back. "You got a packin' mule you can rent me?"

The hostler nodded. "Got a good one. Five bucks a week. Sixty dollars if you don't get back with him."

Schreiber said, "I need a horse for Max, too. One with plenty of bottom."

Less than an hour later Dutch Schreiber and Max were eating their way through two big steaks at Maude's Restaurant. Max knew about the Army detail being wiped out and about Cathy Roland's abduction. He didn't know about the squaws hauling the silver to the border. Dutch filled him in on that and on his belief that Jesse Cogar had been one of the men involved in shooting up the lieutenant and his troops and abducting Cathy Roland.

Max was studying this over when he finally asked, "You say we go after Cogar and the woman? Big reward out for silver. You told me. Why not go after squaws?"

Dutch looked at him in disgust. "Because, you

damned Indian, you can't abandon a woman like Miss Roland to a goddamn renegade like Cogar. May be too late to help her. I don't know. But we got to try.''

Max gnawed on a steak bone. ''Hard thing to decide. Reward buy back the ranch.''

Schreiber drained his coffee cup. ''Ain't nothin' to decide. We got grub for a long ride and plenty of ammunition if we need it.'' He looked at the young Comanche. ''Is that Spencer of yours still in shooting condition?''

Max nodded. ''Pretty good.''

Schreiber grunted. ''If I had any money I'd buy you a .44-40, but after the grub and the hostler, I ain't got enough on me to make wadding for a percussion cap.'' He stood up. ''Let's make tracks.''

There was two hours of daylight ahead of them when they left Two Wells. Schreiber rode tight-gutted, apprehensive, worrying about Cathy Roland, carrying a smouldering hatred for Jesse Cogar.

For one brief moment after his blade had cut the life out of the Apache, Torres, he had felt drained of emotion, free and footloose. Now he was back where he started, on the hunt, the only change being that a different woman was driving him on.

He smiled wryly, wondering if some god, perhaps the one Nochelte called the Great God, had predestined that he would always live his life like this.

Three miles out of town the trail forked and Schreiber pulled up. He looked at Max. ''I'm going back down the ranch road and cut due south toward Cogar's place. You get on to the post and tell the captain I got a lead on Miss Cathy. Tell him I figure the squaws are headin' south by east into the Dragoons. Tell him there isn't a thing he can do for his niece until I cut sign on where

Cogar's taking her. When I do, I'll find the captain, if I need him.''

The young Comanche grunted. "He not want to chase squaws. He want to find Miss Cathy.''

Dutch nodded. ''That's what he wants but he'll get himself court-martialed if that silver crosses the border while he's out on personal business. He's got to leave it to me.''

Max lifted a foot out of a stirrup and scratched an ankle. ''Where I find you, Dutch?''

Schreiber looked at him. ''I'll leave sign even a Comanche can follow. Get on with it now.'' He sat there and watched the youngster pull his horse around and take the road toward the post. He thought, he isn't but about sixteen and he's one of the best men who ever rode with me.

He rode down the ranch road leading the mule and with a lot of things on his mind. All of them were connected with a beautiful blond woman who loved Arizona and was catching hell from it.

On the way back from the Apache camp on Cibecue Creek, Harry Roland had a lot of time to think and he didn't need that. It had been a fruitless ride and he had expected it would be. The Apaches at the camp were passive, seeming to accept this intrusion by the horse soldiers, but he sensed that beneath their calm indifference they were seething with hatred and resentment.

It simply boiled down to the fact that the Army could invade their camp with impunity, but they risked being shot if they left it. Even Harry Roland, thirty years an Army man, could see the inequities in that arrangement.

And he hadn't turned up a thing. He came away convinced that Nochelte had full control over the Apaches there, and none of them were going to ride out on a killing spree without his express orders. The Prophet wasn't going to risk a fight until he had the guns to back it up. Not unless he was forced into it.

It was that simple. Everything depended on the squaws crossing the border with the silver. And he, Captain Harry Roland, had given them an extra two days lead.

He rode into the post, grim-faced, wondering if Schreiber had found anything. When he found out from the orderly that Schreiber had never returned, he got mad and said a few choice words about a goddamned bull-headed Dutchman.

After he got to his quarters and found Ruth Jackson sharing an early supper with the young Comanche, Max, his temper cooled. Whether it was just seeing her there in his home, or whether it was knowing that Schreiber had sent Max to him, he didn't know. He was interested in both of them, and the glum scowl on his face had changed into a smile before he was through the door.

He looked at Ruth. "We didn't find anything. I'm about as sure as a man can be sure out here that the Apaches don't have Cathy."

Ruth rose from the table and moved toward him but before she could say anything Max spoke, over a mouthful of food, "Cogar got her."

Roland felt a cold fury sweep over him, felt the skin tightening in his face. That oily, good-looking, no account sonofabitch had Cathy? Why? He moved into the room, staring at Max. "How does Dutch know this?"

Max wiped a sleeve across his mouth. "Read sign. Cogar's horse behind hill where detail got killed."

Roland scowled. "How does he know it was Cogar's horse?"

Max stuffed a spoonful of stew into his mouth. "Horse behind hill has left front foot that toes out. Cogar got horse whose left front foot toes out. Dutch pretty sure. He say he think squaws will go through Dragoons. He say you ride toward Dragoons. He need you, he'll find you."

Roland felt an uncertainty creeping over him. Suppose Dutch was wrong? Even if he was right, could he take Cathy from Jesse Cogar? What in hell had gotten into Cogar? Did he murder four troopers so he could take Cathy? He looked at Ruth as if asking her for the answers.

She touched his arm. "Harry, sit down. I'll bring you a plate." She shook her head slightly, "If anyone can find Cathy, I'm sure it will be Dutch. And he's better off hunting alone instead of being held up by a bunch of soldiers. As Max says, you'll be where he can find you if he needs you.

Roland said, "I don't like it." He sat down at the table, rubbing his head. The Dragoon Mountains were Chiricahua country, stronghold of the dead warrior chief, Cochise. Obviously, all of the Chiricahuas were not on the reservation. There would be help there for the squaws and old men fleeing toward the border, if they needed it.

The Dragoons held a hundred wild, remote places to hide, to hole up, if the soldiers threatened them. And it was a hundred and fifty miles southeast of the post, a six-day ride for himself and the troops. If the Apaches decided to try and stop him, there were at least a dozen places along the way where he could ride into an ambush. And this they would do, he knew, if he got too close to the silver-laden travois.

He finished his meal in silence, then pushed his chair back from the table and stood up. "Fine stew, Ruth. Appreciate it." When she smiled at him, he felt somehow more relaxed. He fished out a cigar and lighted it. He said finally, "I'm going to ride into Two Wells with a detail. Come back tonight." He looked at Ruth. "Do you want to go along?"

Her face flushed. "Why—well, yes. As I said before you left for the reservation, I need to see about selling the ranch and book passage back to Missouri."

He had said the wrong thing and he knew it. She thought he was trying to get rid of her. He said, unconsciously, "Stupid!"

She looked puzzled. "What, Harry?"

He said, "Talking to myself." He moved over to the window and looked out. "I figured on you coming back. I'll take Second Lieutenant Shafter's quarters tonight. He can bunk with the troops. He needs to get better acquainted with the men anyway."

Roland looked over his shoulder at her. "I'll be out on the job maybe three weeks. Give you time to think and I, well, I'd kind of like to know I'll see you when I get back."

She said gravely, "I'll think about it, Harry. I'll go to Two Wells with you and I'll think about it."

He went outside and found Quincy Shannon sitting on the headquarters' porch. He said, "Get four or five men and let's ride to Two Wells. Saddle a horse for Miss Jackson, too."

The sergeant stood up and saluted. "Yes, sir, Captain." Then he asked, "What's up, Captain?"

Roland grinned faintly, "I'm going to try to take a man away from a very possessive woman, Sergeant. We need a scout."

Shannon grinned back. "Mae Brewer." He shook his head. "It might be a tougher fight than any we've had with the Apaches."

Roland nodded and turned back toward his quarters. "That's for damned sure."

It was late afternoon when the five-man detail escorting Ruth Jackson and the captain pulled up in the Brewers' front yard. Mae Brewer had seen them coming and stood now on the front porch, using the flat of her hand to shield her eyes from the bright rays of the lowering sun.

Roland helped Ruth to dismount and together they walked up to the house. He said in a whisper, "Don't mention Jesse Cogar. Might be accusing the wrong man."

Ruth nodded without answering.

Mae came off the steps toward them. "Oh, Captain Roland! I was so sorry to hear about your pretty niece, Cathy, and the slaughtering of those fine soldier boys. You poor man, you come right on in this house." She led the way and held open the screened door.

Roland said, "Mae, this is Ruth Jackson. She owns Dutch's old ranch. Lost her brother out there a few days ago."

Mae put an arm around Ruth's shoulders. "I reckon you think we don't have nothin' but trouble out here, honey. I'm sorry you sure seem to be gettin' more than your share."

Roland asked, "Mae, where's Joe?"

Mae scurried back into her kitchen and set a cold pot of coffee on the warming burner. "At the freight yard. Not quite time for him to knock off, but if he knew you were here he'd come a-runnin'."

Roland moved back into the kitchen, leaving Ruth sitting in a wicker chair in the parlor directly in front of the breeze from the screen door. He said, "Mae, I'm glad he's not here just now. I need to do some serious talking with you."

She sensed the urgency in his voice and turned to face him. "What is it, Harry?"

He leaned against a big sideboard that lined the kitchen wall. "Mae, Schreiber thinks he's got a line on the men who got off with Cathy."

Mae nodded. "We all thought it was the Apaches, but then Dutch came by and talked with Marshal Welch. The marshal told Joe that Dutch didn't think it was them red heathens."

Roland nodded. "Dutch is out cuttin' sign on those murderers." He paused, "Mae, I've got to take a lot of troopers down into the Dragoons, maybe further. I need a scout."

He saw her stiffen. She turned her back and fussed over the coffee pot. "You want Joe, don't you, Harry?"

"Mae, I got to have him. There's a band of Apache squaws running toward the border. Believe it or not, they're carrying that solen silver shipment with them. If they make it across to Mexico, the Apaches out here will be better armed than my soldiers.

"They'll swap that silver for repeating rifles, ammunition, good horseflesh, and whatever else they want to back up an outbreak. The whole country out here will be in bad trouble."

She took cups out of the cupboard and set them on the table. "Harry, you know how I feel about Joe scoutin', anymore. We been through it before."

He nodded, studying her. "I know, Mae. I wouldn't ask it if it was just for me and the troops. But there's lots of women out here that's going to lose their men if we don't stop that silver." He held up a cup while she poured steaming coffee into it. "You won't be the only woman waiting for a man to come back from this mission."

She looked at him quickly. "What do you mean?"

He smiled slightly and said in a low voice, "Ruth Jackson will be waiting for me."

Mae's face flushed. She laughed. "You old dog, that pretty thing in love with you?"

He shrugged. "I don't know. We haven't had time to really get acquainted. But she's going to stay in my quarters at the post until I get back."

Mae put a hand on a hip. "She'll do no such thing, Captain. She'll stay with me. I couldn't stand being here alone. We'll be company for each other."

Captain Harry Roland sensed he'd won a victory. Still, he had to know for sure, so he asked, "You mean you'll let Joe go?"

She looked away, looking at nothing, a sort of vacant expression in her faded blue eyes. "If he wants to. It's his decision, not mine." She added quickly, "That poor girl needs a cup of coffee."

Mae looked through the kitchen door. "Honey, you want a cup of coffee? I'll be glad to bring it to you in there where it's cooler."

Ruth's voice answered, "I'd love a cup of coffee but only if I get to see your kitchen, Mrs. Brewer."

Mae Brewer laughed. "Come on. Took me a long

time to get that man of mine to build me a few cabinets
and such, but he finally got it done. I'm kind of proud of
it.''

Roland said, ''I'll leave you women to visit. I'm
going down to the freight yard.''

On his way to the freight yard Captain Harry Roland
of the United States Army had a disquieting thought:
What would he say to Mae Brewer if Joe didn't come
back? He tightened his gut, knowing he had no answer
to that question. And for the first time in his career he
wondered if something might happen to him on this
patrol. What if he never saw Ruth Jackson again?

Around a small, dying fire on the banks of Cibecue
Creek a half dozen Apache chiefs smoked their pipes
and oak leaf cigarettes while they waited for the Prophet
to speak.

Nochelte was standing by the fire, staring into it.
Finally he said, ''The horse soldiers will be going after
the squaws with the silver. We must see that they do not
find them.''

Nana sucked on a long stemmed pipe. His wrinkled,
badly scarred parchment-like face glistened in the
flickering light. ''It is a bad thing that the Dutchman got
away from us. If the horse soldiers find the squaws, we
will have to fight them then, with what guns we have.
We will lose many men. But I have faith in the
Prophet.'

Geronimo spat into the fire. ''I will not be in that
fight. I will take my warriors and leave this camp. The
plan of the Prophet like a good dream but now I have
awakened and it is gone. Nahaadah! The Prophet is
playing with our lives.''

Natchez, the Chiricahua chief, stared impassively into the flames. "My warriors are divided. Half are in this camp. The others are in the Dragoons through which the squaws will pass. If the horse soldiers find the squaws, my warriors will fight for them. But they are too few. I want my warriors all together again. I think we shall leave this camp, also."

Nochelte said, "Every Apache child must come through the womb of his mother. It takes many years for such a child to become a warrior or a child-bearing squaw. But the White Eyes do not come from the womb of their mother. They sprout up like seeds flung on the desert in the season of rain.

"If we do not stop them now, there will be no room in this land for the Apache. The Apache will wither and die like stalks of corn in the late summer sun."

He looked at each of them. "We are not beaten yet. We are stronger than we have ever been because we are together. Geronimo and Natchez would destroy the source of our strength."

Juh, chief of the Nednis, stood up. "I have to go back to Mexico. I do not leave because I want to split up this camp. I do not leave because I think the Prophet has failed. I must be in Mexico to trade the silver for guns. I think the silver will cross the border. I believe in Nochelte. Nana believes Nochelte. Nana and I are older than the rest of you and have better judgment."

Nochelte said, "I will go to the top of the mesa in the morning. I will talk with the Great God. I will think on these things. We will meet here again tomorrow when the sun is straight up."

He left them then. He did not know what the chiefs would do. He did not believe that the Great God had abandoned the Apache. Oftentimes it was said that the

Great God tested the faith of his people with adversity. His faith was unshaken and he had not been idle since the Dutchman's escape.

He had sent another scout to join the squaws, replacing the dead Chapparo, with instructions as to how to handle the captive troopers. He had sent two other warriors to establish additional smoke signals so that news of the squaws would travel to this camp a little faster.

Perhaps the wisest thing he had done was to decide to kill the Dutchman. He walked back through the camp toward the meadow. It was nearly time for the dancing to start.

CHAPTER ELEVEN

Jesse Cogar reached the line shack in early afternoon. He had given the cattle broker, Waldo Anderson, power of attorney to sell his cattle. He'd checked out nearly all his money at the bank, leaving a hundred for seed in case he came back. He was taking a hell of a gamble on finding this silver bullion. He knew that. But the stakes were high and he'd never made any money without risking some.

He would have been better off if they had made a clean sweep and killed Cathy Roland, along with the troopers and Chastino. But he knew Whitey Doaks wouldn't go for it and he needed Whitey. So he had her on his hands and if he captured the silver he'd dump her in Mexico, or else get rid of Whitey and keep her around for a spell. She was a damned pretty woman.

He pulled up at the flimsy, weather-dilapidated corral and stripped the saddle from his horse, checked the water in the trough, and then moved toward the shack. Whitey had heard him coming and was standing there in the doorway.

Jesse said, "How's the woman?"

Whitey shrugged. "She won't eat. Just lies there on them blankets."

Cogar pushed past him and went inside. Cathy Roland did not look up. She lay on her side, apparently asleep. He figured she was faking it.

Cogar said, "You and me have got to get a few things ironed out, Cathy Roland. We are goin' to make a long ride, you and me and Whitey, here. We'll travel a lot at night. You ain't goin' to have any privacy. You're goin' to be one of the boys. But you won't get hurt unless you ask for it."

She didn't answer.

He looked at her. He reached for tobacco and rolled a smoke and lighted it. "It's the kind of ride that can kill a person. You got to want to live to make it. It's up to you. It don't matter to me, one way or another." He turned away and went back outside. Hell, it didn't matter to him.

Whitey said, "What do we do now?"

Cogar drew on his cigarette. "We're headin' for Benson. Tot Farrel and his boys still live around there. Good men."

Whitey sucked in his breath. "Bounty hunters. Killers, ain't they?"

Cogar looked at him over his cigarette. "What the hell do you think you and I are?"

Whitey shook his head. "Never thought about it. Them Farrels is tough people. Where'd you know them?"

"Stayed with them a spell when I was hard up. Treated me all right. I can trust them. They can round up another two, three gunhands."

Whitey studied the toe of his boot. "You say we can take that silver. I don't see the hell how. We go chargin' around out there in that Apache country and we get close to them squaws, we'll be lookin' at a lot of

Apache bucks. I don't hanker for the treatment they dish out.''

Cogar tossed his smoke. "We won't do it that way. Them Apaches are going to see a man and his woman taking a couple of wagons across country with a few head of horses. Folks movin' to a place to settle. That's after we reach Benson. Between now and then, you and me and the woman are going to ride low and ride fast.''

Whitey nodded. "When do we start?''

"This night. I got enough beans and coffee and tobacco to get us to Globe tomorrow afternoon. You'll hole up with the woman and I'll go in and get supplies. We'll hit the San Pedro in a couple of days, and ride right down it to Benson. Ought to be there in another day.''

Whitey looked out at the corral. "How many horses we takin'?''

Cogar said, "What we ride and them two grays. They'll pull a light wagon. I'll buy a heavy team in Benson.''

Whitey moved toward the corral. "I'll get things together. You get the woman on her feet.'' He paused and looked back. "You bring any whiskey?''

Cogar said, "No. Forgot it.''

"Good thing,'' Whitey said. "We don't need it on this trip.''

She had heard the men talking and she lay shivering on the filthy blankets in a hundred degree heat, wondering how in God's name had this happened to her, Cathy Roland, whose uncle was a captain in the United States Army? It was a dream, a nightmare, from which she would surely awake and then everything would be all right. The young lieutenant would be hanging around the captain's quarters for a talk with her, she would be making coffee for her uncle, and Sergeant Quincy Shannon would stop by. It had to be so. What she had seen and heard could not be real. Who would believe it?

A rough voice shattered her thoughts. "Get off them blankets, Cathy. You're goin' to take a ride. Get yourself together."

She recognized the voice of Jesse Cogar. Jesse Cogar, whom she had once thought a genial, handsome man, who had even aroused within her a little interest in him. Dear God in heaven! She couldn't believe her stupidity.

His voice came at her again as she lay motionless. "Goddammit, get up!"

Slowly she pulled herself up from the pile of blankets. Her once white blouse had worked free from her black broadcloth riding skirt, her hair was a matted, blond mess. Her Wellington boots felt like twin stoves cooking her feet. She looked at Jesse Cogar.

"Where are you taking me?"

Cogar laughed. "We ain't takin' you anywhere, woman. You're just goin' along because Whitey is squeamish about shootin' women. If I'd had my way, you'd have been laid along the side of the lieutenant.

"Fact is, like I said yesterday, you'll see a lot of Mexico. Don't really know where you'll wind up. Maybe in a presidio with servants and good food and fine wine, maybe in a border whorehouse. Depends on your luck. Who knows?"

She felt a cold fury raging through her at his insolence. "Who knows? Maybe I'll be at your hanging."

His face darkened. "Shut up. I hear any sass out of you again, I'll work you over good." He turned and went outside.

Cathy fought down her feeling of despair and began to tuck in her blouse with swift but sweaty hands. She reached for her black broadcloth riding jacket which she'd removed during the night, and struggled to put it on over her perspiration-drenched blouse. Finally she jerked it off in disgust and threw it back on the floor.

There was no mirror in the line shack so she guessed at straightening her hair. She searched for her stiff black riding hat and put it firmly on her head with an air of defiance.

She must try to keep up her spirits, somehow. Her uncle would know she was alive somewhere. The whole Army would be looking for her. Maybe Dutch Schreiber would be looking for her. Somehow she knew he would be. The thought gave her courage. She'd thought this out. There was hope. She had to believe this to survive.

The post had not seen the bustle of activity now within it for nearly a year. It was like the old days when Victorio and his Mimbrenos were setting the country aflame. Sergeants and corporals barked orders to troopers in wide-brimmed campaign hats swinging McClellan saddles on to the backs of their mounts, loading on their equipment, Springfield carbines, some with Spencer repeaters, canteens, slickers, ammunition.

Three Mexican packers swore softly and fluently in their musical native language as they worked with nearly two dozen pack mules. They put saddle blankets across their reluctant backs, then the *aparejos* or cushions to receive the heavy loads of food and ammunition and other necessities of the trail.

Ruth Jackson stood beside Mae Brewer and watched as Captain Harry Roland came out of headquarters, followed by Joe Brewer. She noted the stern set of Roland's jaw and the flush of excitement on Brewer's face. Men about to lead other men into danger, perhaps death, because they were trained for this kind of work, good at it, and , in spite of the responsibility, enjoyed it. For why else would they do it?

She felt both excitement and apprehension now, but when the troops moved out and she and Mae were escorted back to Two Wells, she knew the excitement would be over. Only apprehension would remain. She began to understand about Mae Brewer.

Joe Brewer smiled at his wife as he walked toward Sergeant Quincy Shannon, and Roland, seeing Ruth, veered toward her. He said, "We'll be ready to ride in half an hour. Where's Max?"

Ruth looked at him, worrying over the tenseness that she sensed held him like a vise. "He's gone. He'll be looking for Dutch."

Roland nodded and said grimly, "And Dutch will be looking for Cathy. God, I hope he gets a lead on her."

Ruth laid a hand on his arm. "Get it out of your mind, Harry. You have to leave it to him. You've got enough on you without that."

Mae Brewer moved closer to them. Her face was tight, unsmiling. She looked at Roland solemnly. "Joe's like a kid out of school. Don't let him do anything foolish, Harry."

Roland patted her shoulder gently, eyes softening. "He knows his business, Mae. If he didn't, I wouldn't have wanted him along. Don't worry about him." He looked at Ruth. "You and I might have time for a quick cup of coffee in my quarters."

Ruth nodded and as Roland moved off to join Brewer, she looked at Mae. "You and Joe are welcome to join us for coffee."

Mae Brewer shook her head. "Thanks, but I want a few minutes alone with Joe. You understand."

Ruth smiled. "Yes. I guess I was hoping you would say that. I—I think I'd like to see Harry alone before they leave." She was surprised at her words and flushed, then turned away toward the captain's quarters.

She hadn't intended to admit, even to herself, that she was falling in love with Harry Roland. But there it was, and now, having virtually admitted it to Mae Brewer, she felt better about it. So what if he was nearly twenty years her senior? He was a strong, vigorous man and should have many good years ahead. A thought sobered her. Perhaps he didn't feel the same way about her.

Ruth had coffee poured and cooling when Roland returned to his quarters, laying his campaign hat on a chair. He pulled her chair out for her at the table and as she sat down he stood behind her for a moment. She knew he was looking at her. Suddenly she felt his hand on her arm and a lump formed in her throat, quick tears springing into her eyes.

He moved around the table and took a seat opposite her, not looking at her, blowing the steam from his coffee. He said quietly, "Ruth, when I get back I'm going to tell you something, ask you something."

She lowered her eyes to her hands, clasped upon the table. She asked, "Does it have to wait, Harry?"

"Yes," he answered, "it has to wait." Then he said gruffly, "Enough of that." He smiled at her over his coffee cup. "I'm glad you are staying with Mae. You'll be good for her. Joe's grateful, too."

She said, "I'll do all I can for her, Harry." She thought, I suspect she'll be helping me as much or more than I help her.

Dutch Schreiber picked up the tracks of three horses going south about noon. He was over a mile off the ranch road when he found them, and he'd ridden in circles all morning to pick them up. One of the horses toed out with its left front foot. So now he knew. There had been only two men in on the ambush of the Army detail. The third horse was being ridden by Cathy Roland.

He pulled up in the shade of a low escarpment and got out of the saddle. He hunkered down with his back against the bank of yellow earth, rolled a cigarette and lighted it. A man on a trail did not always move by the physical sign of his quarry. Sometimes there was no sign. Sometimes the sign was deliberately deceptive.

When trailing a band of hostiles, you tried to figure where they wanted to go and then how they had to go to get there. It was a reasoning process based partly on knowledge of the country and partly on knowing the natural instincts and motivation of those whom you were trying to find.

He looked at his cigarette, frowning. Assuming now that Cogar had been in on the killing and in on the capture of Cathy Roland, why? Where was the reason for it? Sure, she was a beautiful woman, but would a thinking man try to get her for himself like this?

And why, on the same day, would Cogar ride into Two Wells and make a deal with the cattle broker to sell his herd? And why would he let it out he was going to Mexico and be gone a spell? Maybe the story of going to Mexico was simply a ruse, mentioned to muddy the trail. But the tracks were going south, and Mexico was south.

And there was Chastino and the whiskey jug and why was he involved in it? And there was Chapparo, obviously killed by Lieutenant Holcomb. And why? He snubbed out the smoke in the sand and swore under his breath.

He got back in the saddle. A thought struck him and it came so strong and clear and logical that he felt foolish for not seeing it before. Chastino never had money to buy whiskey. He never had anything of value except gossip and information which he picked up, living sometimes with the Apaches and sometimes in the vicinity of the whites. Chastino traded in information and Cogar traded whiskey for favors from the Apache. He knew that. He couldn't prove it. Didn't have to. He simply knew it.

It had to be that Chastino got the jug from Cogar in return for something he told Cogar. And then maybe Cogar decided, later, that he ought to get ride of Chastino, and caught up with him in the company of the Army detail. It had to be. And it had to be that Chastino knew about the silver and was trading the information to the Army after he'd made a deal with Cogar. Nothing else made sense.

The silver was the only thing important enough to warrant wholesale slaughter, and that explained the yarn Cogar was spreading about going to Mexico. He damn sure was, if he could get the silver away from the

Apaches. And Cathy just got caught up in it by being with the detail.

Schreiber's guts knotted up like cold steel had been punched into his stomach. Cogar took Cathy for his own amusement on the trail and he'd treat her like a trail-town whore.

Dutch dug heels into the gray. He turned a little east and rode the horse hard. He needed to see Luis Redoza. He was going to need help. It bothered him that he couldn't find a reason for Chapparo being killed in the ambush, but he dismissed it. He couldn't figure it at all. Maybe he was only half right with what he'd already concluded. Two things he knew, Cogar had Cathy, and they were riding south.

He had all this on his mind so that he was not watching the country around him like he normally would have done, but still he saw the Apache a hundred yards ahead of him, ducking back down into the draw. He was being followed. That figured. Nochelte did not want him tracking the squaws.

Dutch spoke to the gray and reined him due south. The horse responded, stretching out in full run. He rode low, not looking back for half a mile, then cut east on an expanse of level sandy desert that stretched for miles. He did not know how many of them were on his trail but they would not try to close in with him here. They would wait for the mountain and canyon and timber country, where an ambush would be sprung without too much risk to themselves.

He was moving slowly when he rode up to the rancheria of Luis Redoza. He was tired. The horse was tired. The sun was setting on the horizon, still blasting out angry rays of heat. He had not seen the Apaches again.

The door was open and Redoza's Apache wife stood there, looking at him impassively. He dismounted. "I have come to see your husband, senora."

She looked at him awhile, saying nothing. Finally she said, "He is in the garden." Suddenly her face brightened into a wide smile. "Enjuh, Dutch. Good see."

He grinned back at her and walked around the house toward the garden. The Mexican was hoeing a withering row of corn. It came to Dutch, watching silently, that the Americanos knew little of the perseverance required to live in this country. He, himself, had one brief fling at ranching and quit because of a personal tragedy. This man, Luis Redoza, hoeing corn he knew had little chance to survive, had seen many tragedies. Still, he lived and tried.

Dutch said, "Luis, that's a young man's work."

The old Mexican look up quickly, startled, then seeing Schreiber, flashed an ageless smile. "There are no young men willing to do this work, Senor Dutch, mi amigo." He raised the hoe and moved forward, extending his hand. "Word is out that you have killed the Apache, Torres."

"Yes," Dutch said quietly, "that is over." He looked at the Mexican, "I need help, Luis."

The old man propped his hoe against the stone garden fence. "I am your friend. What can I do?"

Dutch moved out into the garden, feeling the wilted leaves of the cornstalks, looking down at the yellowed leaves of the squash vines. He said, "It is a job, Luis. It will pay you fifty dollars when we get back. I have no money now but some coming from the Jackson woman on cattle. I will pay up when we get back. If we do not get back, I will leave a note with your wife to the

Jackson woman who will pay her.''

Doubt hooded the eyes of the old man. He looked
down at the toes of Dutch's boots. He asked, ''What is
this work? Fifty dollars is much money.''

Schreiber squatted on his heels between the rows of
corn. ''It is a dangerous thing, Luis. The captain's
niece has been taken by two men. I think others will join
up with them. I intend to take her from them. Like I
said, I need help.''

Luis Redoza squatted beside him. He took a thin sack
of tobacco from his hip pocket and a package of brown
cigarette papers. Very slowly he built himself a smoke.
He lighted it and looked at Schreiber through slitted
lids. ''This is a shooting job. I do not have many
bullets. Do you have bullets for my Spencer?''

Dutch grinned. ''Plenty. I brought them along for the
Comanche boy. He shoots the same gun. He will join
us.''

The Mexican smoked awhile, staring at his garden.
''Is this all?''

Dutch spread his hands. ''There is more, but not your
concern. Some Apaches are after me. That's my problem. I'm not askin' that you fight Apaches. Your wife is
Apache.''

Luis Redoza stood up. ''How long will we be gone,
Dutch?''

Schreiber got to his feet. ''Maybe three weeks. If we
don't get the woman back in about ten days, she will be
in your country, Mexico. I will go there alone if that
happens.''

The Mexican said, ''I will speak to my wife.''

Dutch moved over to the stone fence as the old man
went inside. Sheep were grazing outside the fence on

sparse grass, perhaps a dozen head. It was a meager living that the man and woman salvaged from this land, but it was a living. Somehow, they got by.

Presently the Mexican returned. He said, "My wife, she say fifty dollars will bring water from the creek to the garden."

Dutch nodded. "It'll buy the tools and lumber. You do the work."

Luis Redoza smiled. "With water in the garden, we will never be hungry again." He looked at Schreiber. "I will go. We will have a cup of tiswin while my woman fixes our supper. After that, we will sleep or we will ride, as you wish."

Dutch said, "We'll get damned little sleep on this trip. We'll ride."

Luis Redoza shrugged. "My wife, she say if Apaches are after Dutch, I fight Apaches. She has no feeling for them. She is not afraid of them."

Schreiber shook his head. "She is Apache, you are Mexican. You are not involved in the war between the White Eyes and the Apaches. That could be dangerous for both of you."

Redoza flashed a gleaming smile. "This Arizona is a bad place, Dutchman. Getting out of bed can be a dangerous thing." He moved toward the house. "Let us wash out our throats with tiswin."

Nochelte and Natchez sat their horses near the boulder-strewn bank of Cibecue Creek a mile north of its confluence with the Salt River. Behind them twenty mounted Chiricahua warriors waited patiently. Nochelte said, "Two suns ago I sent Dalte to replace

Chapparo with the squaws. He is a fine warrior and
scout and has great endurance. He should reach the
band tomorrow.''

Natchez fingered the war necklace of bone beads
around his throat. He looked over his shoulder at his
warriors. ''My followers have great endurance, also,
and they are ready to ride.''

The shaman looked at the lowering sun. ''We will
ride tonight. We will be off the reservation when we
cross the river. I do not think the horse soldiers are
watching us but we will move with caution.''

Natchez made a chopping motion with the edge of his
hand, black eyes glittering angrily. ''I do not like skulk-
ing in shadows like the coyote. This is my land and I am
ready to fight to keep it.''

Nochelte smile thinly. ''The horse soldiers left the
post yesterday in late morning. Chis-sey was on Mule
Peak when they passed under it. He reports that there
are many of them, perhaps three times the number of
your warriors, and they have with them a white scout,
but it is not the Dutchman.''

He looked at the Chiricahua chief. ''I do not think
they will find the squaws. We will get ahead of the
soldiers and confuse them with many trails.''

Natchez grunted. ''But if they find the squaws?''

Nochelte shrugged. ''Then we will fight. We will
need the help of your warriors who are still in the
Dragoons.'' He raised a hand, pointing into the sky.
''The Great God has told me that we must overcome or
outwit the horse soldiers this time without his help. I
think it is a test of our faith. If we do this, then he will
bring back our great departed leaders, Cochise and
Mangus and Delshay, and even others to help us in the
great war if it comes.''

Natchez looked at him sourly, "What is to prevent the great war? You do not think the White Chief in Washington will give up this land without a fight? You do not think he will agree to the terms that you sent back with the Dutchman? If I were the White Chief, I would laugh at you."

Nochelte eyed him coldly. "You are Apache. You do not know the many problems of the White Chief." He neck-reined his horse toward a high, chalk-white knoll. "I will go up there and ask White Painted Woman to favor us on this ride. She has much power and she has long been our protector." He moved away from Natchez.

On top of the knoll Nochelte sat down crosslegged, then pulled his high crowned black hat a little firmer on his head, for there was a stiff breeze up here. He thought about his words to Natchez that the Great God had said he would not help the Apache on this mission, that it was a test of faith.

That had not been exactly true. He simply had not been able to get the attention of the Great God these past few days. He had spent hours talking to the Great God, and after much talking he would put himself into a trance and listen for words from the sky. But the sky was silent. This troubled him.

To the south he could see the Salt River from this height. When they crossed the river they would turn southeast and go through the country of the great canyons which no one entered, not even Apaches, if they could avoid it. But it was the safest route and the shortest. Once in it, they could travel by sunlight without fear of being seen. They would be in front of the horse soldiers within three days. Thirty miles was a full day for a horse soldier. An Apache could cover fifty miles or more and think nothing of it.

He thought about the Dutchman. He did not know why the Dutchman was not with the horse soldiers. Perhaps he was scouting ahead. That was good, for he would be alone when the three Apache warriors found him. He did not doubt that his Apaches would find the Dutchman and kill him. The Americano was a tough fighter, but no one Americano could overcome three Apaches.

He took off his hat and placed it beside him, keeping one hand on the brim so it would not blow away. He leaned back againt a large rock and closed his eyes. He would think now of White Painted Woman. Often when he thought hard about her, she would come to him.

He needed her now. He needed to know that he would still have his rain power and wind power on this mission. He hoped she could tell him that the silver would reach Mexico. It had to reach Mexico with the squaws and old men. If it did not, then the sun was about to set on the day of the Apache.

CHAPTER TWELVE

Captain Harry Roland sat beside the remains of a small cook fire, the embers still glowing in the deep darkness. Beside him lounged Joe Brewer puffing on his pipe, legs outstretched, head propped up on his saddle. Brewer broke the silence. "A man forgets how rough these marches are this time of year. Damned sun doesn't leave a man enough water to spit."

Roland nodded. He did not like the night camps. At night a man had time to think and his thoughts turned to his niece, Cathy. Was she alive? Would she be better off dead? He chewed on the stub of a cold cigar. "We had a chance to cut sign on the squaws today. We're a day's ride from the Dragoons."

Brewer shifted his weight on the saddle. "Didn't see no sign at all. You notice that signal smoke this mornin'? First time it's been north of us. They ain't tellin' us a damn thing. Sendin' their scout at least forty miles away from the band before he sends up his smoke. We don't even know forty miles in which direction."

Roland smiled grimly in the darkness. "I learned a long time ago not to go off chasing signal smokes."

Somewhere in the desert an owl hooted and a coyote answered. Lonely sounds in a lonely land. Roland felt the loneliness, too. He thought about Ruth Jackson and wondered if she missed him.

There was a sudden rush of hoofs moving swiftly over soft ground. The wild, savage cry of the Apache warriors rose above the thunder of hooves. A soldier cried out a warning and then it was pandemonium.

Roland ran toward the main camp, pulling his Colt. Brewer grabbed his rifle and raced after him. And then it was quiet again. No soldier had fired a shot, for there was nothing there to shoot. Just black emptiness and the smell of dust.

Roland looked at his scout. Brewer lowered his rifle, letting it hang at his side. He said, "That was Nochelte, my guess. Just letting us know he and his Apaches are here."

Sergeant Quincy Shannon appeared out of the night. He stood by Roland. "What was that all about?"

Roland holstered the Colt. "I think Joe said it. Nochelte's brought a war party to help out with the squaws. Figured he might. Hoped he wouldn't. We won't take the silver now without losing some troopers."

He looked at Shannon. "Double the night guard. Keep a damned close eye on the horses. We're not foot soldiers and I don't want to become one. We'll break camp early and head for the Dragoons."

It had been bad judgment going to the reservation to look for Cathy. It was a thing he felt he had to do. But it cost him two days and the silver was that much closer to the border. And now Nochelte was here.

They were east of the San Pedro River and moving through rough country west of the Little Dragoons. In the early morning light the bigger Dragoons, twenty miles southeast, loomed in purple silhouette in front of the early sun. Roland rode beside Quincy Shannon, looking back at the troops stretched out behind.

A mile back of the troops would be the mule train with a dozen troopers dropped back of the main force to keep an eye on the supplies. A mile ahead Joe Brewer was covering ground, looking for sign of the fleeing band of squaws and old men and Apache children, looking for sign of travois poles gouging out shallow trenches in the sandy ground.

By mid-morning the desert shimmered and danced in the one hundred-degree heat. The early morning breeze had died. A brightly beaded gila monster waddled from the shade of a decaying saguaro trunk, blinked at the troops, then turned back and lost himself in the shallow pit he'd scratched out under the dead giant cactus. It was a yellow, desolate country of cacti and dwarf mesquite and occasional gray-green patches of salt grass. It was the Sonoran desert at its worst.

The sergeant reached for his canteen and took a meager drink, washing the water around in his mouth before swallowing. He said, "I've never been this far south in the dry season. I reckon we know now what hell looks like."

Roland pulled field glasses from a leather case slung over his saddle. He stopped his horse and squinted through the glasses, moving them in a slow arc, surveying the mountains to the east. Finally he put the glasses back into the case.

He said, "I keep worryin' that Schreiber could be wrong. Maybe they aren't moving toward the Dragoons. They could be thirty miles west of here and just as close to the border." He looked at Shannon. "In which case, we'll never catch them."

Shannon nodded. "No man can know for sure what

route an Apache will take. The Dragoons seemed likely. It's a place where they can rest awhile and cut new travois poles. It's always been Apache country. If they're west of us, it will be up to the troops at Huachucca. We'll be out of the action.'' He looked at Roland. ''Seems like we ought to be hearing from Schreiber.''

Roland didn't answer. This had been on his mind. Dutch was trailing Cathy. He had said he would get word to the troops if he needed help. He was somewhere in this desert. But where? Maybe east or maybe west or maybe dead. A man could overestimate himself.

He rode off from the column of troopers, moving toward Joe Brewer. He could barely see Joe ahead, sitting on his horse, motionless. Joe had found something, or perhaps he was just letting his mount blow.

When he finally pulled even with the scout, Roland had already seen what it was that had stopped Joe Brewer. Travois tracks, parallel ruts disturbing the wind blown earth. Lots of them. And moving toward the Dragoons.

Roland took off his hat and ran a hand over his face, feeling the desert sand scrape against his forehead. He said, ''Well, Schreiber was right. They're heading toward the Dragoons.''

Brewer was studying the horizon. ''I reckon. I don't know. Them tracks end a hundred yards ahead. I checked it out for half a mile. A hell of a wind came through here and there ain't a thing to be seen. Question is, are they going into the mountains or turning south along the flank of the foothills straight for the border?''

Roland rode toward the mountains, still ten miles away. The scout was right. The travois tracks were wiped out and there was only a loose cover of wind-rippled sand, dotted with an occasional cactus. Brewer came up beside him, looking toward the mountains.

The scout said, "Now, would they go into them mountains where they can't make any time at all and take a rest, or would they keep moving south? I don't know a way to find out without riding it out and that can cost us another day."

Roland nodded. "There is no other way. My guess is that Nochelte has been in touch with them, told them to hide out in the mountains while his warriors give us a little hell.

"We don't have the supplies to lay siege." The captain studied the empty expanse in front of him, frowning. "But we can't risk a guess. You'll have to take a dozen troopers and ride it out. I'll move up to the foothills with the main force and wait for your report."

Brewer nodded. "If my detail leaves now, we can cover the flank of the Dragoons and be back tomorrow. If we don't cut sign, then they're in the mountains."

Roland said, "We'll cover another five miles toward the Dragoons, and we might get lucky. If we don't, you peel off with the detail and ride south."

The scout nodded and rode towards the mountains. Harry Roland rode back to the advancing troops, not liking the way things were shaping up.

Dutch Schreiber and the Mexican, Luis Redoza, had been on the trail for three days. The first day had gone slowly, picking up the occasional tracks of five shod horses, always watching for the horse that had a left front hoof toeing out. Finally, deciding he had to commit himself, Dutch headed due south. After that, he didn't bother to look for sign. They got in the saddle early and rode late and they covered ground like Apaches.

They progressed to high ground in late evening, a gentle, swelling slope that seemed to go for miles, but Schreiber could see that the ground dropped steeply ahead. Not a good place to make camp. There was no cover, just small mesquite, some random palo verde and clumps of greasewood.

He rode ahead of the old Mexican. When he came to the dropoff he saw the thick stand of tall mesquite. He sensed he was in trouble. Sunlight flashed on steel. The Apaches were waiting for him, had known where he was going, and beat him there. That was the way it was with Apaches. He fell out of the saddle, drawing his rifle as he fell.

Dutch felt the first bullet burn his neck before he heard the shot. He rolled and lay on his stomach, rifle ready, but there was nothing there. The Apaches were invisible.

He saw a cluster of small boulders a dozen yards away and he scrambled toward them on all fours, keeping his belly low to the ground. To his left, two quick shots broke the desert silence. He waited, worrying about the old Mexican. This was not his fight.

There was a sudden scramble of hoofs over loose rock. A lone Apache raced his horse out from a thick cover of mesquite, brandishing his rifle, yelling defiance. Schreiber dropped him with an unhurried shot. Then it was silent again.

He heard a noise behind him and whirled to see Luis Redoza. The old man was smiling. "Three shots, three Apaches. It has been a good day for hunting, amigo."

Dutch looked at the old man. "Those two shots. You dropped two of them?"

Luis shrugged. "They were huddled together behind the thicket. It was like shooting pigeons in a loft."

Schreiber got up, grinning. "Now I know why I'm paying you fifty dollars." He stood there, looking at the downward slope of the land below. At the bottom of the slope the ground rose abruptly in rocky escarpment, partially obscured by a green line of timbers.

He said, "We will make camp down there, Luis. The Comanche boy will find us tonight. I saw him through the glasses this afternoon, maybe five miles behind us."

They were filling tin plates with beans and side meat when they heard the horse moving toward them. The Mexican picked up his rifle and disappeared into a grove of willows. Dutch eased himself behind a low rock outcropping where he could duck if necessary.

The rider pulled rein on the shoulder of the rise. He called, "Ho, Dutch!"

Schreiber stood up. "Took you a helluva long time to catch up, Comanche. You sleep too late."

The rider came forward and Dutch saw the wide grin splitting the bronze face. Max shrugged, "Hard trip. Not much sign."

Dutch motioned him out of the saddle. "It's ain't supposed to be easy. You learn when it's hard." He grinned at the boy. "Get your butt out of that saddle and have some grub. I cooked enough for you, too. Seen you back there three or four hours ago."

Max slid off his horse and took off the saddle. He moved the animal down to the creek and let the horse water a little from a stagnant pool. Finally he moved the horse up to the small patch of gramma where the horses of Dutch and Redoza were grazing. He asked, "Any sign Miss Cathy?"

Dutch shook his head. "No. We're close, though. I cut tracks running south by east today. Looks like they are heading straight for the San Pedro."

After supper Dutch kicked out the cook fire, poured the dregs from the coffee pot into his cup, then moved off to sit by himself on a low, flat outcropping of rock, leaving Max and Redoza in idle conversation by the ashes of the dead fire. They would let the horses rest while they, themselves, caught a couple of hours of sleep. The San Pedro River ran about ten miles east of this camp. He wanted to reach it by daybreak.

If those tracks today didn't change direction, Cogar would hit the river about ten miles north of Benson. One thing for sure, he wasn't going to ride into that town with Cathy Roland. So what would he do with her?

He felt the hate for Jesse Cogar building up inside him so strong that he couldn't sit still. He got up and rolled a cigarette and walked down to the creek. As he lighted it he could hear the horses moving with slow, short steps in their hobbles. He heard Luis Redoza begin to snore.

Dutch sat down with his back against an aged willow. Maybe Cogar had seduced Elaine. He didn't know. He would probably never know for sure. But Cogar had taken Cathy Roland and that he knew. A young woman down on her luck back East who came out to this godforsaken place and loved it.

He'd heard Roland telling Ruth Jackson at the ranch that Cathy wanted the school-teaching job at Two Wells. He drew deep on his cigarette, feeling the bite of the smoke in his chest. What would she be like after Cogar got through with her?

He pushed his smoke against the hardscrabble ground, snuffing it out. He stood up and moved toward his two sleeping companions. He had lived a rough and violent life and in staying alive he had killed a lot of men, nearly all Apaches. Torres was the only man he'd ever killed and took pleasure from it. Jesse Cogar would be another.

He sat down on his saddle blanket and pulled off his boots and socks and rubbed his feet, letting the night air cool them. Max raised his head, "No sleep, Dutch?"

Schreiber shook his head. "You got another hour, Comanche. Make the most of it."

He thought briefly about Roland. The man could be court-martialed for not taking the trail after the squaws immediately upon learning about the silver. He had tried to tell the captain that it wasn't Apaches who took Cathy. He could understand the captain's feelings, but that wouldn't cut any ice with General Willcox if the silver got across the border.

Lightning streaked and flashed over the Rincons in the west but it was too far away to hear the thunder. There could be a shower in the mountains tonight, but not out here on the flatland. Not unless Nochelte conjured up one with the power bestowed upon him by Child of the Water. Dutch smiled grimly. The Apaches were a very supernatural people. They believed in the powers of their medicine men, perhaps because they had little else left in which to believe.

The Apaches had been dealt a losing hand by the white man, and if occasionally they rebelled and tried to find again the life they once had lived, who could blame them? Yet when you rode upon a burned-out ranch and looked at what was left of a white family who was foolish enough to try to live out here, you left with the stench of death in your nostrils and a burning, loathing hatred for the red devils.

The two races were completely incompatible. Eventually the Apache would be reduced to a handful of miserable, dependent beggars living on scraps from the Americano's table. But that, he knew, was a few years away, and between now and then there would be a lot of killing by both sides.

A cougar coughed a hundred and fifty yards down the creek, and the razor-sharp hooves of a pack of javelinas could be heard running across the loose rock in the stream bed. Everything hunted another thing in the desert. He put on his boots, picked up his rifle, and moved toward the horses. In a few moments now he would be on the hunt, himself.

Cathy Roland sat in the deep shade of a pine grove on the rim of a small canyon. For once in her life she was glad she couldn't see herself. She knew the desert sun had badly burned her face, as only fair skin can be burned. It was painful to the touch. Sometimes she forgot and tried to wipe away the perspiration. It was like rubbing salt into an open wound, and her dead skin rolled off her face after she'd wiped her hands over it.

Her hair was a tangled mess, bleached even whiter than its natural blond color. She sat there exhausted, not caring anymore, watching the two men who stood a dozen yards in front of her.

Jesse Cogar's dark face was partly obscured as he pointed to the canyon down below. She heard him say, ''I'll be back tomorrow evening with Farrel and his men. We'll have a couple of wagons and plenty of supplies. We'll cut southeast and hit the south slope of the Dragoons. I think that silver will walk right into us.''

Whitey Doaks listened silently. He took off his hat and ran a hand through his thin, silver-blond hair. He said, "I got a feelin' we're in trouble."

She saw the anger darken Cogar's face. "You're actin' like an old woman, Whitey. What the hell? Where's the trouble? We got it made."

Doaks put his hat back on his head slowly, carefully, like a man who was coming to a decision. He said, "I got a feelin' we're bein' followed. Had it for a day now. I ain't usually wrong about that feelin'. It's been tested plenty of times before."

"Christ sake!" Cogar started to walk away, then turned. "Who the hell? Nobody knows about the silver except us and the Apaches."

Whitey turned around and Cathy felt his pale eyes on her. She felt a tremor run through her pain-ridden body. Doaks said, "We got her on our hands. Maybe they're after her. Schreiber could read our tracks like a book, if he's on the trail."

Jesse Cogar laughed shortly. "No chance. He's huntin' his own Indian. Maybe found him now and got himself killed. No way he'll get off that reservation without an Apache knife stuck in him. They'll say his Indian killed him, whether he did or not."

Cathy saw Cogar moving toward her and her hands clenched. He was an animal. Worse than an animal because he walked in the disguise of a human being but he had no mercy and no soul.

He smiled down at her. "I'm goin' into Benson. Be back tomorrow afternoon with a couple of wagons and more men. You rest yourself. You'll be bouncin' on a wagon seat across rough country."

She forced herself to look at him. "Maybe Whitey Doaks is right. Maybe Dutch Schreiber is on our trail."

Cogar scowled. "Don't get your hopes up on it. I left a good story behind about goin' to Mexico. No reason he'd follow me." He smiled thinly, "Course if he knew I'd slept with his wife, he would come after me. Way it is, he's meat for the Apaches. He's got nothin' goin' for him, anymore."

He looked at her critically. "Your face looks like you're part Indian." Cogar shook his head. "You sure don't look like no prize package, anymore. I'll be lucky to get anything for you in Mexico."

He turned away and walked back to Doaks. "I'll see you tomorrow. You want to have a little fun while I'm gone, go ahead. It don't bother me none, not the way she looks. Hell, she's goin' to be dumped in Mexico, no matter how little I get for her."

Cathy watched Cogar move off toward his horse. She saw him mount and ride off into the scattered pines. Only when she could no longer hear the movement of his horse did she allow herself to relax a little.

Whitey Doaks moved toward her. He stood near her awhile in silence, looking down in the canyon. He said, "There's a pool of spring water down there. It'll be cold, but you can take a bath if you want it."

She felt her stomach tighten. Her bathing, him watching. She said, "No, thank you."

He walked away from her and fiddled around his horse for a long moment and then he came back. There was a sort of feverish excitement in his eyes. He looked straight at her. "You want to be my woman?"

A shudder ran through her. She swallowed hard and

forced herself to remain calm. She remembered he
didn't like to see women abused. She put her hands
together as if in prayer and looked directly at him, her
eyes pleading. "No! Please, please leave me alone!
Please!"

He studied her thoughtfully. "Wouldn't have you
unless you're willin'. We can get out of here while he's
gone. Be better for you than Mexico. Them greasers are
hard on white women."

The implication behind his words struck her speech-
less. She fought against a sudden dizziness, her eyes
glued on him like a bird watching a snake.

He smiled loosely and reached a hand out to touch
her arm. "I can make us a livin'. I'm a pretty good all
around hand. Plenty of work out here."

Cathy screamed when she felt the touch of Whitey
Doaks. She sprang to her feet and ran blindly, still
screaming, into the pine grove. She didn't see the man
standing in her path until she ran into him. The man said
gruffly, "Get down on the ground. Quick!"

Schreiber! It was Dutch Schreiber, just standing
there. Coming out of nowhere. It was a dream. She had
lost her mind. Oh, dear God in heaven, she had lost her
mind! She cried out, mouthing words with no meaning,
tears streaming down her face. A heavy hand pushed
her to the ground.

She heard the choked voice of Whitey Doaks,
"Schreiber! Goddamn."

Then she heard the rifle blasting overhead, two shots
so fast they seemed as one. She was afraid to look up.
She kept her face against the ground. A hand took her
arm, gentle but with firmness. Schreiber said, "We've
got to get out of here."

She stumbled to her feet, looking at him, not believ-

ing it. She heard her stammering voice, "How—
how—"

Schreiber shrugged. "They weren't very careful.
Man wantin' to live out here has to be careful." He
looked over his shoulder. Max and Redoza were riding
out of the timber. He said, "That's far enough. Keep
them horses back. We'll stash Doaks's carcass somewhere and kill any sign we've left.

"We'll take both horses. Could be that Cogar will
think Whitey ran off with Cathy. He won't give much
of a damn if he's after that silver." He looked at Cathy.
"I watched Cogar ride off but I was too far away to get a
shot at him. Reckon he was goin' into Benson."

She nodded mutely.

Schreiber stuffed two cartridges into the magazine of
his rifle. "He knows about the Apache squaws and the
silver?"

Cathy nodded again. She felt faint. Her legs trembled
and she was biting her lip. Finally she was able to say,
"He's going to get some men to help him. He was
going to get two wagons, one for the men to hide in
when they started after the silver."

Dutch looked around at Max. "You and Redoza put
Whitey on his horse and saddle up Miss Cathy's. We
got a thirty-mile ride to get her to her uncle and the
troops. We'll dump Whitey somewhere along the
way."

Cathy felt his eyes appraising her. "You're used up.
Can't blame you. Can you ride? We need to stay in the
saddle at least half the night."

She found herself smiling at him. She didn't think
she remembered how. She didn't think she'd ever smile
again. She put her hands to her hair and removed the

tight, stiff riding derby. She shook her hair, then smoothed it back from her face.

"I can do anything that has to be done, Dutch. Anything. I'm all right now."

He grinned at her. "Well, now, that's good news. I was bad worried about you." He turned and drew his knife and walked off into a dense clump of pines. Presently he returned with two long pine boughs. He looked at Cathy. "You get on your horse and you lead Whitey's horse out of here up to the top of that slope. Max and I will clean up all the prints on the way out."

She nodded and turned away and walked toward Max who was saddling her horse. She had a silly thought and it brought a wry smile to her sun-cracked lips. Was this sudden feeling of warmth and elation due to being free again, or was it from hearing Dutch Schreiber's concerned voice saying that he had been "bad worried" about her?

They rode hard, passing north of the Mormon village of St. David, heading straight into the Dragoons. At sunset they pulled up and Dutch Schreiber said, "We'll rest a spell here."

Max took care of the horses, unsaddling them, taking the pack off the pack animal, talking to all of them as only a Comanche can talk to a horse, rubbing them down and then hobbling them so that they could not stray far. The horses were tired, hungry for grain, irritable with the long, hot miles behind them. They gentled under the Comanche crooning.

The Mexican, Luis Redoza, walked up a steep rise to the top of a low mesa and looked around. His Spencer was cradled in his arms. Schreiber moved in behind him. Redoza said, "I do not like this place."

Schreiber shrugged. "Hell, I don't like it, either, Luis. But we got to rest and eat. It's near twenty miles to the Dragoons."

Redoza did not answer. He stood there sniffing the air, moving over the mesa rim. "It has the smell of Apache."

Dutch said shortly, "They're out there." He turned around and went back down the rise to Cathy Roland. He said, "We'll have a snack. Not much. We'll rest three or four hours, and then ride toward the mountains. Your uncle and his troops are there if they are on schedule."

She took her riding hat and dropped it at her feet. She tried to smile but the smile didn't come. "What if he's not on schedule, Dutch? What do we do then?"

He returned her look, noticing the clear blue of her eyes and the hair like cornsilk spilling to her shoulders. He smiled at her, noting her badly burned face and wanting to touch it, but not doing it. He remembered how she had looked at the post with her hair all done up and resplendent with the aura of the captain's niece. There was something much more attractive about her now, in spite of her peeling face and cracked, sun-baked lips.

He smiled at her again, trying to reassure her, in spite of his own misgivings. "Well, Miss Cathy, it's a big country. We got lots of choices. We'll take care of it. Don't worry about it."

They did not make a fire. They ate cold beans from a can, together with morning biscuits, then washed the food down with brackish water from the canteens. When they were through, Dutch took the saddle blanket from Cathy's horse and also his own, then laid them over a smooth patch of sandy soil. He said, "You can get three hours sleep, if you will. We've got to find the Army by good sunup.''

There was a quiver in Cathy's voice but her eyes were steady on him in the fading light. ''What's out there, Dutch? What about Jesse Cogar?''

He took off his hat and ran a hand through his hair. ''Cogar ain't lookin' for us. He's lookin' for thirty thousand dollars in silver. It's Apaches that are out there. Nochelte and no telling how many are with him. We've got to make the mountains without running into them. It can be done, with luck.''

Her hand touched his arm and a feeling of warmth ran over him. She said quietly, ''You'll do it, Dutch.''

He didn't answer. A man riding this country in darkness needed more luck than sense. He slapped on his hat and got to his feet, then walked back up the mesa and looked over the flat country below. There was nothing to see but shadows and streaks of light from the setting sun.

Yet there were Apaches out there. Nochelte would have led a band of warriors to follow the troopers. The question was whether the Apaches were between him and the troops. That would be answered by morning.

Dutch rolled a smoke and sat down and let his mind drift. When it came back to Elaine and the ranch, he stubbed out the cigarette. He stood up and walked down to check the horses. He hoped to God that Roland was flanking the Dragoons.

A shadow moved in behind him and he said without looking around, ''Max, goddammit, you should be asleep.''

Max moved beside him. ''It is hard to rest in this country, Dutch. Someday maybe I go home.''

CHAPTER THIRTEEN

Captain Harry Roland and his horse soldiers had been gone exactly one week. There had been no word of them. None was expected. That was the way things were out here. Maybe Tucson would get word of some battle or skirmish between the soldiers and the Apaches, and the word would work its way up to Globe and the stage would bring the Globe newspaper to Two Wells. The news would be history by then.

Ruth Jackson was thinking about this now as she sat in the swing on the Brewers' front porch, snapping a mess of green beans for the evening meal. Inside the house she could hear Mae Brewer singing to herself in a tuneless voice. Every day that Joe Brewer was away, Mae became a little more apprehensive, a little more nervous, and her doubts and fears were showing in her eyes and the set of her mouth.

Ruth had to admit that she was not holding up much better than Mae. She tried to keep busy. First, there had been the stage trip to Globe to see the Brewers' lawyer there about settling her brother's estate. She had to establish her identity as his only heir in order to get the cattle money out of the bank and clear title to the ranch.

She had gone one day and came back the next, but the trip hadn't helped much because all there was to do on the twenty mile ride was sit and think. And her thoughts always came back to Harry Roland.

He wanted to retire from the Army. He wanted to raise good horses and write about this country, and the Apaches and the white men who took it from the Apaches. It would be a wonderful life for him. He deserved this time to reflect and remember and to do the things he liked.

By tragic circumstance she owned a ranch that would be ideal for this life. The house was too small but it had been built by a man with a dream, also, a man who thought ahead to better times. And it was so constructed that it would be easy to add on a couple of rooms. A room for the study of Captain Harry Roland. And he was not too old to have children. She blushed at her thoughts.

Mae Brewer stuck her head out of the open door. ''If them beans are ready, I'll put them on. We can eat a little early.''

Ruth moved out of the swing, carrying the pan of snapped beans in one hand and a straw basket of strings and bean tips in the other. ''They're ready, Mae. I think I'll change into an old dress and work in the garden awhile after supper.''

Mae smiled briefly. ''Good idea. I'll join you. Tired of being cooped up in the house and in the freight office. Joe always said this country was made to move around in.''

Inside the house Ruth moved to the ever-present coffee pot and poured herself a half cup. Sipping at it, she looked at Mae adding side meat to the beans. ''You know Captain Roland pretty well, Mae. Do you think he will ever retire from the Army?''

Mae smiled at her. ''You been talkin' to him, I

reckon. Sure. He's a man that knows his own mind. He's mentioned it to Joe and me a time or two. I just hope he gets the chance.''

Ruth looked at her quickly, ''You mean he might get killed?''

Mae shrugged. ''There's that chance. When your man leaves you to go huntin' Apaches, don't count on him comin' back until you see him. But the captain's got another problem.''

Ruth said, ''I knew he was troubled when he left. What is it, Mae?''

The woman wiped her hands on an apron and turned to face her. ''He may get himself court-martialed if he doesn't stop that silver from reaching the border. He took two days to go look for Cathy when he should have been on the trail of them squaws. Leastways, that's the way the Army will look at it. Me, I don't blame him.''

Ruth looked at her cup. ''That's why he didn't ask me.''

''Ask you what, girl?''

Ruth smiled unsurely. ''He said when he got back he had something to ask me, but he couldn't do it until he got back.''

Mae nodded curtly. ''That's Harry. If he comes back with that silver, he'll ask you to marry him, my guess. If he don't come back with the silver, he'll forget what it was he was going to ask you.''

''But why?'' Ruth frowned at her. ''Whether he gets the silver or not, he's still Harry Roland and I love him, Mae.''

Mae shrugged. ''I ain't sayin' you don't know him as well as I do. Maybe you know him better. Ought to, if you aim to marry him. But he's a proud man and he's a reasoning man. That's why he's a captain. One thing for Captain Roland to ask you to marry him, and another thing for a disgraced Harry Roland to ask you. Besides, he might have to serve some time. It must be weighin' heavy on his mind, Ruth. Thank goodness Joe hasn't got any problem except just stayin' alive and gettin' back.''

Ruth got up from her chair at the table. ''He didn't tell me any of that. I wish he had. Why are men like that? We could have talked about it, planned around it. He should know I'd marry him, no matter what happened. He's carrying the load all by himself and it's not right.''

Mae moved forward and placed an arm around her shoulders. ''Ruth, remember he's a captain. That's what captains are for. They carry the load.''

Ruth said, ''I know, Mae.'' She moved out of Mae's arm and went to the room where she had been sleeping at night. She would change her clothes and put in a couple of hard, physical hours in Mae's garden. She thought better when she was working outside.

She would find a way around Harry Roland's pride, if that was necessary. For the first time in her life she had found a man she could love and she would not give him up. Arizona had taken one man from her. Bill Jackson, her brother. In restitution Harry Roland had walked into her life. She intended to make sure he was there to stay.

Nochelte sat apart from the Apache camp in the Dragoons. He was roasting two succulent wood rats by a small fire for his evening meal. The squaws were working, some cooking, some trimming new travois poles to replace those that had given up their usefulness on the desert journey. The children were playing, the old men were resting. It was a peaceful place here in the mountains.

Natchez and some of his warriors were out on the desert hauling rocks on travois, heading west from the Dragoons. It was not the work of a warrior, doing this thing, but the trail might well throw the horse soldiers off course. Nochelte was counting on this because the squaws and children and old men needed a day of rest. The mules and horses pulling the travois needed rest also.

White Painted Woman had been faithful to the Apache. When the silver was tracking toward the Dragoons, she had given him the power to make the big wind. The tracks had blown away. His scouts reported the Army bivouacked near the north tip of the mountains a half day ride away from this place. The scouts said a patrol was moving south, searching for sign. Nochelte smiled at this. Natchez and his braves would give them sign, and if they followed it, all was well.

He turned the meat on a wooden spit, adding a small amount of wood to the fire. He wondered if the captain at the post had gotten his message to the Big White Chief in Washington? It would be a small thing for the Americanos to give back to the Apache a fragment of their mother land. It could be done with less loss to the white settlers than another Apache war.

But the white man was greedy. He did not easily give up that which he already had. He did not live much beyond the next sunrise. The choice was always that of the Americano. The Apache had no alternatives. More land, more room to hunt and live, a right to move with the seasons to avoid the bitter winter cold of the White Mountains. This was all the Apache wanted. This is what the Apache would die for, if need be.

The repeating rifles would add weight to the cause of the Apache. Fresh horses, good, long-legged, deep-chested horses would enhance the Apache position. Food and new blankets would give them endurance and hope. It all depended upon moving silver across the border into the arms of Juh.

They had an easy day journey ahead out of the mountains, moving down a watered valley for perhaps ten miles. Then they would have to move back into the flatland, still thirty miles from Mexico.

It would be the task of the Apache warriors to keep the Army at bay. Nochelte did not want to start a shooting war with the horse soldiers. That could cancel out any chance for a peaceful solution of the predicament of the Apache. But some lives would be lost, both Americano and Apache, before this thing ended.

He lifted the wooden, meat-laden spit from the glowing coals. He poured water from a bag made of a goat's stomach into a gourd. Nochelte sipped the water, letting the meat cool. The Apache did not need much to live in this land. They had learned to do with what was at hand and to do without the many things that the Americano thought of as necessities. There were no necessities for an Apache except a little food, a little water, enough warmth for the body, and clean air to breathe.

Darkness in the Dragoons came like the dropping of a black velvet curtain. Nochelte chewed off the meat from the last bone of the rats in the pitch blackness of the mountain night. He wondered if Natchez had encountered any horse soldiers. He did not think so. The troops were north of them now and the two dispatch riders to Huachucca did not make it. One lay now on his back with an Apache arrow in his chest. The other was wandering in the desert without a horse. He did not think there would be any horse soldiers south of them, cutting off the silver from the border.

A sound behind him turned his head and he waited. A tall, lean figure moved out of the night and stood before him. He tossed away the last bone, getting to his feet. He said, "You will leave by daybreak in the morning. Take the band to the draw leading out of the mountains, but do not come into the desert until you are told that it is safe."

The tall Apache nodded in the darkness. "Dalte will do as the Prophet says to do."

Nochelte said, "You are young. Chapparo was older than you, and wise. I trusted Chapparo, but now he is dead. You must take his place. Your scouts are young and full of excitement. They are supposed to hunt game for the squaws and children and old men, but they would rather be hunting White Eyes. Do not let them disobey you. Nothing matters but getting the silver load across the border. That is the only reason for being here now. Do not forget it."

The tall figure grunted assent and moved away. Nochelte sat back down on the dead trunk of a giant cedar. They were so close and yet they were not there. And he wondered about the Dutchman. Did his Apaches kill him or was he still loose?

If he were alive, he was dangerous to the Apache. The Dutchman would not be drawn off the trail by travois hauling rocks. He would see that there were no footprints of small children following the travois. He hoped the white scout with the Army would not notice this.

Cogar unsaddled his horse in the evening shade of a giant cottonwood tree, whose roots surfaced and spread desperately toward the small, seeping spring. He reached for tobacco and looked at the small man standing a dozen feet away.

Tot Farrel stood a half head shorter than Cogar. Two sixguns strapped his thick waist. He leaned his weight on a carbine, then said flatly, "It ain't the same deal it was the way you told it in Benson."

Cogar flared a match and lighted his smoke. "What's changed?"

Farrel's eyes narrowed, milky blue, settling on Cogar, and Jesse felt the chill of them. Farrel said, "First, the girl and Doaks. They ran out. Now I got to wonder why. Is he goin' to the law with his story?"

Cogar laughed shortly, drawing on his cigarette. Tot was supposed to be a manhunter. He was acting like an old woman. He said, "He was in on the killing of four troopers. I don't see him huntin' up any lawman to tell that story to. I figure he got an itch for the woman and took off with her. That crap he was feedin' me about abusing a woman was his way of keepin' me off her until he could get her for himself."

Tot Farrel took out a cob pipe and stuffed it with stringy tobacco. "Trouble is, Jesse, you're always figuring and not knowing. Man's got to know to pull off something like this."

He had a lot of respect for Tot Farrel. Cogar had a lot of respect for any man that could ride beside him. But he was goddamn tired of Farrel's nit-picking. He said shortly, "You don't like it, you don't have to ride. Me, I think you're spooked."

Farrel grinned, a mean, thin grin that caused Cogar to fumble and drop his smoke. Farrel said, "Hell, yes, I'm spooked. I've always been spooked, Jesse. That's why I'm still alive." He lighted his pipe. "Price is goin' up. We split fifty-fifty and you pay the expenses. It ain't no bargain at that.''

Jesse Cogar scowled. ''I always figured you a square shooter. We made a deal. You get a third.''

Tot Farrel sighed, looking at his pipe. ''Like I said, Jesse. You're always figuring and not knowin'.'' He looked at a half-dozen riders squatted around a cook fire. His eyes moved to the two wagons and then to the dozen head of horses grazing on thin grass. ''I don't need you, Jesse. I know what we're after. I know where we ought to find it. Them are my men, not yours.''

Cogar shrugged. ''Like you said, fifty-fifty.'' He turned back to get his saddle blanket when he heard the hard click of metal against metal. He looked over his shoulder at Tot Farrel. The little man held a sixgun lined on Cogar's stomach.

Farrel grinned. ''Just testin', Jesse. I ain't shot a man in near a year now.''

Cogar got his blanket and spread it away from the fire. He filled a plate of beans and side meat and poured himself a cup of coffee. Fifteen thousand was some different than thirty, but it was still a wad of money.

He said, ''I got a notion that them squaws will come out of the south end of the Dragoons, Tot. Chastino said they'd lay up a day or so in them mountains. I figure the west side because it would take a hell of a long time to move over them and come out the east flank.''

Tot Farrel filled his own plate. ''If it's just us and the squaw band, that's one thing. What troubles me is we don't know if Schreiber is in on this, and that's another thing if he is.''

Cogar scowled. He spooned beans into his mouth, then said over them, ''I told you he's huntin' his Indian. Damned fool went right on to the reservation after him. How's he gonna come out?''

Tot studied him over a cup of coffee. "That's what worries me."

Cogar wiped his mouth on a sleeve. "You can quit worryin'. I told you I killed the only men who knew about the silver. No one chasin' after them squaws but us."

Farrel took a swallow of coffee, pale eyes looking past the wagons to the flat horizon beyond, lying gold and purple in the early twilight. "The halfbreed wasn't the only man who supplies drinkin' whiskey to the Apaches. Must be three hundred Indians know about that silver by now. It's too big a story to lay quiet for long. We got to get to the squaws first. We got a good start but from here in we're just guessin'."

A little uneasiness drifted over Jesse Cogar. Farrel was right that whiskey had a way of getting to the reservation. The medicine man couldn't keep it all off. And what got there would find its way into some young buck's gut.

That's how Chastino picked up the story on the silver. If he did it, others could, too. He got up restlessly and walked over to the big covered wagon. The wagon was heavy. Extra timbers had been nailed to the sides, thick enough to stop a bullet. Blankets covered the bed where six men rode during the day, each armed with repeating rifles. The few Apache scouts riding with the fleeing band of squaws wouldn't have a chance. All he had to do was find them.

Cogar moved to the smaller, flat-bedded wagon and raised the canvas tarp that covered it. Saddles and bridles for their horses so they could make a quick getaway if something went wrong, extra ammunition, extra harness if needed, and plenty of food. He had planned this well. Farrel was acting like an old woman.

He moved away from the wagons and rolled a

cigarette and lighted it, looking over the horizon. Nothing moved out there. Where was the squaw band? Twenty miles away or fifteen? Or had they come out of the east slope of the Dragoons? That would put them forty miles from this camp. He puffed nervously on his cigarette.

A fresh thought sent a chill through him. What if Whitey Doaks let the girl get away? Cathy Roland's story would bring the Army and every white man able to ride with a posse down on him. He threw down his smoke and stomped it with his heel. He hated the goddamned waiting that came with nightfall. He wanted to move.

CHAPTER FOURTEEN

It was near midnight when Schreiber touched Cathy Roland's arm. The sleeping women opened her eyes slowly, looking at him, then smiled. "Is it time, Dutch?"

He nodded. "Max and Redoza are saddling the horses. I made a little fresh coffee."

She sat up with a leisurely movement, then stretched and got to her feet. "Coffee sounds good. Smells good."

He walked to the dying embers and poured two cups of the strong brew. "It will have to hold us until we hit the foothills. We can find a little timber cover there, make camp, rest awhile."

Max moved up and poured his own coffee. "How far, you reckon?"

"Too far," Dutch grunted. "We'll have to do a little daylight ridin'."

They moved to their horses and walked them slowly off the high swell of ground at the foot of the mesa and down into the flatness of the desert floor. Max led the pack horse, bringing up the rear. The half moon was high, bathing the land with its soft, faint light. They rode silently, single file, moving like dark phantoms across the desert's empty screen.

He did not like riding blind like this. He was a man who liked to see where he was going and what had been over this ground before he came along. But there was no choice. It was one thing to ride this country, realizing that you might run into Apaches. It was another thing to ride it, knowing they were out there.

They had only the darkness for cover. Once the sun rose on this flat, barren land, there would be no place to hide. They would have at least an hour of exposure before reaching timber cover. He hoped to God they made it.

He wondered if Roland was still moving his troops or whether he had bivouacked and sent out patrols to look for sign of the squaws. Maybe he had caght up with them. He hoped so.

Time was growing short for the captain. He had not mentioned Roland's predicment to Cathy. No use in it. If her uncle was court-martialed, she would blame herself for coming out here. He was glad she had come.

He hadn't realized it then, but the first time he saw her, it had done something to him. Made him feel better, somehow, like walking out of a stuffy cabin and feeling the first touch of a spring breeze laden with the scent of pine and cedar. It made a man feel clean and alive. She did the same.

He dropped back from the lead and rode beside Cathy. He said, "Another couple of hours, and we'll get a little light. Sun won't get up, though, for a spell because of the mountains."

She looked at him. "What is your first name? It can't be Dutch."

"Andress."

She smiled. "I like that. It has a good sound."

He shook his head. "Call me Dutch."

She laughed softly. "And Max? Is that his real name?"

He shook his head again. "No. I fastened it on to him after he told me his Indian name, Mah-e-yah. Indian names were not made for the white man's tongues. So I call him Max." He moved away to ride lead again.

Dawn comes quickly on the desert. Even with mountains blotting out the rising sun the cool light seems to encompass the land all at once. The light had come now and the risk increased a dozenfold.

Max rode up beside him. "How far, Dutch?"

Schreiber fished for tobacco. "Another fifteen minutes and you'll see the mountains, Comanche. My guess is under six miles."

They were less than an hour away from the mountains when they heard the gunfire. It rolled up from the south foothills of the Dragoons and spread across the silence of the land. The sharp, staccato bark of repeating rifles came so fast as to seem one continuous sound. For perhaps a minute or two it was so, and then the firing languished into a few sporadic shots and suddenly died.

Dutch pulled rein, stopping the others. Luis Redoza fingered the small metal cross chained around his wrinkled neck, then pulled his rifle from the saddle boot.

Fear flashed across Cathy's face. She asked tightly, "What is it, Dutch?"

He shook his head. "Whatever it is, it's two miles away. Maybe a patrol caught in an ambush. Those shots didn't come from Army Springfields." He moved his horse forward. "Maybe Cogar and his men caught up with the silver."

They came to a dry creek bed flanked for a short

distance by a green grove of leafless palo verdes. He
said, "Luis, you and the woman get into that grove and
wait for us." He looked at Max. "Let's see what we
can find out."

He rode off with a tightness in his guts. Whatever it
was, it couldn't be good.

Dalte was leading the squaws and children and old men
out of the south pass in the Dragoons to the desert floor.
They had rested a day and eaten well. He knew that
their spirits were good. The six captive horse soldiers
were not faring so well. Their arms were beginning to
rub raw with the rawhide thongs that bound them. Their
beards were long and caked with dust and their boots
were worn out. Perhaps when they reached the border
Nochelte would kill them and end their misery.

He was proud of the trust that Nochelte had placed in
him. He would do his job well. Nochelte was not being
critical of him when he pointed out that the dead Chapparo was an older and wiser man than he. For most
men, wisdom came with age. He would be older soon
and he would be wise.

In the meantime he had much energy and he had done
well in the last war against the White Eyes. That was
why Nochelte noticed him and singled him out for this
mission. He would be the one to lead his people across
the border. When the silver arrived there, he would be
singled out again and all the chiefs would praise him.
But it was still nearly three days walk to the border.
Three days was a long time. Much could go wrong.

In front of the moving band of Apaches six young
scouts covered the ground ahead, searching for any sign
of trouble. It was their job to find this trouble and report

it to Dalte. Behind the band, perhaps fifteen miles, the warriors of Nochelte formed a barrier between the silver bullion and the horse soldiers.

One of the scouts rode toward him now and Dalte felt a twinge of apprehension, but the scout was not riding fast. He was taking his time, so the news could not be urgent. The scout slid from his horse beside Dalte. He said, "I have discovered a good thing."

Dalte looked at him questioningly. "Then let me hear of it."

The scout was young, in his late teens, and he stood proudly erect in front of Dalte. "A small distance ahead, perhaps two miles, there moves two wagons and a fine herd of horses."

Dalte blinked. "And what of this? If there were White Eyes around, I do not see that it is good."

The young scout smiled. "There are only three Americanos with these wagons and horses. Two of them drive and one handles the herd. I think they are looking for land upon which to settle."

Dalte said thoughtfully, "Only three of them?" He took his time, thinking this thing through. "With the wagons we could move the silver much faster. It is flat country ahead and the stream bed runs through the canyons. We could be across the border by tomorrow when the sun is high."

The young scout nodded agreement. "It would be a great accomplishment. The Prophet would be pleased."

Dalte walked over to a large rock and sat on it. Finally he said, "But Nochelte does not want any Americanos killed unless it need be to save the silver."

The scout shrugged. "You are the leader." He looked beyond Dalte to the small cloud of dust that marked the progress of the squaws and children and old men. "I do not think the Americanos would resist us. We are too many. We could take the Americanos and their wagons and horses to the border. Nochelte will say whether to turn the White Eyes loose. The silver will be safe."

Dalte thought in silence. Finally he stood up. "It is my decision. We will take the wagons."

Quickly the squaws, old men, children, and the scouts were bunched on the downside of a steep slope in the desert floor. The wagons were moving slowly toward them. Dalte looked at his charges. "I will talk with the Americanos. If they make a hostile move, the scouts will take care of them. I do not think we will have any trouble."

When the wagons were two hundred yards away the Apaches, all of them, moved up the slope to stand exposed on the flatland of the desert directly in front of the wagons. Dalte dug heels into his horse's flanks, moving smartly toward the wagons.

Fifty feet away he raised a hand. He said in a strong voice, "We are here to take the wagons and the horses. You will come with us." He looked at the three Americanos staring at him. "You will be safe enough. We only want the horses and wagons."

A small, heavy-set man on the seat of the big wagon took off his hat and ran a hand through thin, red hair. The man looked at the rider who was handling the herd of horses. "Jesse, by God, we didn't have to find them. They found us."

Dalte did not fully understand the words of the man. He knew some Americano, but not much. He motioned to the Apaches behind him and they moved forward slowly, leading the mules and the horses with the travois. He said again, "We will take the wagons and horses."

The big wagon had moved a little, broadside to the advancing Apaches. The horse wrangler, a tall, bronzed-face man, waved to the wagon driver. The driver laughed. "You won't take a damn thing, Apaches."

The canvas cover rolled up suddenly and a terrible noise fell over the desert. Apaches were on the ground, squaws, old men and children, bleeding out their lives in the sand. Horses and mules were falling, screaming and kicking.

For a moment Dalte was stunned motionless. He heard this noise, this crashing fire of guns. He saw his people writhing on the ground, others running before the sound of the guns. He did not know what to make of this. The scout had said only three Americanos but the guns roared and blasted and his people were dying, and there were many Americanos in front of him.

A panic seized him and gave way to a wild, savage ferocity. This was war. He knew about war. He had killed many White Eyes in the last big fight. But the screams and moans and falling bodies wiped out his judgement and he gripped his rifle by the barrel and swung it over his shoulder like a club.

He cried the Apache war cry and touched his heels to his horse, charging the wagon. He was six feet from the wagon when he fell, riddled by a dozen .44-40 slugs.

Jesse Cogar dismounted and turned Dalte's body over with a foot. He said shortly, "Let's load the silver."

Schreiber took a lot of time covering the distance toward the gunshots. Every patch of cover, every lone withered mesquite was a stopping point, a listening place. Max moved like a brown shadow behind him, knowing instinctively where Dutch was going and what he would do.

When they were perhaps within a mile of the place where the gunshots erupted, Dutch pulled up in a narrow, steep-banked arroyo. He looked at Max. "We go in from here on foot."

The Comanche boy nodded, sliding out of his saddle. "Go in on belly."

Schreiber agreed. "Damned near it. There's not enough cover out there to hide a ground squirrel." He drew his rifle and moved forward on foot, walking crouched over, close to the ground, eyes searching every foot of the expanse ahead.

When they had covered a quarter mile, he drew up and motioned to a clump of greasewood standing some four feet in height. He said, "We need a rest." They crouched on the shady side of the scant cover and breathed the hot desert air.

Schreiber thought about Cathy and wished she was with her uncle and the troops, but she was not. That was another problem. Another responsibility. She was too fine a woman to lose herself in this godforsaken country. She was due better than that. He wanted a smoke but decided against it, not knowing what was ahead.

Max took off his battered black hat and ran his hands through his coal-black hair. He was relaxed. Dutch Schreiber was leading the way. This was his life, following Dutch. He grinned slightly, pulling a knife from a belt sheath. He ran a finger over the edge. "You reckon it's Cogar?"

Dutch shrugged. "Who the hell knows? Let's make tracks."

They carved a crooked trail like two sidewinders over the desert sand. The minutes became an hour and the hour brought forth the answer. A desert tragedy spread itself before them. Four young Apache scouts sprawled on their backs with the red blood of their lives sucked up in the brown sand. A few yards in front of the scouts another warrior lay under his horse, still gripping a single shot rifle by its barrel. Behind these bodies lay a half-dozen squaws, an old man, and two children, all shot to pieces by repeating rifles. Strewn across the flat land was the carcasses of many horses and mules.

Schreiber's lips tightened. He looked at the Comanche boy beside him. "It was Cogar. They walked right in on him and his killers. He has the silver now."

Max nodded. "He in for one hell a time. Nochelte hear about this pretty quick. Be on Cogar's butt pretty quick."

"Cogar ain't got a chance. But we got to get to him before the Apaches do, else we lost ourselves a captain and a lot of white folks that think this is a good place to live."

Dutch reached for his tobacco and rolled a smoke and handed the sack to Max. "Maybe you ain't too young. You got a man's job ahead of you."

He lighted his own cigarette and drew deeply on it. He watched Max struggle with the brown paper and tobacco. He said, "You got to get back to Cathy and Luis. Tell Luis to cut back west a couple of miles and then head north. He'll miss the Apaches if he does that. Tell him to head back east toward the mountains when he hits their north flank. He'll cut Army sign by then if Roland is out there and I know he is."

Max licked the edge of his loosely rolled smoke. "What I do then?"

"Well, goddammit, Max, you come back here and

see if you can follow my trail. You don't figure on me
handling that bunch of killers all by myself, do you? I
need a little help. Not much, but some.''

Max eyed him cautiously, touching a match to his
cigarette, puffing on the tobacco. ''First time you ever
said it. Big fight coming up, I think.''

Nochelte was troubled. Two days ago when the horse
soldiers were overtaking the squaws and the silver load,
he had made the wind blow. He had stood out on the flat
expanse of loose sand and cacti and salt grass, and
picked up a handful of the gritty soil. He had thrown a
pinch of it in the air and blown on it toward the east,
toward the mountains.

The winds had come, sweeping down from the distant Rincons and racing across the desert toward the
Dragoons. The tracks of the squaws and old men and
children had been wiped out. Not a travois rut remained
to be seen. He thought then that the Great God was
hearing him again.

But today it was not so. The moving Apache band
with the silver treasure had rested a day in the cool
mountains, eating well from fresh game supplied by the
Chiricahuas who still held forth in the mountain fast-
ness. New travois poles had been cut. But this morning,
as they moved out of the southern pass back to the
desert, he had not been able to blow out the tracks.

This was a bad sign. He climbed a steep, rocky slope
in the Dragoons and settled himself to talk to the Great
God. If he received no response, he would talk with
White Painted Woman.

Nochelte sat for a long while on a wide ledge of stone
in the shade of a small grove of cedar. He looked at the

noon sun and waited patiently for word from the Great God or White Painted Woman, but he heard nothing. It was his fault. Always when he failed to get word from the Great God or White Painted Woman or even Child of the Water, it was his fault. He could not concentrate. He could not hear them because his mind was on the moving band of Apaches with the silver.

He had made a bad mistake. He had convinced himself that the future of the Apaches rested with the silver treasure. By His silence, the Great God was perhaps showing him that it was not so.

In the past he had accepted the power that had been bestowed upon him. But when he could not call up these powers, his faith in the Great God dimmed. The Great God was testing him, trying his faith. Faith was more important than the silver.

He could see this now, thinking it over, but his followers would be hard to convince. He was a shaman, the Prophet, and he had sold his people on the importance of getting the silver across the border, on the necessity of arming themselves for a final desperate war if need be.

He could not explain to them that perhaps he was wrong. The Great God worked through him, and if he lost the confidence of his people there would be no way to get the word to them. They would not listen to him any longer. And so it was. The silver had to reach the border without the help of the Great God and without any words of wisdom from White Painted Woman.

In the horizon a small object was moving. Nochelte stood up. The object became a rider throwing up a narrow trail of dust behind him as he moved toward the mountains. In a moment the rider became an Apache scout. The shaman moved off the rock ledge and hurriedly made his way to the base of the slope.

The rider slid from his horse as he reached the timber cover of the slope. A half dozen Chiricahuas gathered around him. Nochelte, running and sliding to reach level ground, moved in among them.

He looked at the young Apache rider who had fallen exhausted to his knees, head bowed. He asked quietly, "Is there trouble with the band?"

Slowly the scout looked up. "Many have been killed. The silver is gone. It was trick of the White Eyes. There were two wagons and some horses moving across the desert. Dalte thought we might use the wagons to haul the silver. The wagons were full of Americanos with repeating rifles, but we could not see this." He grimaced, looking at Nochelte. "Dalte is dead."

Nochelte looked at the Apaches around him. He had been a warrior once, before becoming an Army scout and then a shaman. He felt like a warrior at the moment. He said, "We will go after the Americanos. We will retake the silver."

He looked around him. "There are twelve of us here. We will leave now." He pointed to an older warrior, standing back on the edge of the group. "You will go after Natchez and his braves. Tell him to bring all of his warriors. Have the squaws gather new travois poles and follow."

CHAPTER FIFTEEN

The troops had been moving south since early morning. They rode in the arid desert flanking the Dragoons, the heat and dry wind sapping the moisture from their bodies, plodding onward toward the border.

One worry was off of Captain Roland's mind. Cathy had ridden into the Army camp last night, escorted by an old Mexican. She was exhausted, disheveled, dirty, and faint from the heat and long hours in the saddle, but she was physically and mentally sound. Given a chance to rest and clean up, she would be the same woman he had known on the post. For that he was thankful.

He mulled over in his mind the story told by the Mexican. Someone, probably Jesse Cogar, had ambushed the band of squaws and taken the silver away in wagons. Many Indians were killed. The wagons were taking the silver to the border.

Roland looked now at Sergeant Quincy Shannon. "Those killers with the silver will never see the border, Sergeant."

The sergeant ran a sleeve over his dust-coated red face. "Don't seem too likely. The wagons move pretty fast in this country, but not as fast as Apaches. Way it works out, they are just helping Nochelte get the stuff across. We lost a day and a half waiting on Brewer and we got no chance to catch up now.''

Roland thought about that in silence. It was true. He had decided this morning to push on without his scout, and he had driven the column as hard as he dared in this heat. It would still take a freak stroke of luck to capture the silver bullion, and he did not believe in luck out here. Not in Apache country.

He pulled away from the column and looked back. Cathy rode in the rear beside the old man who had brought her in. She had said that Schreiber and the Comanche boy were tracking the wagons. Still, it helped some to know Schreiber was scouting for him again. But where the hell was Joe Brewer? He could not bring himself to face Mae Brewer if he didn't bring her husband back.

There was movement on the western horizon. He pulled his field glasses and focused on it, picking up the tiny haze of dust and dark figures churning under it. He pulled his horse out of line and sat there studying the land, unrelenting in its grim gray and brown mantle shimmering in the heat waves.

Riders appeared out of the dust, a dozen of them, and finally the riders became troopers. Brewer's scouting detail. And there was Brewer and another man in civilian garb riding with them. Roland felt a great sense of relief. Cathy and the old Mexican passed him and she smiled at him wearily but said nothing. He waited there for the patrol, and when they were a quarter of a mile away he rode toward them.

Joe Brewer was used up. His face was etched in fatigue and pain, he slumped forward in the saddle. He tried to grin as Roland pulled rein in front of him. The captain saw that a sleeve had been torn from the man's shirt and wrapped around his left hand. The sleeve was stained with blood.

Brewer said huskily, "Made a mistake, Captain. Thought I'd cut sign on the travois. Plain as day it was, them tracks coming out of the south pass of the Dragoons, headin' west instead of south. Figured I'd find out why." He paused, steadying himself in the saddle. "Ran smack into an ambush. Nobody hurt but me." He held up his cloth-wrapped hand. "Caught an Apache broadhead arrow right through the palm."

Roland's lips thinned. "Take care of the hand, Joe. My guess is they made that trail for you. The silver went south. We have word that Cogar and his men have taken it from the squaws."

Brewer shook his head. "Ain't been much good to you, Harry. I've lost my touch. Them damned red bastards kept us pinned down for near a day. Didn't seem to be tryin' to kill us particularly. Just holdin' us there, and buyin' time." He nodded toward the man beside him. "Meet Bud Norwood. He was ridin' dispatch out of Fort Thomas lookin' for you. He heard the gunfire and found me instead."

The dispatch rider nodded and handed Roland a leather pouch. He said, "Don't worry about any Apaches comin' up on you from the rear, Captain. Between Thomas and Fort Apache they've put five hundred troops out patrolling the south end of the reservation. They'll hold the Apaches on it or there'll be a helluva lot of dead Indians stinkin' up the country."

Roland took the pouch and rode off a short distance and read silently the communication inside. It verified what the dispatch rider had told him. The Army had decided that the Apaches were not as peaceful as they had hoped and was now in the field in force.

Word had it that Indian sympathizers in the East were putting the heat on President Arthur to do something for the Apaches. The Commissioner of Indian Affairs was coming out with a representative of the War Department, perhaps Sherman himself, to meet with General Willcox.

But that was not all. Willcox was critical of Roland for letting the silver get off the reservation. He was more critical of Roland's delay in getting his troops out to retake it. If the silver reached the border, there would be an official inquiry, and no help could be expected from Fort Huachucca. Geronimo and his followers, with some help from the Nednis in Mexico, were raiding around Patagonia, burning ranches, stealing stock. The troops at Huachucca had their hands full.

The captain put the report back into the pouch and pushed it into a saddle bag. He rode back to the patrol. He said to Norwood, "Tell the colonel at Thomas that we are near the south end of the Dragoons. I think the silver is at least twenty miles ahead of us and about thirty miles from the border. We will do our best."

He watched the rider turn his horse north and ride off. He thought about Ruth Jackson. Strange that he should go through life a bachelor, without a blemish on his Army record, then meet a woman for the first time that he wanted as a wife and find himself facing disgrace as an officer.

He looked at Brewer. "Cathy's back, Joe. You won't recognize her, maybe, but she's all right."

Brewer managed a smile. "That's good news, Harry. I'll get the details later. You've got a lot on your mind."

Roland nodded and turned his horse toward the troops. "You are right about that."

It was an easy thing for Schreiber to follow the deep ruts left by the wagon wheels. He rode hard, pausing twice to rest his horse while he swept the desert ahead with his field glasses. Within an hour he had picked up the wagons lumbering along about four miles ahead.

He slowed his mount to a walk now. He was close enough. The wagons could make another six to eight miles before night camp. There would be no attempt here to drive the wagons in darkness. Soon they would be in canyon country again, and south of the canyons loomed the Mule Mountains, split by deep gulches and even more shallow arroyos. Cogar and his men would have to have daylight to pick their way over that country. The gunmen were riding their saddle horses now as there was no longer need to stay cooped up in the wagon.

He rode slowly, worrying about Cathy Roland. Had Redoza found the troops? Was it possible that Nochelte had brought along enough warriors to wipe out the horse soldiers led by Roland? He didn't think so. Nochelte would do all he could to delay the troops, short of open conflict. The shaman didn't want a war. Not yet, anyway.

He remembered the way Cathy had smiled up at him when he had awakened her in the dark hours of early morning. It had done something to him, given him a lift. Given him something to think about on lonely rides like this.

He kept looking over his shoulder for some sign of Max. He wasn't really worried about the kid. Max was careful. He'd been raised in Apache country. Still, he wished the Comanche was riding beside him. Max was a good man to have along in spite of his young years.

The sun was a bright ball of fire setting on the rim of the desert. He picked up his pace a little and after a while he stopped and used the glasses. He was closer to the wagons now, perhaps only three miles away. He turned and swept the land behind him and picked up the solitary figure of a rider coming toward him.

Dutch grinned slightly. That would be Max. He began to look ahead for a place to make camp. An hour later, just as the sun was sliding below the horizon, he found what he wanted. A small, deep sink hole that held good water most of the year but was dried up now, except for one small pool. At one end of it was a stand of dried reeds, and higher up a stand of greasewood, some of them dead.

He pulled rein and unsaddled his horse. The horse drank a little from the pool, not liking it much. Schreiber tethered him with a rope, knowing they would not be in this camp long. He was hungry but he had left the pack horse with Redoza and Cathy. He hoped Max remembered to bring some grub.

Max moved into sight, having already spotted Schreiber's horse. He pulled up beside Dutch and slid out of the saddle. He opened a saddle bag and pulled out two cans of beans. He heanded one to Dutch. "No make fire, no need coffee."

Schreiber nodded. "We won't be making a campfire. That's for sure." He looked at the boy. "Miss Roland all right?"

"She hold up pretty good. Scared, maybe. She and Redoza do like you say."

They wolfed down the cold beans in silence. Finished, Schreiber got to his feet and walked over to his saddle and cut two long rawhide thongs from a metal ring on the saddle skirt. He drew his knife and walked

into the patch of dried reeds. He motioned to Max,
"Gather up some of that dead greasewood. Nothin'
bigger 'round than your thumb."

He cut an armload of reeds and laid the stiff, straw-
like vegetation on the sand. He spread it out into two
piles and waited for Max to bring the greasewood.
When the Comanche laid the dried sticks in front
of him, he carefully selected a half-dozen pieces and
put them on top of the reeds, then laid more reeds on top
of the greasewood.

Schreiber took a leather thong and bound the reeds
closely around the dead wood. When finished, he had a
bundle about two feet long and six inches in diameter.
He made another just like it.

Max shook his head. "What the hell? You make
fire?"

"Yeah. But not here." Dutch jerked a thumb toward
Max's saddle. "You get a couple of hours on the
blanket, then you let me take my turn. We'll be riding a
little after midnight."

They rode very slowly as they neared the spot where
Schreiber figured the gunmen would make camp. They
rode carefully, picking their way in the shallow light of
the crescent moon, pausing often to listen. They could
not afford to stumble into a camp of gunmen armed with
repeating rifles. It was a chancy business but the
chance had to be taken.

In the distance, off to the east, a horse snorted and
stomped. They pulled rein and waited, but there was no
further sound. The horse had not been far away.
Schreiber dismounted and handed Max the reins. He
eased ahead, trying to force his eyes to pierce the
shadowy darkness. The horse snorted again and he

stopped, judging the distance. He crawled forward on his stomach.

Suddenly, less than fifty feet away, the camp took shape. Men sprawled on blankets, lying in a half circle, some snoring softly. Two wagons were side by side less than twenty feet from the men. The horses were picketed some hundred feet in front of the camp.

Watching closely, Dutch saw the solitary night guard move away from the horses toward the camp. He crawled backwards, keeping his eye on the night guard, then turned and made his way back to Max.

He said, "The horses are due left of you, maybe two hundred fifty feet. The night guard has gone into camp, probably to get himself a drink of whiskey. You think you can spook them animals?"

Max grinned in the moonlight. "Comanche old hand at stealin' horses."

Schreiber took the bundle of straw and greasewood from behind Max's saddle and the other bundle from behind his own. "You be damned careful, Indian. Them are mean men out there."

Max dismounted and pulled his knife. "Comanche pretty mean, too."

Schreiber grinned tightly, "Then get after it."

He waited a long time. He was worried the guard would return to the herd. Seemed like he was always asking the kid to take chances with his life. The youngster never complained. That was the kind of country it was. That was Schreiber's line of work, taking chances, and Max was with Schreiber.

A Comanche war whoop screamed against the silence of the night. A horse squealed, hooves thundered against the dry ground. Men yelled and ran around wildly, reaching for guns, cursing into the darkness.

Cogar's voice shouted, "Goddammit, stop them horses!"

Schreiber moved out of the darkness toward the wagons. He touched a match to one of the reed bundles and held it inside the covered wagon. By the flaring light he could see the silver bars bunched toward the front of the wagonbed. He held the flame against the covering canvas. When it flared, he tossed the blazing bundle into a pile of blankets and wooden boxes on the far side of the wagonbed.

He moved deliberately to the other, smaller wagon and lifted the back end of the tarp that covered it. He lighted the other bundle of tinder-dry reeds and greasewood and held it under the canvas until it smouldered and blazed, then shoved the bundle against the side of the wagonbed.

A man's voice screamed, "Look at the damn wagons!"

Schreiber pulled back into the shelter of darkness. A man ran into the bright ring of firelight, heading for the big wagon. Schreiber's sixgun exploded and the man went down, clutching his leg, rolling in pain. Schreiber called out, "Next man gets near them wagons, gets lead in the belly."

He heard Jesse Cogar yell, "Schreiber, is that you out there?"

Dutch grinned thinly, "Damned sure is, Jesse. Just happened by."

Another voice said thickly, "Only about two hours to daylight. We'll stretch his hide then."

Cogar's voice came again, taunting him, "Dutch, I been tellin' the boys how I used to sleep with your wife when you was gone."

Schreiber felt the cold rage threaten to smother him,

threaten to blot out his reason. He walked around in a small circle fighting against it. Finally he was able to say in a steady voice, "I'll bury you beside her, Jesse. You can sleep with her forever."

Cogar laughed. Schreiber heard him say, "You men stay after the horses. We can ride into Tombstone for another wagon."

He wondered if he should tell the men about Nochelte and the Apaches who would be paying them a call come daylight. He decided against it. Whatever they got, they more than deserved, but he did not want to be around to hear their tortured cries. When he was sure that the wagons were destroyed, he would ride on south into the canyon country and pick a place to watch it through the glasses.

When the bed of the big wagon caved in, sending sparks fifty feet upward into the dark sky, Schreiber moved back toward the horses. Max was already there. He looked at the youngster. "That silver will stay put. They got no way to haul it now and neither have the Apaches. It'll take the Indians more than a day to get back to the mountains and cut travois poles and get them back here."

Dutch got into the saddle. "You cut west a couple of miles and then move north. That ought to take you around Nochelte's warriors. Find the captain and tell him how things are. I'll be along when I can."

Max looked at him curiously. "What more to do here? Why you hold back?"

Schreiber shrugged. "Cogar might get lucky and get away from the Apaches. If he does I want to be around to meet up with him."

Max nodded. He reined his horse around. "Ho, Dutch. Good luck."

Schreiber rode south and when he had covered a half-mile he began to hit the rough country. He rolled a smoke and waited for daylight. When it came he spotted a high slope, not too steep, and took his horse upon it. He pulled his glasses and focused on the gunmen's camp, waiting for it to happen.

He did not wait long. He never saw the Apaches moving in on the camp. They came in on foot and suddenly they were there. From this distance he could not hear whether they were screaming out their shrill battle cries. Most likely, he figured, they were not. They would move in like a dozen red ghosts in the pale dawn light, and the butchery would be a terrible thing to see.

And then he saw two men riding, racing their horses almost directly toward him, and he recognized Jesse Cogar and another man he either didn't know or could not make out. They had been smarter than the others. They had found their horses and had them saddled and close by. Likely the Apaches would be satisfied with five dead Americanos. Besides, they would not want to leave the silver.

Schreiber watched the riders coming, studying their course, then he pulled off the summit of the slope and rode down the backside. A wide, sandy wash wound past the foot of the slope. In the rainy season it would carry a bankful of foaming, muddy water filled with desert brush down its crooked course.

For a rider wanting to put miles behind him, the sandy bed offered an unobstructed path of firm sand as far as a man could see. Schreiber rode the rim of the wash until he came to an arroyo feeding into the main channel. He put his horse down the bank of the arroyo and pulled up under cover of the arroyo's steep bank.

He would wait here for Jesse Cogar.

He heard them coming, running their horses, too frightened to care that they might soon break their horse's wind and be left afoot. He had the rifle in front of him, across the saddle. He rode out of the arroyo when they were scarcely fifty feet away. He said, "Hello, Jesse."

The red-whiskered man beside Cogar pulled rein so hard that his horse slid back on its haunches. He said, "He aims to kill us." The man's hand streaked for the gun on his hip.

Schreiber fired across the saddle, squeezing off the shot, knowing it was dead center, yet bewildered by the speed of the bearded man. A shot from the man's gun spewed sand a dozen feet in front of him, and he recognized the man now. Tot Farrel, the gunslinger, the bounty hunter, you name it and he'd do it, just so long as he was paid. He watched briefly as Farrel fell from the saddle, but his attention was mostly on Jess Cogar.

Cogar said, "You ought to give a man a chance." His left hand held his horse's reins, his right hand was palm open, shoulder high.

Schreiber looked at him. "You want a chance, Jesse? I'll give it to you. Better than the one you gave the lieutenant. Better than the chance you gave the Apache squaws and old men. Get off your horse."

He would have given Cogar a chance. He wanted to look at him when he killed him. He wanted him to know what it was like to look at death and know it was not to be avoided.

But Cogar didn't see it that way. When he swung out of the saddle, he ducked behind his horse and pulled his gun as he moved. He snapped off a quick shot under the horse's neck, but he was moving and hurried and the shot was wild.

Schreiber fired again across the saddle with the .44-40, and Cogar screamed and spun around and staggered to keep his feet. Cogar raised his short gun again but he was hurt and he was slow. The next bullet caught him center and stretched him out on his back, his eyes staring at the bright morning sun.

Schreiber stuck the rifle in the saddle boot. He had killed Torres for Elaine. Killing Cogar meant a lot of things. It meant, most of all, self-respect.

CHAPTER SIXTEEN

For the first time since he had left the post, Captain Harry Roland began to feel some hope that he might successfully complete his mission. He thought about this as he listened to the young Comanche, Max. The boy was taking his time spreading the picture of the situation, partly because he had an inborn awe of official authority and partly because he had the natural Comanche aptitude for drama.

"Silver bars, they are on the ground, Captain Roland. No way to move. Dutch, he burn wagons. Apaches come. They maybe kill all Americanos but they no can move silver bars on the ground. They go back to mountains for travois. No travois poles in desert."

Roland pointed to the south. "How many miles?"

"Miles?" Max shrugged. "I no understand miles. I left this morning before daylight." He squinted at the westering sun. He shrugged again. "A day ride." He added with a little arrogance, "For a Comanche."

Sergeant Shannon shifted in his saddle, looking south. "Take us near half again that time, Captain, unless we ditch the pack train and pick a patrol of good troopers."

Cathy Roland, seeing Max, rode up beside her Uncle. "Where's Dutch?" She looked at Max.

The Comanche shrugged. "I think he in the canyons. I think he all right."

Roland said, "We got a break, Cathy. The silver is grounded. No way the Apaches can move it for a day or two."

Cathy looked at him. "How did this happen?"

He smiled faintly. "Schreiber."

He saw the look that spread over her face, the eagerness in her eyes. She said, "He has given us a chance. Let's make the most of it."

Roland nodded. "I aim to do that." He looked at Shannon. "We can't divide our forces. We'll ride all night if we have to." He touched Cathy's arm, eyes softening. "Can you take that kind of ride?"

She nodded. "After what I've been through, I think I can take anything."

"Good. Get the men moving, Sergeant."

Captain Roland rode at the head of the column with the Comanche, Max, at his side. The boy had changed horses, picking a gray gelding. He looked now at the captain. "You think, this over, Dutch settle himself down?"

Roland was surprised by the question. He thought it over. "I always figured him a settled man in his own way. He knows what he's doing. I think he likes it."

Max shrugged. "He not been right since wife killed. Maybe he gettin' over it. I think so. But what a man like him do except hunt Apaches?"

Roland speculated, "Maybe ranch somewhere. He did it before."

Max shook his head. "He been on the move too long. Besides, he got no money."

Roland smiled at the boy, feeling the concern the Comanche had for Dutch Schreiber. "A man can lose a lot of time for nothing, worrying about the Dutchman.''

The boy's grin was small, uncertain. "Maybeso."

Joe Brewer had been ranging out south and west of the troops. He rode up beside Roland now. He said, "There's a dust haze southwest of us, maybe five miles. Figure that'll be the band of broncos that had my patrol pinned down. They've got word about the silver now."

Roland looked over his shoulder at his horse soldiers, slumped in their saddles, bodies swaying slightly with the plodding walk of their mounts. Cathy was riding in silence beside Shannon. They would go another hour, then make a rest stop for a couple of hours, and eat a cold supper. After that, there would be no more stops.

He jerked a thumb toward the scout's bandaged hand. "How's it feelin', Joe?"

Brewer grimaced. "Throbs like hell. If it would stop the pain I'd wish the damned thing would fall off."

There was movement far out on the horizon east of them. Roland pulled his glasses and focused on the tiny dots crawling across the land. He handed the glasses to Brewer. "See what you make of it."

Brewer studied the horizon through the binoculars a long moment. "More Apaches. Maybe twenty of them. Always knew that there was a big bunch of Chiricahuas in those mountains. Some said they had gone to Mexico, but Dutch and I never believed it. They like the Dragoons, just like Cochise did in the old days."

Roland put up the field glasses. "That will give Nochelte about forty fighting men. We've got sixty. Those are not good odds in Apache country."

Brewer nodded. "And don't forget the squaws and kids and old men. They'll be coming back for the silver, and they can kill a trooper just as dead as a warrior can.'' He looked at Roland thoughtfully, ''You reckon Geronimo is pulling off those raids just to tie up the troops at Huachucca?''

Roland shrugged. ''Doesn't matter, does it? We fight this battle with what we brought with us. We know there's no help coming.'' He motioned with a hand. ''Ride out and find us a place close by to make a short camp. I'll go back and alert Shannon that Nochelte is getting reinforcements.''

He watched Brewer ride off, then wheeled his horse around and rode back toward the sergeant. He had taken all of the men out of the post that he dared to take. He had to leave enough to defend the post if necessary, or form a patrol if trouble developed elsewhere.

He had not really expected to have to fight another major engagement with the Apaches before he retired. But there was one coming up. He thought about Ruth Jackson and wondered if he would see her again.

They camped at twilight on a slight rise that would give them a view of the country in all directions. It was a dry camp, for there was no water here in this desolate land. They did not make coffee but hoarded their precious water supply against the long, dry miles ahead. They ate canned beans and canned peaches and called it supper.

Joe Brewer rose and walked around the edge of the camp because his hand hurt so badly he could not sit still. He was looking south, wondering if Nochelte now had all of his warriors around him, when he saw the lone rider. He walked over to Captain Roland. He said quietly, ''Dutch is comin' in.''

Roland got to his feet and walked out from the camp,

looking in the direction that Brewer had pointed. After a while he said, "That's him. Know the way he sits a horse."

Schreiber moved in slowly. He had covered a lot of ground this day. He pulled up by the troops' mounts and ground-tied his own horse. He walked into the camp and saw that Brewer and Roland were waiting for him. Max and Cathy moved into the small group. Then Shannon moved up and they all stood there, waiting for Schreiber to speak.

Dutch smiled at Cathy. "You all right?"

She nodded.

He looked at the troops scattered around on the rise, resting, not knowing what would come next. He said, "You're short-handed, Captain."

Roland looked at his troops. "They're good men, Dutch. Not many, but good soldiers."

Schreiber looked at Brewer, noticing his hand. "What happened?"

Brewer's face was gray, lined with wrinkles of fatigue. "Caught an arrow, Dutch. Ten-man patrol and I'm the only casualty."

Schreiber took the scout's arm and peeled off the bloody bandage. The hand was swollen, full of puss. He looked at Cathy. "You got on anything white under that skirt?"

She blushed. "Why—why, yes."

Dutch pointed to the downside of the slope. "Get over there and take it off." He handed her his pocket knife. "Make up some bandage."

Roland frowned uneasily, "It's bad?"

Schreiber looked at him. "You may be bringing home a one-handed scout." He went to his horse and dug in his saddle bag and brought out a pint bottle of whiskey, nearly half full. He walked back to Brewer and handed him the bottle. "Have a drink, Joe."

Brewer gulped a swallow of the liquor and handed the bottle back. He said, "Thanks, Dutch," and Schreiber hit him. A hard, savage blow on the jaw that sent the man to the ground, landing on his shoulders.

Shannon moved in, grabbing at Dutch, but Roland caught him by the arm. "He knows what has to be done, Sergeant. Let him do it."

Schreiber straddled the fallen scout, drawing his sheath knife. He made a deep slice across the puffy palm that also crossed the hole left by the arrow. He spread the palm and the putrilage squirted from Brewer's hand. He looked at Shannon. "Give me a hand. He's got a piece of that arrow shaft still in him. You hold his wrist and I'll bend his hand back, maybe fish it out."

The sergeant grabbed Brewer's wrist. Schreiber probed with the knife point for a long while. Finally he grunted and straightened up, holding a piece of wood a half-inch long and almost a quarter-inch thick. He poured more whiskey on the wound.

Cathy came up, still blushing, handing Dutch the bandage and together they wrapped the hand. Brewer groaned, pawed at the air with his free hand, and struggled to a sitting position. Dutch handed the whiskey to him and he took a long drink. He looked at his freshly bandaged hand. He grinned. "Thanks, Dutch." He turned up the bottle again, emptied it, and lay back down.

They lounged on the coarse sand of the rise, talking, resting, waiting for riding time. Roland looked at Schreiber. "No help coming, Dutch. It's up to us. The Commissioner and maybe Sherman are coming out here to check out the Apaches' condition. The president is getting some heat by the Eastern do-gooders.''

Schreiber rolled a smoke in silence. Finally he said, ''Maybe it's time. When I can forget that Torres was an Apache and look at him like he's just a man, I can make a case for the Apache myself.''

Roland stood up and fished for a cigar. He lighted it. ''How far to the silver?''

Dutch blew smoke. ''You'll get there by mid-morning, if your horses hold out.'' He was silent a. moment, then added, ''I want to talk a little strategy with you, Captain. You're the boss and I've been with you on enough of these patrols to know that you can fight Apaches. But this maybe is a little different.''

Roland looked at him. ''Different? How?''

Schreiber straightened to a sitting position. ''Well, start with the six missing troopers. I think the squaws have them. Nochelte said they did. I think you'll get a choice of letting the silver through or watching those men die one at a time.''

Roland sat down. ''I figured that myself. Tried not to think about it. They could be dead by now.''

Dutch nodded. ''There's that chance but we don't know.''

They smoked in silence. Finally Roland said, ''Dutch, I couldn't let those men die. I'd always wonder if I sacrificed them in an attempt to save myself from a court-martial.'' He looked at Schreiber. ''I didn't mention it, but I'm in trouble with Willcox.''

Schreiber said finally, ''We all got problems, Captain. I went after Torres when I could have gone after the silver. Lots of folks are dead because of that. Cathy went through hell because of it. But I couldn't have done it any different. I made my choice. A man can't think beyond what is most on his mind. Leastways, I can't.''

Roland studied the glowing end of his cigar. ''That's behind us. What are our chances?''

Dutch pinched out his cigarette. ''I did some ridin' yesterday after I killed Cogar.''

Roland's head came up. ''You killed him? I thought the Apaches got him.''

Dutch smiled. ''Turned out to be my pleasure, Captain. But, like I say, I did some ridin'. The only way the squaws are goin' to get the silver to the border is to follow that stream bed in the canyons. Runs about ten miles, then the land flattens out and it's only fifteen miles or so to the border. But they have to take the stream bed and there's high bluffs along the way, where a half-dozen men could drop anything moving along that bed. I'm thinking of horses and mules pullin' travois.''

Roland puffed on his cigar. ''I'm listening.''

Dutch rolled over on an elbow, stretching out his legs. ''Nochelte is figurin' that you'll head straight for the silver. That's my guess. He'll have all his men dug in and waitin' for you. You won't see them until you're right up on them. He'll figure to empty a lot of saddles before you can get in fighting position.''

Roland shook his head. ''I've been out here a long time, Dutch. You know I wouldn't fall for that. I'd have my reconnoitering done before we get in rifle range.''

Dutch nodded. ''Yeah, but he don't know it. Maybe best to play it like he thinks it ought to be.''

''What do you mean?''

Dutch grinned thinly, ''Ride right up on them with most of your troops. Not close enough to give them a shot, but close enough to make them think they'll get a

shot. But give me ten troopers. I'll put half of them on
high points along the stream bed.

"I'll take them out tonight and ride around the
Apaches and we'll get into the canyons by morning
without them knowing it. Then I'll take three or four
troopers and try to catch them squaws, who'll be
comin' out of the mountains with new travois poles.
Maybe I can take them six soldiers. If I can, we got
ourselves a damn strong position."

Roland let his cigar grow cold. He thought a long
moment. Finally he said, "There's no other way, is
there?" He jabbed the cigar at Schreiber. "You got it
all thought out while ridin' back here." He grinned. "If
you were in the Army you would be a general."

Schreiber grunted. "If I was in the Army I'd be
loco." He got to his feet. "I know the troops. Can I
pick my men?"

Roland nodded. "Take the best. Be sure they have
repeaters. Those damned Springfields are made for
soldiers that have all day to get off a shot."

Nochelte and Natchez were pulling away the dead timbers of the burned-out wagon that held the silver. The
bars of bullion were intact, not affected by the fire.
There were over twenty of them, their dull, gray-white
color absorbing the heat of the desert sun. Nochelte
looked at the warriors behind him.

He said, "Spread them out on the ground. Make a
long line of them so that the mules and horses may be
loaded quickly when they arrive." He looked at
Natchez. "How was it, you suppose, that the wagons
caught on fire?"

The Chiricahua chief shrugged. "Who is to know? It

is a bad thing, else we could take the wagons on across the border. It is only a ride of a day in a wagon."

Nochelte stood, head down, hands clasped behind his back. "The Americanos with the wagons did not set the fire. There was no lightning to cause a blaze." He raised his head and looked southward into the canyons. "I sent three warriors after the Dutchman and they have never joined us. I think they are dead. I think this is the work of the Dutchman."

Natchez shrugged. "What is the difference who did it? It is a small delay. Our squaws will be here tomorrow with the mules and horses and new travois poles. We will hold off the horse soldiers until they cross the border."

Natchez strode toward the mounted Apaches. "Move away from the silver. Move forward so that the silver is beyond the range of the rifles of the horse soldiers." He pointed toward a small rise of ground a half-mile away. "Some of you take the horses behind that small hill. The rest of you dig holes in the desert floor so that you will be invisible when the soldiers arrive. We will empty many saddles when they ride in upon us."

Nochelte found the shade of a small mesquite and settled under it. He watched the warriors scooping out their shallow trenches, cutting yucca leaves to tie around their heads. There would be a big fight with the horse soldiers and Natchez would be in charge because he was a war chief, and most of the Apaches out there were his own Chiricahuas.

The silver had been the idea of Nochelte. The salvation of the Apache people had been placed in his hands. But his medicine had grown weak. The Dutchman had somehow come between him and the Great God. And now Natchez was taking over. He did not like this.

The night came and the warriors ate cold venison
jerky and drank a little tepid water. This was not a
hardship to them. This was the way life was lived in the
Territory. They had grown to manhood on it. And
perhaps tomorrow they would slaughter some
Americanos.

Morning came quickly. Nochelte stirred on his blanket and sat up. The others still slept. He moved quietly
from his resting place out into an area of open ground.
He raked the soil with his fingers and picked up a
handful of brown, gravelly sand. He tossed a pinch of it
into the air and blew northward toward the horse soldiers.

Four times he did this and then he stood there, studying the empty horizon. Nothing was happening. The air
was clear in the pale light of dawn. There was no dust
storm, not even a small dust devil in the making. He
shook his head. He had lost his power.

Schreiber rode out of the Army camp with Max beside
him and ten troopers following. By early morning they
were in the canyons. Halfway down the stream bed,
Dutch pulled rein and looked at Jack Rockland, the
oldest trooper.

He said, "You can see it all from here. These bluffs
over the stream gives a man a place to shoot from.
There's no cover for the squaws coming down the
stream bed. Get your men scattered along these bluffs.
If the squaws show up, drop every animal pulling a
travois. It's hell on horses and mules but it may save
some human lives."

Dutch looked at Max. "You and me and about four
troopers are going to take a ride right into Apache

country.'' He picked out four soldiers and then looked at them coldly. ''Anybody don't want to make this ride?''

There was no answer.

Schreiber grinned. ''You're damned liars. Nobody wants to make it. I don't want to make it, myself. But six of your compadres are coming out of the Dragoons and either we take them or the Apaches will carve them up like turkeys.''

He looked at Max. ''You afraid, Comanche?''

Max grinned. ''Always afraid, Dutch, that you forget and leave me behind.''

Schreiber scowled. ''Time our rumps was poundin' leather. Let's go.''

It was a scary thing, riding east through the canyon country. You rode knowing that a couple of miles north were gathered forty-odd of the most savage fighters on earth. You rode knowing that over the next sharp rise you might blunder into a party of them looking for fresh water, or scouting out the route the squaws would take with the silver. And you rode knowing that the horses under you had traveled all night and were already worn out.

Schreiber wiped a sleeve across his sweating face and looked back at his men. They rode quiet and tight-faced, knowing the chances.

By noon they were out of the canyons and moving over a flat bench of land. They had let the horses rest a half-hour before moving out on flat ground. Out here, there was no cover from which to make a stand, if a band of Apaches spotted them. Schreiber was gambling that the Apaches would all dig in around the silver, but he had been wrong about Apaches before. If he was wrong now they would have to make it to the Dragoons to find cover and those mountains were ten miles ahead.

Max rode up beside him. ''You got plan, Dutch?''

Schreiber shook his head. ''None at all. Can't figure a thing until we see the squaws. Got to know first whether they have the troopers. It's my guess they do, unless they've died off on this march. Got to know how many scouts they've got with the squaws. Got to know whether the troopers are bunched in the middle of the band, or walkin' up front or in the rear. When we know all that, we can make some plans.''

Dutch looked ahead at the mountains. He needed to get his men into them as fast as possible. He said, ''Whatever we do has to be done fast. First sign of trouble, the squaws will be holding knives against the troopers' throats.''

They were in the foothills by mid-afternoon. They had found a spring of water and drunk their fill and replenished the canteens. The horses had drunk, too, and were picketed in a shallow swale carpeted with grass. The men stretched out in the shade of an oak grove. Schreiber climbed to the peak of an upthrust of red rock. He took out his field glasses and studied the blue haze of distance stretching east.

Anytime now the squaws and children and old men would come out of the mountains. They would stay as close to their mountain haven as this land would permit, and they would move south almost to the canyon country before cutting west toward the silver and Nochelte's warriors. They would have to do this to make sure they avoided Roland and his horse soldiers.

Roland should have his men in place by now. Dutch hoped that Joe Brewer had been able to spot the area where the Apaches were dug in. If he hadn't, Roland would have lost some men already. One thing was in favor of the horse soldiers. Once the Apaches rose out of their holes like red ghosts and the initial shock of ambush was over, the odds evened out, and perhaps even favored the troopers. The Apaches would be exposed. There was no cover for either side and Apaches did not like to fight in the open.

A half-mile to the north they came out of the mountain pass like a swarm of red ants. Looking through his glasses Schreiber saw the thin, undulating line of figures moving out of the high country into the desert flats. Waiting, he saw the squaws and old men leading the horses and mules with empty travois.

Behind them three Apache boys kept their distance on their horses. Each Apache had two troopers stumbling along behind, each with a leather reata around their necks. Behind the troops, one lone scout rode with a rifle across his horse's back.

Schreiber looked at Max. "They raised you. You're goin' to be one of them again." He pulled a sack of tobacco and rolled a smoke and handed the sack to the Comanche.

"You'll have to strip. Leave hat, pants, and boots on the ground. Make a breechclout out of your shirt. Take the saddle off your horse. Wish we could take the shoes off the animal but we can't." He grinned tentatively. "We're rollin' dice, Comanche. It's you against six troopers."

Max grinned back. He rolled his cigarette and lighted it and coughed on the first drag. He looked at Schreiber. "You lay it out, Dutch. Me do best."

Dutch felt a tightening in his guts. He looked at Max and looked away. It was not the kid's fight. But the kid would fight it because he was that kind. And there were white folks in the Territory who thought the only good Indian was a dead one.

Schreiber said, "You'll have to ride in on them." He

pointed to a deep slope off to the south. "From there. You speak Apache. Don't get it mixed up with Comanche, goddammit. Pure Apache. Tell them Nochelte sent you to guide them."

Max took a final drag off his smoke without coughing. "What then, Dutch?"

Dutch shrugged. "Only show we got is to hit them all at once. You check in with that scout bringing up the rear. Ride off toward the troopers and hold there a minute or so." He looked past Max into the emptiness of the desert.

Finally he said, "I'll cut the scout down. The troopers will down the horses those Apache kids are ridin'. You got to be there to cut them lariats else the horses will choke them troopers to death just thrashin' around."

Max smiled. "I do it. Comanche good for something out here."

Dutch smiled back. "Maybe so. I ain't figured out what yet."

Sometimes a white man fighting Apaches can have a little luck. Later when Schreiber thought about it, and he thought about it often, he admitted to himself that it was mostly luck.

Max came up the rise of the slope with one hand up. He cajoled the squaws, insulted the kids, and checked in with the scout. The sun of tomorrow, he explained to the Apache, by the sun of tomorrow the band would be with Nochelte. He would lead. He paused by the troopers, hands bound behind them, shuffling along, more dead than alive.

And then the shooting started and the scout behind him rolled off his horse and the three Apache kids leading the horse soldiers were on the ground scrambling around, their mounts kicking and thrashing in the agony of their death throes. Max moved in and cut the leather thongs around the necks of the troopers. The squaws and old men were beating their animals with the travois into a run.

With the squaws running south Schreiber moved in with the four troopers. In no time the six captive horse soldiers were riding for the first time in many days, and Dutch, Max and the four troopers were walking beside them.

Schreiber managed a grin. "It's due west for maybe ten miles, then south another ten. We'll join Captain Roland there." He looked at his men. "And we'll walk every damned mile.

"These men," he motioned toward the exhausted, emaciated captives, "haven't sat a horse in the last two weeks, and they've covered a hundred and seventy miles."

Captain Harry Roland was heading the column of troopers and packers moving south. Constant use of the field glasses had not discovered any sign of the burned wagons, nor of the Apaches guarding the silver. But he was picking up some of the rough edges of the canyon country, and he knew that somewhere between here and there the Apaches were waiting for them.

Joe Brewer and Sergeant Quincy Shannon flanked him on each side. The sergeant said now, "Give me a small patrol and I'll flush the red heathens, Captain. Let's get them off their bellies where we can see them."

Roland did not answer. He looked at Brewer. "What do you think? Are they lying out there waiting for us?"

Brewer shrugged. "I think so, but I don't see anything.'' He looked at Roland. ''They got to have water same as a white man. We might wait them out.''

Roland nodded. ''Might work if Dutch did his job.'' He looked at Shannon. ''I can't give you that patrol, Sergeant. If something happens to me, then you are the man in charge.''

Shannon swore quietly, ''That goddamned Dutch!''

Roland looked at him sharply, ''What about Dutch?''

Shannon grinned crookedly, ''Bastard is never where you need him.''

Brewer rested his bandaged hand on the pommel of his saddle. ''We need him too many places. Give him time.''

Roland said, ''We'll pull up here. There's no sign of the squaws and the silver can't be moved without them.'' He motioned to Shannon. ''Dismount the men and spread them out doubles about twenty yards apart. Turn the horses over to the packers but keep them saddled.''

He swept the flat land with his glasses. It was a creepy feeling, knowing you might be standing within a hundred yards of forty Apaches who had no place to hide and yet a man couldn't see them.

Twilight came and the desert began to cool with the breeze off of the Dragoons looming up in orange and purple hues in the distant horizon. One of the packers had stretched a sheet of canvas over two small creosote bushes, and Cathy Roland had avoided much of the afternoon heat sitting in its shade.

Several times she had dozed but real sleep would not come. Her body ached. Her eyes were swollen from the glare of the sun. Fragments of thought slipped through her mind, but she could hold to none of them for fatigue had affected her mind as well as her body.

Most of these thoughts were on Schreiber, disjointed, with no sequence, but on him, nonetheless. She hoped he was alive and once today she had said a small prayer for him.

Without really watching, Cathy was aware that the soldiers were in battle position. The time was at hand for the red men and the white men to make war on each other. She thought abstractly that this had been going on for years out here. Likely it would continue for years to come: the white man struggling desperately to keep what he had fought for so hard; the Apache grimly determined to take back that which he had lost.

She was an Eastern woman. She knew nothing of this kind of living. Could she really make a life for herself out here? For the second time she felt some doubts.

Her uncle stopped by and spoke to her, quietly reassuring. He seemed such a sensitive and gentle man. Yet it must be that he was not entirely what he seemed. How could a man lead men whom he knew, for whom he had regard and friendship, into a death battle and watch them suffer and die, and still remain a sensitive and gentle man? This was not a new experience for Captain Harry Roland. He had done this many times before.

One of the packers stopped by with a plate of beans and a small, opened can of tomatoes. She ate the beans and tomatoes, then drank the tomato juice. She lay back on the ground and watched the stars begin to appear in the sky, as darkness overtook the desert.

Somewhere in the distance a coyote wailed and the plaintive cry was answered by another. Closer by, a desert fox barked. The sounds seemed natural to this country and soothing to her troubled mind. She slept without knowing that the Apaches had been talking.

By dark Dutch and the troopers and Max had covered ten miles, with only two short stops when a little shade could be found to escape the searing heat. By early dawn his glasses picked up Roland's soldiers spread across the flats. An hour later they shuffled into the Army camp, hungry, bone-tired, craving rest and water.

Roland and Brewer moved out to meet them and immediately began to visit with the former hostage soldiers, shaking hands, checking them over, listening to their stories. Dutch and Max headed for the packers who were in charge of the food and water when the Army was in camp. They wolfed down beans and hardtack and tepid water.

Dutch ran a hand over his whisker-stubbled face. He looked at Max. ''Get some sleep, Comanche. Soon as I shave, I aim to do the same. Gonna be a long day, I reckon.''

Roland moved up, looking fresh, confident. ''That was good work, Dutch.''

Schreiber shrugged. ''Thank the kid. He took most of the risk.'' He looked toward the mountains, barely visible in the early light. ''The squaws will be gettin' here about noon. That's when the ruckus will start.'' He looked around the camp. ''How's Cathy holding up?''

The captain smiled slightly. ''I think she's worried about you.''

Dutch flushed. ''Aw, hell.'' He took off his hat and beat the dust out of his pants and shirt. ''I'll catch some shut-eye.'' He walked off, wishing he could catch a glimpse of Cathy Roland but he knew she was still asleep. Maybe someday they could sit down together and talk like any normal man and woman without the fear of impending violence smothering their words.

He was fishing in his saddle bag for his razor when Joe Brewer came up beside him. Brewer said, "The red heathens were moving around some last night. I figure some of them have settled in closer to us."

Dutch nodded. "Wouldn't be surprised. We'll know soon enough."

It seemed to Schreiber that he had barely closed his eyes when a rough hand shook his shoulder. He opened his eyes to look into Quincy Shannon's sun-blistered face.

The sergeant said, "The squaws are here. About a mile in front of us. Captain says they've already started loading the silver."

Dutch got up slowly, rubbing his hands over his face. He found his hat and put it on. He looked at the sun and judged the time to be about noon. He said, "Let's go see the captain."

Roland was moving along the line of his positioned soldiers. They had dug shallow troughs and settled in them, packing the excavated earth in front of them.

Roland looked at Schreiber. "The Apaches are wondering what we're waitin' for."

Dutch nodded. "They want us to come chargin' in after the squaws. We'd lose half the men tryin' it." He pulled his field glasses and studied the flats. The squaws were moving towards the canyons.

Time passed slowly. A hot breeze sprang up and blew sand in front of it, dusting the troops with yellow grit. A solitary buzzard circled in the yellow sky, wings outstretched and motionless as a thermal draft carried it in an upward spiral. Then the desert silence was broken by the sound of distant gunfire rolling up out of the canyons.

A tall Apache raced a spotted horse from behind a small rise a half-mile away, yelling, making signs with one hand. The desert came alive. Brown-skinned figures seemed to grow suddenly where a moment before only scattered yuccas had flourished. They came forward, yelling their hatred and defiance, firing rifles, filling the air with arrows. Behind them, another scattered line of Apaches ran for the canyons.

Roland barked a command to his troopers and rifles crashed and flung their leaden messengers of death into the charging warriors. Apaches fell and writhed on the ground. A soldier cried out in pain. And then the charging hordes of Indians seemed to melt and fade away. They veered to either side of the embattled troopers, then turned and raced back toward the canyons, following others who were already nearing the broken country.

Roland was shouting orders and horses were being led up, fully saddled and ready to go. The troopers rolled out of their holes and mounted up. Captain Roland gave the order to charge.

Roland and Dutch led the troops, sixguns in hand, bearing down on the running Apaches. Two of the warriors, each with rifles, whirled and threw themselves on the ground and poured a volley of shots into the troops. Horses stumbled and went down, men shouted, guns blasted in a wild crescendo, and smoke drifted low like a storm cloud. And then it was quiet.

Roland halted the troops. He rode among his men and then came back. He looked at Dutch. "They must have lost over a third of their warriors. We've got one trooper dead and three wounded. None seriously.''

Schreiber studied the rough country ahead. Finally he said, "It's time we talked to Nochelte."

Roland frowned. "Why talk? They're on the run. We outnumber them two to one."

Schreiber rolled a cigarette. "They'll start figurin' out ways to get at our men on them bluffs above the stream bed. Brewer and I will have to take a couple of details into them canyons to protect those men. It'll be rough in there. Both sides will lose a lot of men. Now's a good time to parley before it starts."

The captain thought it over. "Do you think he will talk?"

Schreiber lighted his cigarette. "I'll find out."

Nochelte moved among the squaws and children and old men, talking with them, praising them, trying to quiet their panic. They had suffered much these past days. Some had died from exhaustion, many had been killed by the Americano, Jesse Cogar, and his outlaws. Their destination was close now but the horse soldiers were upon them and they were afraid.

Natchez maneuvered through the midst of his warriors, giving orders, exhorting them to find and destroy the soldiers hidden on the bluffs. Nochelte heard his words and moved toward him. He said, "The Chiricahuas are brave fighters but we have lost many warriors. What chance do we have against the horse soldiers now?"

Natchez grunted, studying the terrain. "We are in the canyons now. We fight best in this kind of country. We cannot match the guns of the White Eyes in the open, but in this land," his eyes swept the jagged, broken buttes and mesas, "the horse soldiers can lose many men and never see an Apache."

Nochelte was silent. Finally he said, "I am not thinking so much of killing horse soldiers. Can we protect the travois carrying the silver?"

Before Natchez could answer a warrior came running up to them. The warrior said, "The Dutchman is coming. He is riding alone."

Nochelte moved toward the rim of the flats, Natchez beside him. When Natchez saw the rider, he raised his rifle, but Nochelte pushed downward on the barrel. "Let him come. He brings a message from the chief of the horse soldiers."

The rider pulled rein a hundred yards from the point where the flats dropped off into the canyons. The rider called, "I come to ask if Nochelte will talk with the captain?"

Nochelte moved forward. He did not feel good inside. He did not think the chance was good for the silver to reach the border. If it did not, then he had failed his people and caused the death of many. Things had turned out in a bad way but he would not surrender. Talk? Yes, he would talk with the chief of the horse soldiers, but he would not go back as a prisoner.

He stopped in front of the Dutchman. It was this man who was mostly responsible for the trouble. It was this man who had told the horse soldier chief about the silver. It was this man who had burned the wagons that by now would have been in Mexico with the silver. It was this man who had retaken the captive horse soldiers.

Nochelte said, "Bring the horse soldier chief. We will talk."

A short time later Schreiber and Roland rode up to

within a hundred yards of the dropoff into the canyons and waited. Presently Nochelte came riding over the rim. Natchez was with him.

Dutch said, "Let him see the dispatch first thing. He'll know then that the Apaches will maybe get some help from Washington."

The captain nodded. "Maybe he'll believe it, maybe not. The Apaches are a suspicious people when it comes to promises from the white man."

Dutch shrugged. "Got a right to be."

The shaman and the war chief stopped their mounts a few yards away. Schreiber got out of the saddle. He said, "Let's sit. May be quite a palaver."

They sat down on the hot ground under the glare of the mid afternoon sun. Roland handed Nochelte the dispatch from Fort Thomas, and the little Apache sat there and read it over carefully.

The shaman looked at Roland. "What does this mean for the Apache? So the big chiefs in Washington come to my country. They talk among themselves and decided what the Apache should do. The Apache does not get to tell his story. He does not make any decisions."

Roland was cautious. "How do you know? The Commissioner is a new man. I hear he is concerned for all of the Indians. I cannot see him coming all this way just to talk to Army people. If that was all there was to be to it, he would have them come to him and save himself the trip."

Nochelte was silent. He looked at Natchez but there was nothing to read in stoic face of the Chiricahua chief.

Nochelte said, "When the big chiefs in Washington get here, they will hear about the silver and about the

Apaches leaving the reservation. They will be angry
with us and want to punish us.''

Roland shook his head. ''Not if it stops now. Not if
you go back to the reservation. There have been no
settlers killed, no ranches burned, no livestock stolen.
Only a patrol of sixty men has been involved, and it has
lost only one man.''

Nochelte shook his head. ''We cannot go back and
tell our people that we have failed. We cannot tell them
that we bring them nothing but sorrow for the squaws
whose wickiups will be empty because their men died
under the guns of the horse soldiers.''

Schreiber looked at the medicine man. ''You've still
got the silver.''

Roland looked at him sharply. ''That has to be turned
over to the smelting company in Globe.''

Dutch nodded. ''Sure. But it brings a three
thousand-dollar reward. Nochelte didn't steal it. He
took it off the men who did. We got proof of that. If you
tell the company that Nochelte brought it back voluntar-
ily, he'll get the reward. That's the way I see it.''

Roland studied Schreiber. ''Dutch, I figured you
would get the reward. The Army can't take it. You
grounded the silver and led us to it.''

Schreiber shook his head. ''I ain't got it, have I? I
ain't goin' to get it without a bunch of men gettin'
killed, maybe me included. If he gives it back and calls
this thing off, let him have it. That ought to raise the
Apache up considerable in the minds of the settlers
when they hear it.''

Roland grinned. ''You've been thinking about this
for a spell, haven't you? And if the settlers are pleased,
that will go good for the Apaches with the Commissioner.''

Nochelte said solemnly, "That is much Americano money."

Roland nodded. "You'll buy no guns with that money. That's my stipulation. You'll spend it under our supervision for anything you want except guns and ammunition."

Nochelte smiled faintly, "I have the hope that we will not need guns. We will see if the Commissioner intends to help the Apache before we seek guns again. The money will be spent for food and seed and plows. We need sheep so that the squaws can work the looms again and make blankets."

He looked again at Schreiber. "Why do you give up your claim on the reward? Your claim on it is strong."

Dutch shrugged. "Like I said, shaman, I find I ain't tired of living yet. Ain't sure I'd make it through another scrap with Natchez there."

Nochelte looked at the war chief. "What do you think?"

Natchez shrugged indifferently. "It was your plan. It is your decision. There is some sense to it." He looked into the canyons. "It would be a great fight. But we would lose some more warriors."

Nochelte looked at Roland. "My squaws and old men and children are worn out with the silver. It will take a long time to haul it back on travois."

Roland took cigars from his pocket and handed one to Nochelte and one to Natchez. "I will send to Tombstone for wagons."

Nochelte leaned over to catch the flare of Roland's match. He puffed with appreciation on the Havana tobacco. He said, "I can tell my people that we have made a good treaty with the horse soldier chief. That we bring them many good things."

He eyed Roland sharply, "Can I also tell them that the big chiefs in Washington are going to meet with me?"

Roland nodded. "I'll promise that. Willcox will back me."

Nochelte stood up. "We will end this thing. Send for the wagons." He walked out on the flats. He reached down and picked up a handful of loose sand. He tossed a pinch of it in the air and blew on it. He did this three more times, then stood back, and looked out over the flat country toward the mountains.

A small spiral of dust rose from the desert floor. It raced and whirled and grew larger until it was a raging storm, sending its yellow color two thousand feet upward into the sky.

Nochelte smiled. His power was regained. The Great God was pleased. Somewhere he had lost the message. The Great God did not want the Apache to retake his land by violence, but by patience and endurance and negotiation with the Americano.

Dutch Schreiber watched the dust storm racing toward the mountains. Somehow he sensed Nochelte had created it, and yet in his practical mind he found it hard to believe. He knew much about the Apache, perhaps more than any single man in the Territory. He watched the storm die against the mountains and he turned away, knowing he still had much to learn.

CHAPTER SEVENTEEN

Schreiber was feeling used up when he rode into sight of the post. It had taken eight days to wagon-haul the silver to Globe.

The superintendant of the Globe Smelting Company could hardly believe it when he saw the silver. He was so overjoyed by its recovery that he had his wife prepare a dinner for Captain Roland and Cathy. He also invited the medicine man, Nochelte. At Roland's suggestion the editor of the local paper was invited also to assure good press coverage.

The Apaches left Globe with three wagonloads of corn and beans. Nochelte bought three plows, harness, and bolts of bright cloth for the squaws. He held back a good part of the reward money for sheep. Roland had agreed he could go north to buy them from the Navajos, because they would sell cheaper than the White Eyes.

Schreiber rode his weary horse through the gates of the post and pulled rein in front of headquarters. Sergeant Quincy Shannon was on the porch of the building, leaning against a post. He said, "You're late, Dutch."

Schreiber nodded. "Got hung up at the Smelting Company." He grinned at the Sergeant. "Got myself a payin' job, Quincy. The company is goin' to haul its own bullion from now on and I'm in charge."

Shannon grinned back. "Pay good, Dutch?"

"Yeah. Hundred fifty a month. Never figured this mother's son would make that kind of money." He looked at Quincy. "What's goin' on?"

The sergeant shrugged. "Not much. The captain is retiring within a month or two. He's marryin' up with the Jackson woman come Saturday. Big affair. Most of Two Wells is invited."

Schreiber blinked. "He don't waste much time, does he? Where is Miss Cathy?"

"In Two Wells. She and Miss Jackson both stayin' with the Brewers until the wedding."

"Where's the captain?"

The sergeant smiled. "At Fort Apache with the Commissioner and Willcox, and a top man from the War Department." His smile broadened. "Guess who's with them?"

Dutch grinned. "My thinkin', Nochelte."

Shannon nodded. "You think good. He'll talk them out of their socks. Some Indian."

Dutch reached for tobacco. "Where's Max?"

Shannon said, "In Two Wells. He's at the Brewers, too."

Dutch scowled. "Christ sake! If I want to see anybody I know, I got to go to the Brewers." He turned away, "See you, Quincy."

The sergeant came off the porch grinning. "Guess what I'm goin' to do, Dutch."

Schreiber looked at him. "What you been doin', I reckon. Bossin' men and horses."

Quincy laughed. "Not me. I'm goin' to Washington. Goin' back with the Commissioner."

Schreiber looked at him suspiciously. "That don't make any sense. You all right, Quincy?"

Quincy Shannon drew himself up proudly. "Dutch, the Commissioner needs a man who knows this Territory, who knows Apaches. A man who can read and write intelligently. That's what the Commissioner said. I'm self-trained but I read and write pretty good.

"I'll screen all reports coming into his office from the military and the Indian agents in this country and evaluate them." He grinned again. "Besides, the Commissioner is an Irishman and he wants company."

Schreiber stuck out his hand. "Good luck, Quincy."

Shannon gripped the offered hand. "I'll miss you, Dutch."

Schreiber got back on his horse and headed for Two Wells. He had been out of touch just three or four days, and the whole damned world had changed. The horse was tired but he was in no mood to humor it. The ride to Two Wells was one of the shortest he'd ever made.

He pulled up in front of the Brewers' house and walked up on the porch. Mae Brewer heard his boots and was waiting for him. He smiled, "Hello, Mae."

She looked at him. "You took a long time gettin' here."

He shrugged. "Business in Globe, then rode out of my way to the post. No one but Quincy there. Everybody's stayin' with you." He added quietly, "How's Joe?"

She smiled and opened the door for him. "Joe's all right. He's got a bad hand that isn't ever goin' to be as good as it was, but he can use it some, thanks to you."

"He here or workin'?"

She moved into the kitchen. "He's at the office. Max is with him."

He walked to the kitchen and stood with hat in hand, feeling suddenly ill at ease. Mae poured a cup of coffee and handed it to him.

Schreiber said, ''Quincy said Miss Cathy was here.''

Mae smiled. ''Quit callin' her Miss Cathy. The way that girl has been moonin' over you.''

A clear, feminine voice interrupted Mae. ''Now, Mae, you promised—''

Dutch saw her then. Her hair was shining like gold and her face was full of color. She was, he reckoned, the prettiest thing he'd ever seen.

He moved forward involuntarily, instinctively, reaching out a hand, ''Miss Cathy—''

She came to him, laughing. ''Mae is right, Dutch. It's just Cathy.'' She walked right into him, unabashed, naturally, in the way of a woman who loves a man. She said softly, ''Let's go out to the swing.''

No one disturbed them. They talked of many things. Dutch was proud of his new job. When he got his money from Ruth Jackson on the cattle, there was a little place outside Globe a man could buy. Not much land, but enough to raise a few cows on the side. He wanted Cathy to see it before he decided.

She had her job here in Two Wells teaching school. She would stay with the Brewers. Unless something special was going on, Dutch could leave Globe on Saturday afternoon, then have the Sunday mornings to visit here at Two Wells.

Two figures moved into sight. They were riding slowly, hats pulled low against the glare of the late evening sun. Dutch recognized Joe Brewer and Max. Brewer dismounted and led his horse around the corner to the corral. Max stayed in the saddle. He grinned at Dutch. ''Ho, Dutch. All over now.''

Dutch grinned back. ''All over, kid. I'm goin' to work. Got a place for you, too.''

Max studied Dutch for a long moment. He reached in his shirt pocket and pulled out a sack of tobacco. Quietly and expertly he rolled a smoke. "I go home, Dutch. My country." He rubbed his stomach. "Gettin' older, Dutch. Got big burn for squaw. Comanche squaw."

Dutch started out of the swing and then relaxed. He put an arm around Cathy. "It had to come, kid. You got good sense. Never suspected it before, but you have. Make sure it's a Comanche squaw. One of your own."

Max lighted his smoke, studying Dutch over the flame of the match. "Good times, Dutch. Maybe see you again."

Schreiber felt a lump in his throat. He pulled a bandanna and blew his nose. "Maybe, kid."

Max pulled his horse around and rode off under the red glare of the evening sun. He never looked back.

Cathy put a hand on Dutch's arm. "Why did he leave so suddenly?"

Dutch watched the young rider drift out of sight. "It's the only way, I guess. You do it or you don't."

"Will he come back when he finds the woman he wants?"

Schreiber shrugged. He said thickly, "Who knows what a Comanche will do?"

Winners of the SPUR and WESTERN HERITAGE AWARD

☐ 08390 **The Buffalo Wagons** Kelton $1.75

☐ 13907 **The Day The Cowboys Quit** Elmer Kelton $1.95

☐ 22766 **Fancher Train** Bean $1.95

☐ 29742 **Gold In California** Todhunter Ballard $1.75

☐ 34272 **The Honyocker** Giles Lutz $1.95

☐ 47082 **The Last Days of Wolf Garnett** Clifton Adams $1.75

☐ 47493 **Law Man** Lee Leighton $1.95

☐ 48921 **Long Run** Nye $1.95

☐ 55123 **My Brother John** Herbert Purdum $1.75

☐ 56027 **The Nameless Breed** Will C. Brown $1.95

☐ 71154 **The Red Sabbath** Lewis B. Patten $1.95

☐ 74940 **Sam Chance** Benjamin Capps $1.95

☐ 80271 **The Time It Never Rained** Kelton $1.95

☐ 82091 **Tragg's Choice** Clifton Adams $1.75

☐ 82136 **The Trail to Ogallala** Benjamin Capps $1.95

☐ 85904 **The Valdez Horses** Lee Hoffman $1.95

Available wherever paperbacks are sold or use this coupon.

Ⓒ ACE CHARTER BOOKS WAREHOUSE
P.O. Box 400, Kirkwood, N.Y. 13795

Please send me the titles checked above. I enclose _____ .
Include 75¢ for postage and handling if one book is ordered; 50¢ per book for two to five. If six or more are ordered, postage is free. California, Illinois, New York and Tennessee residents please add sales tax.

NAME_____

ADDRESS_____

CITY_____STATE_____ZIP_____

125

Sharp Shooting and Rugged Adventure from America's Favorite Western Writers

Page-turning Suspense from
CHARTER BOOKS

CHARTER
BOOKS

SUSPENSE TO KEEP YOU
ON THE EDGE OF YOUR SEAT

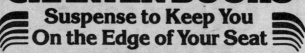